HAVEN'S INDIGO

SARAH BYRD

THIS LITTLE BYRD
BOOKS

Publisher's Note: This is a work of fiction. Names, characters, and incidents are a product of the author's imagination. Locales and public names are sometimes used for atmospheric purposes. Any resemblance to actual people, living or dead, or to businesses, companies, events, institutions, or Time Servers are completely coincidental.

Jacksonville / Sarah Byrd — First Edition

Hardcover ISBN 978-1-7366166-0-4

Ebook ISBN 978-1-7366166-1-1

Cover Art: Rachel Bostwick

Edited by: Lizzie V. Appel and Agata Antonow

Printed in the United States of America

This Little Byrd Books | www.thislittlebyrd.com

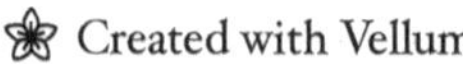 Created with Vellum

For my Creator,
Who saw me when no one else did.

CONTENTS

IT HAD BEEN a day since Haven had eaten anything, and her stomach was angry. The dusty air in Five Points in Jacksonville, or Jax as the locals called it, smelled of seasoned meat and toasted bread that came from a food truck parked on the corner. Haven's stomach yelled for her to stop, but she willed her feet to move forward.

Just hours earlier she had seen Aiden, her six-year-old friend, sick among the moth-eaten blankets at the dump, shaking uncontrollably because of the fever. It was scary high; Haven could tell because he was hotter than the sidewalk in the southern summer heat.

"First medicine, then food," Haven whispered to her stomach, which rumbled at a dull roar.

The clinking of coins on the pavement rang to her left and she saw that the old woman who had dropped them struggled to bend down. One of the quarters rolled to her feet and Haven picked it up, staring at it in her hand. She sighed. Even though she needed the money, it wasn't in her to steal.

She scooped up the rest of the coins that were on the pavement around her and placed them—all of them—in the woman's dry, cracked hands; hands that felt like old play dough that had been left out too long.

"Bless you, dear," the old woman croaked.

"Yes ma'am," Haven replied. "Thank you."

She turned away and kept a quick pace, dodging two men that spat insults to each other, stinking cigars hanging from their mouths. A shop owner swept a door stoop and paused to stare at Haven, who nodded hello, but they gave a hard glare in return. Most older people didn't want teenagers like her around their stores, especially if they wore backpacks big enough to steal stuff.

Haven adjusted her own pack and pushed her greasy hair behind her ears. She hopped off the sidewalk, a piece of duct tape holding her shoe together scraping the pavement as she did so, and crossed the road to Twigette's. The bell rang when she pushed through the front door that read: Twigette's Treasures N' Things. It was a glorified pawn shop—the only place in Jax that would even let Haven trade junk for cash.

The strong smell of sandalwood assaulted her nostrils as soon as she stepped into the shop. To her left, different umbrellas with decorated handles hung haphazardly, wooden radios with worn outer boards from ages past sat on a dusty shelf, a set of bobblehead dolls with creepy faces bobbed up and down as if invisible hands moved them, and a framed dollar bill with the saying, 'First Fair Trade' hung over the doorway to the back.

Haven wiped her sweaty palms on the side of her pants as she reached Twigette. She needed a sale for money to buy medicine for Aiden. The trouble was she didn't have anything of true value to sell and Twigette didn't just give things away. You had to give her a fair trade.

"Hey, Twigette," Haven said, unsuccessfully hiding the quiver in her voice.

The woman was hunched over an old tape recorder with ribbons of tape spurting out like an octopus trying to escape. Twigette clicked the pause button on the dented machine with her nails that were always painted deep, cardinal red. She looked up at Haven through her high density reading glasses before rising to her full height of over six-feet tall. Her inky hair was in a bun, and the name Twigette described her build.

"My favorite trader! You find anything good for me on your walks through the landfill?"

After a deep breath, Haven set her bag on the counter and laid out the old radio dial, radio case, and the broken watch she found the day before. With a pained expression, she glanced up. Twigette hovered over each item, moving a piece or two from time to time with the end of a pencil. At last, she stood with a puzzled look.

"Haven . . . really? There is nothing here of any value to me. It would not be a fair trade."

She knew the shopkeeper didn't give in to sob stories, but Haven had no choice. Steadying herself, the girl shoved her hands in her pockets and started to explain, "I thought—"

A tiny metal circle bumped her left pointer finger as she wiggled her fingers in her jeans pocket. With a furrowed brow, Haven pulled out the object and glanced down. A weighty platinum ring with a deep indigo stone in the center lay cradled in her palm. Haven held her breath.

Attached to the ring, a torn piece of paper read, '2 Bestie' with both Es written backward. Haven pushed down the sob that caught her throat, for she knew the little boy who wrote this was the reason she was at Twigette's in the first place.

"What about this?"

She lifted the ring with the purple-blue stone for the shopkeeper to inspect.

Twigette's faced drained of all color as she whispered, "The

Indigo." She leaned close to Haven, her voice shaky, "Where did you get that?" The top and bottoms of her eyes were larger than the reading glasses she wore.

"Aiden—" Haven forced her voice to remain steady, "—Aiden must have found it at the dump. He put it in my pocket."

Twigette stepped back to glance around the store and at the door. "How did it end up at the landfill of all places? And for you, of all people, to find! The Time Servers—" Twigette cleared her throat and moved so close to Haven that she could see the vein popping out of her left temple. "Listen, I cannot trade anything for that and I cannot keep it. Matter of fact, do *not* give it to anybody."

"Wait, what do I—?"

The bell rang, signaling another customer had entered the store. A stout man with a grayed goatee, leather boots, and jacket to match ambled up to the counter almost in perfect time with the pendulum clicks of the grandfather clock in the corner, his every step making a soft squeak of leather brushing leather.

He eyed Haven and the ring she held, then spoke gruffly to Twigette. "I need parts for my 1940 Indian Four motorcycle that my half-wit mechanic is too dumb to find. You have any?"

Twigette smoothed her hair and drummed her fingers on the glass countertop.

"Yeah, I have a few; what do you need?"

The man handed her a list and she scanned it carefully. "I have a couple of these in the back, hold on." Then with a sharp look toward Haven that clearly told her to go, she stated in her usual businesslike tone, "I think we are done here."

Haven hung her head and moved to put the ring back in her pocket.

"Wait there, girl," the man growled. "You trying to sell that ring?"

"I—"

"She wasn't," Twigette interrupted. "It is just a family heirloom she wanted to show me."

"Family heirloom, huh?" he grunted as he eyed the tough woman. "If you want to sell it, you can have this." He slammed two one-hundred-dollar bills on the counter.

Haven's heart pounded fast and hard in her chest. That was like winning the lottery. She opened her mouth, but Twigette made a slight move towards her that made her shut it again. Haven trusted Twigette more than anyone and if she told her not to give the ring to anyone, then she shouldn't.

"No sir, it is not for sale," she willed her cheeks to raise so that a sweet smile beamed from her face.

The man wiped his nose with the back of his hand, hiding a scowl. "All right, your loss."

Haven hesitated, looked at the shopkeeper who was unusually interested in the parts list, pocketed the ring, and nodded tersely at the unkempt man, sneaking one last peek at the two bills on the counter. She grabbed her pack, left the junk on the counter, and exited as quickly as she came.

The door clanged behind her as Haven released a breath she didn't know she was holding. She searched the busy city street for a hiding place and found a sprawling oak tree across the street in front of a church.

After scaling high to blend amongst the leafy boughs, Haven rested her head against the trunk of the tree, letting her heartbeat return to normal.

Why did Twigette freak out when she saw the ring and why didn't she let me sell it? Who are the Time Servers?

Letting curiosity get the best of her, Haven slipped her hand into her pocket and pulled out the perfect piece of jewelry, holding it close for inspection.

It had one tiny dahlia as the stone rested in the center. Haven squinted her eyes; she didn't remember the dahlia being there before, but she didn't mind. It was her favorite flower because of the way the petals curved upward and seemed to keep building on each other. She slipped the ring on her grimy finger, tanned from her days of trash digging. It fit perfectly, as if melting into her skin. Such a lovely thing. She had never worn jewelry before. She imagined her father giving this to her for her birthday, with a loving smile on his face, and he was proud of her. So different from her actual father who left her at the landfill like an abandoned puppy and peeled out in a cloud of dust.

Her shoulders tensed as her hand gripped the tiny rectangles of bark on the oak tree. Haven willed herself out of that memory and took a breath. The smell of fresh greenery helped her relax as she closed her eyes to listen to the people chatter and the cars driving past her on the streets below.

What am I supposed to do? I gotta figure something out. Think, Haven.

Okay, so there is no way Aiden is going to get better without medicine.

But to get medicine I have to trade for money—and no stealing!

So where can I get something to trade in the next five minutes?

Haven glanced down at the ring then watched the street below her. A woman pushed a rambunctious toddler who twisted and turned in his seat. An elderly man in a frayed jacket sat on a park bench and looked about every minute or so while he fed the ducks at Riverside Park across the way. A bus rumbled down the street filled with passengers.

The mother with the now-crying child stopped in the crosswalk to pick up the sippy cup the boy had thrown in aggravation. Haven saw the trouble before anyone else did. The bus driver was not paying attention as the bus came barreling down towards the poor woman and her impatient son. Three more seconds and they would be pancakes in the middle of the street.

Haven opened her mouth to scream in desperation, but instead, time paused.

Haven's scream echoed through an entirely quiet city block.

The bus, ten feet from the woman, paused in the middle of the street. A man was mid-laugh and looked like his nostrils could park a motorcycle inside, they had flared so much. A dog was in the middle of jumping on their owner and his ears looked like they could take flight, just like the birds in the tree next to Haven. The leaves on the tree next to her were unmoving, but soft, pliable. *Weird.*

Out of nowhere, a chestnut-colored circle, small like a mousehole, appeared as if it were floating mid-air. It grew larger until it looked like a huge circular stone gate in the middle of the street. A man wearing a long green overcoat down to his calves bounced out of the gate. His shirt read, 'Will Break for Food,' his sequined socks had pockets at the ankles, and he wore bright purple tennis shoes.

He hummed a song to himself as he pulled out a small pocketbook from his overcoat and ran his finger down the page.

"Ah," he said, carefully closing the pocketbook. "The bus."

He bounded over to the bus and opened the door, popping in with a wide smile on his face as if he were greeting the passengers who sat still, like wax figures in a museum. The man turned the wheel slightly to the right and threw away a cup of coffee that hung in midair beside the front passenger who had been chatting to the bus driver. Then, he leaped off the bus, pulled out what looked like a tiny ball of glass from his pocket, ran down the sidewalk, and turned the corner.

As if announcing herself to the city, a woman flounced out of the gate. She wore black wedge shoes with hearts on the tips, a coattail jacket that had bunny rabbits on them, a scarf that wrapped three times around her neck, hiding the lower part of her face, and a fedora hat with the word, 'Cheers!' printed on the side. Her sequined notebook shimmered in the sun, and Haven could see her long fingernail paging through it before she found her place.

The woman skittered mid-street, her ebony shoes snapping to her heels every time she took a step, making her sound like a crab moving quickly to the ocean. The woman popped her right foot into the air, posing as if for a picture, then easily slid the mother and wailing son about three feet further down the cross-walk as if they were on pads of melted butter. Then with an air of pizazz, she popped a lollipop in the boy's tiny fist—just as something whizzed by Haven's tree.

What was that? A hummingbird? It was so fast that Haven had to follow very carefully with her eyes until the movement came to rest in the trash can near the tree she had climbed. Haven was checking for feathers but instead noticed a minuscule leg stuck out of the trash pile. Wriggling, the lone leg struggled until it found something to brace itself against, pulling the rest of the body with it.

A fairy in a pin-striped pantsuit? The tiny creature looked as if she could have been a lawyer in Ponte Vedra, the wealthiest area around the city. In her hand, she grasped a golden chain which was almost as large as she was.

The Fairy cruised to a crack in the sidewalk at the base of the tree where Haven pretended to be one of the frozen. After hovering for a minute, the Fairy flew off to the floating gateway of stone and vanished into the darkness beyond. The man and woman, like the Fairy, jumped through the circle while Haven craned her neck, trying to get a peek at where the gate led. Smaller and smaller the circle shrank until nothing was left.

As soon as all evidence of the three unusual beings was gone, it was like the play button had been pressed again as everyone started to move. The bus driver's eyes grew huge as he noticed the woman and toddler on the road. But the bus had already turned to the right thanks to the unknown man that had turned the wheel moments ago, and the driver slammed on the brakes, screeching onto the sidewalk near the elderly gentleman feeding the birds. The empty coffee cup bounced off the front windshield and rolled to the side while the bus hissed to a stop.

The mother glanced behind her and realized that she had almost met her maker. She jumped, crossed herself, and moved along while her fussy son stopped crying immediately. He sucked on the lollipop that the skittering woman left in his hand.

"Oh no!" wailed a teenager with her group of friends, "I accidentally threw my mother's bracelet away in the trash back there! She's gonna kill me!"

The girl and her friends dashed to the trash can that the Fairy was digging around in. They made faces as they pushed aside hamburger and chip wrappers. "I can't find it!" the girl wailed.

Haven jumped down from the tree while the girls continued to dig. Now that she thought about it, wasn't the Fairy carrying a golden chain? Could it be . . . ? But what would a Fairy do with a lost bracelet?

Fairies? Doorways appearing out of nowhere? Am I going crazy? Haven held her head in her hands, massaging her temples and staring at the ground. There, wedged in the crack of the cement, where the Fairy had been hovering moments ago, was a rolled-up piece of paper.

Slowly, Haven pinched the paper and wriggled it free from its hiding place. Her mouth dropped open. A message written in curly lettering on the edge of a ten dollar bill.

'For the medicine.'

Haven held the money to her chest, the ring pressed into the palm of her other hand.

Could it be, thought Haven, *that those people were helping us? Why would they do that? Where did they come from? How did they know that things were going to happen? Better yet, how come I wasn't frozen?*

She pulled the ring off as a group of older boys passed, gawking at her, probably because of the twigs she could feel had made a home in her hair. Putting the ten dollars in her back pocket, and the ring in her front, Haven ran to the store to get the medicine for Aiden's fever. Before she turned the corner, she heard a young woman speaking to the elderly duck-feeding gentleman, "I'm sorry for being late Grandpa. Forgot where we were meeting!" It wasn't lost on Haven had the young woman been standing next to the elderly gentleman, she would have been hit by the bus.

THE THREE MEN

"Heya Haven, were they frozen like this?" Aiden called as he had just been tagged in freeze tag. He tried to remain still, but Haven saw he couldn't help smiling.

"Sort of," Haven called as she tinkered with a contraption of homemade aqueducts and bowls. "Only they didn't smile. They were frozen like this." Haven made a weird face and Aiden giggled.

Hearing him giggle made Haven's shoulders relax a little. She looked at him as a doctor would inspect her patient. He was still a little pale and thinner than normal, but he looked so much better than the sunken-eyed boy he had been two weeks ago. Haven had spent three days giving him dose after dose of medication. Even now, she pushed down the memory of how weak he had looked—and the memory of how she got the money for the medicine.

"Got you!" Hannalee, a girl knee-high to a grasshopper glee-fully screeched. Her coils of brown hair stuck out wildly around her head.

"No way you touched me!" yelled Finn, a wiry boy with straight ebony hair. "I've got on my invisibility force field!"

"No force fields, Finn!" Hannalee wagged her head back and forth, her hands on her hips. Grasped in her dirt-caked hand was her favorite unicorn, dangling beside her leg. "Besides, it's Freeze Tag and you're frozen so it don't matter if we can see you!"

Finn huffed and crossed his arms, trying to prevent himself from exploding. "Fine!" he said, his face reddened. "If somebody could please tag me to *unfreeze* me? Somebody?"

"Yeah, yeah, I got you, little bro," Fletcher, his twin brother, said, as he dodged Hannalee's attempt at tagging him and rounded a fence pole poking out of the ground. A sign hung from the top that read, 'Haven's Place' which flapped as he passed. Hannalee was quick to follow and grabbed the pole to swing around faster, missing Fletcher by inches.

"Can't catch me, Harmonious Hannalee!"

"Watch me," she replied, shaking her unicorn around. "I'm smarter, and faster, and more beautifuller!" She lunged forward, grazing Fletcher. He zigged out of the way, lost his footing on a plastic tarp, and slid feet first, landing on his back.

Hannalee pounced on her prey, and Fletcher lay in his pretend-frozen state, legs halfway in the air, looking like a puppy on his back waiting for a belly rub.

"I win!" Hannalee said as she bounced up and down, hugging her unicorn tight. "Look, Unie! I'm Queen of Haven's Place!"

"Liora, help us," whined Finn. "You aren't going to hang us out to dry, are ya?"

"Yeah, I am," she replied lazily as she relaxed in the shade against the incline of the mound of trash, braiding a piece of her flaming red hair.

"Oh, come on!" Fletcher joined in. "We need help! Hannalee can't be the queen of us!"

Liora made a mock yawn, "When are you going to learn that girls are better than boys?"

Finn stood up indignantly. "Crazy talk!"

Fletcher agreed. "Yeah, that's bat-crazy talk! Come play with us or we'll make you with our mind control powers."

"Yeah, mind control," Aiden agreed. He squinted his eyes to see if he could actually do it.

Liora rolled *her* eyes and continued to braid, her tall build making it impossible for the boys to move her to do anything, and they knew it.

Haven laughed at them as she continued to tinker. "When I'm done, I'll come play if you want," she said.

"No fair! You're the fastest!" Finn argued.

"Yeah, no tipping the scales cause you're a dame," Fletcher said.

Haven furrowed her brow. "Which movie is that from again?"

"His Girl Friday," Fletcher answered, and kicked part of a plastic bag sticking out of the ground. "Mom watched it on late night TV."

"When are you two ever going to talk normal?" Liora asked as she stretched out her long legs. "Calling a girl a dame is weird."

"It's not weird," Finn muttered as he looked down and stuffed his hands in his pockets.

"Besides, weird people are cool cats, right Haven?" Fletcher added, glancing at his brother.

Haven smiled at the twins. "The coolest."

Both boys grinned at Haven as if someone had given them a store full of candy.

"Whatever," Liora said as she shrugged and picked up another piece of hair to braid.

"Hey," Haven said, "maybe you guys can get Jairus to play."

She nodded towards an older boy who trudged from the forest to the edge of their home in the landfill.

Jarius grunted as he set a scuffed five-gallon plastic bottle on the ground next to Haven. With great care, he looked at the river water inside the bottle, where a tiny dark sphere clicked against the bottom of the container. It was a trade from Twigette's that kept their drinking water clean.

Jairus wiped his forehead with his sleeve, squatted down and inspected Haven's work. "You missed the right screw."

"I'm not done, get outta here," Haven said as she waved him away and continued her work. "Go play freeze tag."

"You're not gonna finish if you don't put the right screw in," Jairus said, trying to conceal a smile.

"Jairus, won'tcha come play?" Hannalee begged. "We get to pick teams and you can be on mine!"

Jairus knocked his head against a wooden pole that jutted from the ground as he looked up. His pale blue eyes almost glowed against his deep olive skin.

Hannalee clasped her miniature hands together and pouted her full lips, "Pul-lease?"

"After I finish helping Haven."

Hannalee cheered while the twins groaned.

"Didn't know you had it in you," Haven teased. "You are usually grumpy with the Youngers."

He stared at Haven while he handed her a wrench, the tool she needed but didn't ask him for. At last, he shook his head and mumbled, "You don't know a lot about me."

Haven nodded and went back to tightening the last bolt of the water sprayer she and Jairus invented together. It was true: Jairus didn't reveal much about himself.

She glanced around at the others who ended up finding this place after she did. Liora, her closest friend, was the first. She was the one to name their home Haven's Place and survived for a year with Haven before more children came. While Haven had been glad to no longer spend the chilly nights alone, Liora could be more cantankerous than an eighty-year-old man.

Hannalee was next and wandered there from the woods. She was unable to speak for the first few months, so it was a while before they found out that her mom was gone and she didn't know her dad.

The twins' mom drank 'too much of the sauce' as they had put it and was unfit to take care of them so they ended up in a foster home. After many nights of being whipped and locked in a closet, they left and took Aiden with them.

No one knew where Jairus came from except that he showed up and never left. He was like a stray cat; you could never be sure if he actually liked you or was just there for the food. The only clue as to what happened before he found them was a deep scar on his forearm that traveled past his sleeve. Who or what caused it, Haven didn't know.

"Finished, Bestie?" Aiden, who had a messy cowlick and missing front tooth, asked as he picked a dead moth out of old cereal. He had given up on Freeze Tag and was up for a snack.

"Yup," she replied. Haven stood up, stretched, and pulled down a wooden lever made from a bedpost. Gallons of water trickled from a metal washing tub to dozens of tubes which sprayed out a fine mist at different times as the Youngers ran screaming in excitement. Jairus ducked under his tent and tossed the wrench into the cracked tool bucket as Haven raised her hands triumphantly.

"Hey, where's the treasure I got you?" Aiden said as he wiped his greasy hands on the soaked superman shirt Haven found for him in the dump days before.

Liora glanced at Haven.

"I, uh," Haven stammered. She couldn't tell the young boy that the ring had been hidden safely in her pocket on purpose.

"Put it on!" he stood in front of her expectantly.

She reached into her pocket and let it slip onto her finger, a move she had perfected over the last several days. Haven had secretly loved wearing the ring that day two weeks ago; it made her feel special. Which was saying something because, as a person whose parents dropped her off at a landfill demanding she should never return home because she was trouble, feeling special wasn't something that usually happened to her.

"Here," she said, as she held out her hand for him to inspect.

He nodded, his cowlick swaying forward and back. "That ring's got superpowers. Now you can go fight crime with me!"

Aiden darted through the hydrating spray, shouting that he was the greatest superhero of all time. Haven followed at a slower pace and plopped down next to Liora.

"Why don't you just keep the ring on? Everyone agreed that we couldn't sell it, and you look at it all the time!"

Haven laughed, "Not *all* the time!"

"Whatever, genius," she nudged her friend. "Like, every five minutes."

Haven hesitated as she twisted the ring around her finger. Should she keep it on? She didn't quite understand how the ring worked. What if time froze again?

"You think time will freeze again?" Liora laughed.

When Haven had told Liora the whole story of what happened, she looked at her like Haven had hallucinated from hunger.

"You still don't believe me?"

"I'll believe it when I see it," Liora quipped.

At that moment, Jairus yelled, "We've got snoopers!" Haven looked up in time to spot a dust cloud rise up from the road just past the edge of the landfill. Jarius threw the water lever off and grabbed his pack.

"It's The Fuzz!" Finn yelled.

The van drove like nothing was going to stop it from reaching where they were.

"They're moving too fast," Jairus glanced around. "Can't outrun them."

"Don't panic," Haven said calmly. "We aren't doing anything wrong. Just hanging out." She looked pointedly at Liora. "We aren't running."

Liora nodded and stood her ground, sweat beading on her forehead. The van reached its destination and three men dressed as security guards exited the van. They left the doors open behind them.

"What are you kids doing out here?" spat one of them—a man whose hair looked like an oil slick slid down the center of his head.

Liora, who was always ready for a fight, clenched her fists and replied, "Just having a campout. It's a great spot for it."

"Ain't you the girl who the police are looking for?" Said a man with dyed blonde hair and freckles that covered his face. It made him look like he was a pop art painting. He pointed at Liora. "Yeah—the murder case," he added.

Liora looked like she would explode, and Haven quickly touched her arm to calm her. "Why do you care about some kids way out here?" She asked through clenched teeth while staring down the blonde, dotted-face man.

"Have several reports that there were a bunch of you living out at the dump. Selling old parts to a junk dealer at Five Points. That wouldn't be you, would it?" Oil-Slick Man flanked the left side of the group. Meanwhile, Jairus and Hannalee inched toward the landfill.

Haven remained calm as she straightened up to look older than she was. Unfortunately, with her small stature and round face, she looked about ten, despite being fourteen. "We do find interesting things out here, sir. Is it a crime to try to make money off of what others throw away?"

A menacing man with spiky gray hair made a beeline for Haven as if he had just been waiting for her to speak. His gruff voice and stubbly, peppered beard made him look like a snow leopard ready to pounce. "I'm sure you do find interesting things. But stealing isn't finding." The overwhelming smell of aftershave and something else—*Was it motor oil?*—surrounded Haven as he leaned close. "We heard that you may have stolen something and tried to sell it."

With a flick of the eye, he spotted her ring. A thin smile grew on his face. Haven shifted her weight as the man continued to smile as he whispered, his spittle flecking her cheek, "Where did you get the ring, girlie?"

"Family heirloom," Haven said calmly. She remembered the excuse Twigette gave Haven when the leathered motorcycle guy wanted it.

"Liar," he whispered.

The man grabbed Haven's wrist, held up her hand. He wrapped his bulky fingers around her small ones and pulled on the ring.

Haven's hand began to shake violently, and so did the man who was hanging on to her like a limp banana peel. A sharp indigo colored electrical current circled the stone and then shot up the man's arm where it blasted him forty feet into the air higher than a school building. When he landed with a heavy thud, he was doused in purple slime that dripped from every part of his body. He was an indigo swamp monster, frozen in time.

"Whoa," whispered Finn. "Remind me not to nick Haven's ring."

"Sketch!" the dotted-faced man screeched. But Sketch couldn't answer because he was frozen in goo.

"Forget him!" the greaseball yelled, seeing his compatriot couldn't move. "Get the garbage rats!" he shouted, and grabbed Aiden who wailed and kicked his little legs. Haven jumped on the greaseball's back but he threw her to the ground, knocking the wind out of her. Liora landed a swift kick to the man's knee. He howled in pain and dropped Aiden. She went in for his nose, but the man pulled out a balisong knife with a blade shaped like the curved bill of a hawk and grabbed Liora's wrist.

She glanced around for help but Haven was still trying to shake off the pounding in her right ear from being thrown.

Just five feet away, Dotted Face held both twins as they struggled under his grip.

"I'mma give you a knuckle sandwich!" Finn yelled.

"Bite him! Biiiite him!" Fletcher hollered.

Both boys went in on his forearm and the man tried to shake them off, but they were like two snapping turtles, latched on for good.

Haven couldn't breathe. Her worst fear was coming true. Her little family—all of them—being taken away from her. With a desperate cry, she shrieked, "Stop!"

Time stood still. This time, however, it wasn't only Haven who stayed unfrozen.

"Get away from me!" Liora hissed, trying to free herself from the greaseball's grasp. She was successful, but not before she saw the frozen look in the man's eyes. "What the—"

"Jeepers!" marveled Finn after he freed himself and turned to the man's face, inches from his own. He sniffed the air. "This guy has bad breath! Did he eat garlic for lunch or what?"

Fletcher joined his brother, leaned in for a sniff and agreed. "Putrid."

Aiden jumped into Haven's arms, not wanting to let go, his body trembling.

"It's okay, Aiden. It'll be alright," Haven said, soothing him.

"Okay, I believe you, Haven!" Liora said, glancing at her friend.

Haven stroked Aiden's hair to calm him and gave Liora and I-told-you-so look. "Not hallucinating are you, Lior?"

"Shut it," Liora quipped as she stood back and surveyed everyone. "Wait, where are Hannalee and Jairus?"

Everyone looked around. In the driver's seat of the van, Jairus sat smiling from ear to ear, and next to him, Hannalee.

"Jairus!" Liora called out. "What, you going to learn how to drive today?"

"Learn?" he shouted out the window. "I've known how to drive since I was seven!" He stepped out of the van. "It won't start even with the keys in the ignition."

"We're gonna rescue you," Hannalee said with a broad smile. "Jairus said that when the meanies put you in the trunk, we'd take off with the van."

Finn strode up to the greaseball, who was in mid wrangle with air, yet frozen like a squishy statue. He puffed and pounded his chest, "Whatcha going to do now, huh, punk?"

"We have to move. We can't stay here," Jairus pointed out, as Hannalee clung to his leg with her unicorn dangling at her side.

Haven took a deep breath and sighed. Jairus was right: they couldn't stay here. But where would they go? She glanced to her right. In the distance, she saw something glimmer.

A circular gateway had opened.

AROUND THE WORLD IN EIGHTY SECONDS

"YOU WANT us to go in *there*?" Jairus asked incredulously. He eyed the floating circle of stone like it was a prison cell.

"Listen, I know it sounds weird but it's the only thing we can do," Haven urged.

"No," he argued. "The woods is an option; they'll never follow us."

"I won't follow you either," Liora glanced at the woods then at the three men in their frozen state. "If we go where Haven wants, there's no way the police can find me. Uh, I mean us."

"You have no idea who lives in there!" Jairus said as he practically flung his arm out toward the gate.

"What I saw a few weeks ago convinced me that kind people do," Haven said. "Think about it, they saved that woman and her baby's life. The bus, remember?"

Jairus stared Haven down with his piercing eyes. "You have too much trust."

Haven stared right back. "You don't have enough. We can't stay here—what happens when those men unfreeze? What happens if more guys like that show up? Besides, aren't you curious what is in there?"

"Not really, no."

"Me!" said Aiden as he slid a cracked flowerpot to Fletcher who waved his arms toward him like the foreman of a construction site.

"Jairus," Hannalee said sweetly as she put dried flowers in Dotted Face's hair. "Don'tcha wanna go someplace new? Unie and I don't like the stinky trash."

Jairus looked at her, the twins, and Aiden. "You're going to drag the Youngers in there?"

"Youngers?" Finn said indignantly as he slid the grease ball man to the right of the van. "Who you calling Youngers?"

"We're old enough to do what we want, and The Boss has got our vote!" Fletcher said as he scrawled something on old cardboard.

Jairus shook his head. Hannalee tiptoed to him furtively and slipped her tiny hand in his rough one. "Jairus, Haven says we're family so we gotta—"

"—stick together," Jairus mumbled. "Yeah, I know." He surveyed the scene. Finn was putting an old bra on the leader of the three men as Aiden was stacking dirty diapers underneath another.

"Fine," Jairus conceded. "But if it gets weird, I'm leaving."

* * *

Beyond the floating gateway, a room waited for them that had a stone floor tinted the color of dark chocolate. Billions of stars dotted the black sky overhead. Circular glass pieces that spread out like massive petals of a flower hung on a far wall with a brilliance of oranges, blues, and purples. Haven ran her fingers along the smooth glass. It was cool to her touch.

In the back of the room, polished gold nameplates were screwed to the stone above openings that lined the wall. Haven adjusted her pack and leaned close to one of the smaller slots to read 'Keys' on the nameplate. Intrigued, she went to the next. 'Glasses,' 'Toys,' 'Homework,' and 'Jewelry.'

"Time restarted." Liora's voice snapped Haven's attention. The gateway opening had spun around until it shrunk and seemed covered with a thick layer of glass, making the wall a large movie screen they could see through.

In the world outside, the play button of time had been pressed again. The Youngers had gone to work on all three of the men. An old bra covered the eyes of the menacing leader, who was still covered in purple slime but now unfrozen. The dotted face man whose hair had been decorated with dead flowers tripped on a mountain of dirty diapers, fell, and ended up with one in his mouth. The greaseball held a sign that read 'I Smell' and when he realized what he was holding, he threw it away in disgust.

"Where'd they go?" he said as he paced in frustration.

Their salt and peppered leader replied, "Job this took we normal weren't they already when."

"What? You ain't making sense, Sketch!" Dotted Face whined.

Sketch moved his mouth around and spoke again, "Speak can't I come how?"

"What in peanut butter's name are you sayin'?"

Sketch shook his head again, and rounded the van, "Keys?"

"I don't have your keys," the greasy man retorted. "Check your pockets."

Sketch began to pat his pants frantically, "Wallet where's my?" He groaned and spoke slowly, "Where. Is. My. Wallet?"

All the children looked at Finn and Fletcher. The twins grinned and Finn held up a leather wallet.

"Sometimes I like you two," Liora whispered.

"Maybe in the van?" suggested Dotted Face.

A wad of trash came flying at his head. "Them look . . . Arghhhh! Look. For. Them. It. Has. The. Shop. Key." He knelt to look on the floorboards.

"But it smells out here, Sketch!"

"Sissy!" the greaseball cackled and wiped his hooked nose as a fly buzzed around it.

"If you don't shut your mouth—"

Sketch pounded the dashboard and yelled, "I'll shut both of your mouths if you don't find those keys!"

"Hey! You're talking' straight now!" Dotted Face clapped his hands.

Another wad of trash came at his head.

"We shouldn't have taken this job!" The greaseball muttered as he moved trash out of the way with part of the cracked flowerpot.

"Took this job?" Haven felt as if her stomach would jump out of her body. "Did someone hire them to kidnap us?"

Jairus and Liora stared at Haven.

"They did seem interested in that ring," Liora said.

Haven glanced down at her ring. Was it her imagination or was there another row of petals that had formed around the stone?

"No, I want to try it, I got here first!" whined Hannalee as Finn grabbed her by the backpack and pulled her to the ground. She grabbed his leg and pulled him right along.

Fletcher had taken that opportunity to try the contraption they were fighting over. He poked his finger at a water-encased sphere that looked like a globe sitting on a pedestal in a rich person's library. The room jumped.

"Whoa!" Aiden said, his mouth agape. He crawled to Haven and grabbed onto her arm.

Haven's mouth matched Aiden. *The room could move!* She clasped her hands together and looked at Fletcher, "Again, but gentle this time."

"Wait, what?" Liora said.

Fletcher nodded, licked his lips, and gently ran his finger over the water, causing a bit of it to splash. The room glided on the earth's surface, and Liora grasped a chair in the corner of the room. Gold plated numbers on the wall clicked softly as they flipped, while the colorful circles below them moved in different directions to reflect the position change.

"Okay, that is enough!" Liora said, turning a light shade of green as she buried her head in her pack.

The room halted near the Town Center, a busy outdoor shopping and dining area of the city. Muted honks, whistles, and people in the busy palm-lined street were overtaken by the sound of metal scraping against stone, which came from the openings at the back of the room. Two pairs of sunglasses, a set of keys, and a wristwatch slid down each chute.

Jairus grabbed the wristwatch and turned it over in his hands. "These aren't cheap," he said.

"Not yours," Haven answered gruffly.

"Sure, Mom," Jairus rolled his eyes but replaced the watch where he found it.

"And Finn, don't think I forgot about the wallet," Haven turned to the twins, "We have to return it at some point."

"Got it, boss!" Finn said. By this time, he had squirmed out of Hannalee's grip and wrested control over the sphere. He jerked his whole finger over the glowing water encased orb so fast, everyone was pasted to the right side of the room, hanging on for dear life. Images of cities passed by. At one point Fletcher yelled, "I'm losing my lunch!"

After a speedy trip over an ocean, the room came to rest in the countryside. Vineyards spread out far—farther even than their own landfill—and beyond the glass, they could see families enjoying the early afternoon sun of a late spring day.

A pair of pruning shears, a very old book written in a different language, and a locket slid down the stone chutes after the wristwatch and other earlier items fell through a discard shaft below.

"Why do these things keep showing up?" Liora asked as she pulled herself up by the slot openings.

"They are lost things that will be returned to their owners."

Everyone whipped around to stare at the stout middle-aged man with a black curly beard, deep brown eyes, and full cheeks as he casually leaned against a doorframe. Underneath his mustard tweed overcoat, he wore a shirt with a picture of a sail-boat on it and the words: 'Sailing's The Life.' Black and green striped suspenders held up the baggy purple jeans which he had stuffed into his combat boots.

"I come back to shut my room down and find it full of chil-dren! My job got infinitely more interesting today!" he scratched his furry beard.

Nobody moved.

He cleared his throat, "We help people by placing these items where they can be found at the right moment. Timing is everything, you know," he said as he patted Liora's shoulder. She stiffened and slightly moved away from him.

Haven spoke up, "Please sir, we don't want trouble. We didn't steal anything, well, except for a creepy guy's wallet. But it was only because he was really terrible to us. We tried to get away, and time just sort of froze I think because of this ring Aiden found and . . . "

The man's eyebrows raised so high that they looked like fuzzy black caterpillars trying to climb a shiny mountain, "That is a special treasure you have, young lady."

"I didn't steal it, I promise," she said in earnest. Haven began to take off the ring, "Here I can return it—"

"No, the Indigo is yours!" he backed up as if she were trying to give him a nest of angry yellow jackets. "*Please* do not give it to anyone else."

Haven furrowed her brow at the odd reaction. It was the same as Twigette's at the shop a few weeks ago. Was there something wrong with her? Or . . . with the ring?

A woman with short, maroon-tipped ebony hair tromped down steps that had appeared behind the man. Her business suit was crisp and pinstriped. "Eutychus, the reports I received of a missing building—"

"We have guests, Charity," Eutychus said as he took the papers in her hand as if everything were business as usual.

Charity's shining dark eyes grew wide; stunned by the unexpected guests. "Skeevers to heaven! I mean, look at this . . . Otherworld children in our workroom. Isn't it the oddest thing, Eutychus? They look like they are carrying everything they own! And how thin! You need a good meal. Hasn't anyone fed you? Oh, you poor things!" Charity cried as she bounced into the room and hugged Finn and Fletcher.

"Lady microbes!" Fletcher said, trying to squirm out of the rotund woman's grasp.

She kept her smothering hold on the two. "All of you have dirt-stained faces! And your clothes don't even fit you! Has no one has taken care of these babies? Where are your parents?"

Aiden approached the curvy woman who had the twins in such a squeeze that both of them had given up and were letting their feet and arms dangle from the woman's grasp. "We don't have mamas or daddies."

"We don't need 'em!" Finn said in a muffled voice and kicked his legs in a last-ditch effort.

"Jumping Junipers! How have you seven survived? Where do you live?"

"Haven's Place, in the trash," Hannalee said, her unicorn pointed toward Haven.

Charity glanced at Haven, and her eyes traveled down to the ring. "Bushy Bobbins!" She dropped the twins and tripped over Jairus in the process, "Sorry, young man. It's just—I just—"

"Don't want to be blasted back like one of the kidnappers?" Fletcher said, rubbing his elbows after being dropped.

"Kidnappers?" Eutychus raised his voice.

"Uh huh," Hannalee said. "Three meanie guys, right Unie?"

"Yeah, they tried to get the five-finger discount on that ring," Fletcher said.

"Five-finger what?" Eutychus whispered to Haven.

"He means they tried to steal it. Finn and Fletcher learned English by watching old reruns on late night television. Their parents weren't around much," she answered him.

"Haven blasted him!" Aiden shouted, pumping his fist in the air.

Eutychus cleared his throat. "Yes, anyone who tries to steal one of our rings will get a nasty shock. Indigo slime with electricity I presume?"

Haven smiled, remembering the way Sketch looked shocked in mid-air, "Yeah. Something I definitely didn't expect."

Eutychus looked at every child. "Do you have anywhere else to go?"

"Yes," Jairus said. "If you can drop us off at the woods, I can take care of us."

"By yourself?" Charity fanned her face rapidly.

"No, Jairus!" Liora yelled. "We can't go back to the woods. Who knows what they'll do if those guys find us."

"Stop freaking out, Liora. No one will turn you in." Jairus matched her tone.

Charity and Eutychus exchanged glances.

Eutychus cleared his throat, "Why don't you stay with my family for a bit, until you can get your next move sorted out? Anyone up for crispy fried chicken with mashed potatoes and a bit of buttered rolls?"

Finn and Fletcher jumped to their feet and shook his hand. "I'm Fletcher," said the oldest twin enthusiastically.

"And I'm Finn. Do you have lumpia?"

Laughing merrily, "I bet we can scrounge up something of the sort."

Aiden stepped timidly to the older man, "Mr. U-t-kus?"

"Yes, little one?"

"Can I have chocolate cake?"

Eutychus's merry eyes danced with the reflection of orange light of the nearest glass circle. "Of course!"

Haven's insides seemed to vibrate with an energy she didn't know she had. Liora shrugged her shoulders in approval and the Youngers were all clustered around Eutychus and Charity. Jairus was the only one left to convince.

"Listen," she whispered to him as the twins peppered Eutychus with food questions. "Let's at least get some food. We've worked for years to get that, and here is this guy who seems so kind . . . "

Jairus turned to look at her. "I don't want to rely on people we don't know for food. We can figure out another solution, Haven."

Haven sighed. "Look—you and I are always good at figuring stuff out together, but when we do, we use what is in front of us. Right now, this is the only thing in front of us. Let's try it and see what happens."

Jairus eyed Eutychus then Charity who were working on flipping switches and turning lights off. "Strange people," he said to himself. "You sure you want to do this?"

"Have I ever steered you wrong?" Haven smiled.

"The marshmallow popper."

"Besides that. Plus, you put out the fire, so it worked out. Come on! We may need you to protect us if a dragon tries to eat us," Haven added, poked him in the ribs as he hid a half-smile.

"Protect you, huh? I think you can protect yourself, Haven."

"Maybe, but it wouldn't hurt to have backup."

"We are laying our hat down?" the twins asked Haven. She nodded.

"But we can leave anytime we want right?" Jairus asked Eutychus.

"Goodness gracious you are not prisoners!" Eutychus chortled.

Charity giggled and shook her head as though the idea was completely absurd. "We love you Otherworlds, and serve your kind daily! We would never . . . " She giggled again.

Eutychus gently put a hand on Charity's shoulder. "My family will host our guests and you notify the Council. They will want to know about the Indigo's reappearance."

Charity swallowed, her giggles disappeared. She put a hand to her upper arm where a silver cuff inlaid with the pattern of a rose encircled her bicep. At the center of the cuff was an opaque stone. When she pressed the stone with her palm, a whirring noise filled the room, and great wings attached to tiny gears spread from her back.

Hannalee jumped up and down with excitement and Jairus' eyes grew wide in disbelief. Charity smiled and twisted the stone to the right. Instantly she shrunk to be the size of a humming-bird and hovered in mid-air.

"A tiny Superman!" Aiden gasped.

"I want one!" the twins begged. "Please, please, please?"

Eutychus bellowed with laughter. "Charity is a wingless Fairy, you have to go through rigorous training from the Fairy Federacy to allow one of those contraptions!"

"I'll make hoppity-haste to the council!" Charity yelled in her little Fairy voice as she zoomed around the twins who tried to catch her like a butterfly. "The council will know about the Indigo! You can count on me!" and she disappeared up the stone steps.

Eutychus slapped his hands together. "I do imagine you have an interesting story in how you got the Indigo, er—Haven, is it?"

"Yes, sir."

He held out his hand to shake hers. "Eutychus," he said and then chuckled. "I'm one of the workers of this room, 450A68. Seen lots of good stuff happen in this room. Lots of good stuff."

"Uh, sir? Am I in trouble? For this ring I mean?"

Then he bellowed a hearty laugh, "Oh, dear girl, no! Though you arriving with the Indigo is certainly a surprise. Come now, let's get you fed."

Aiden tugged the man's sleeve and Eutychus bent down so the boy could hang onto him. The boy's tiny arms wrapped around the man's thick neck as if he had known him all his life. As they ascended the stairs, Aiden whispered to Haven, "I think this is Santa Claus' brother."

04:00:17

THE SERVING DISH

"Welcome to Time Server City, the city that serves!" Euty-chus spread his hands out as if introducing an old friend.

Haven's eyes adjusted to the bright sunshine as the scent of vanilla and coffee teased her nose. A cobblestone street lined with thatched roof buildings bustled with people. They moved hastily out of circular gateways and into the traffic flow of others in the street. They all wore overcoats that whipped around them, especially when one person dodged another moving too fast. It reminded Haven of I95 during rush hour as people cut in front of each other, merging into traffic. Only here, people didn't seem to mind as much.

"Vote for keys?" Jairus mumbled as he squinted his eyes.

Haven followed Jairus' gaze. 'Vote for keys,' 'Coughing is good for the Soul,' 'Dog Surfer on Board,' or 'Broccoli Cupcakes are Divine!' Slogans as far as Haven could see were printed on shirts, hats, pants, and shoes. Almost everyone in this place wore something with a saying on it. She laughed at the last slogan. Aiden hated broccoli. Come to think of it, had she not been hungry she may have passed on the tiny little trees too.

"Oh ho! That is a Time Server's favorite thing! To wear clothing with statement!" Eutychus said dramatically.

"I'm gonna be a Slime Server!" Aiden said, pumping his tiny fist in the air.

Finn snorted as he patted Aiden's shoulder.

"Time Server, little Aides!" Fletcher said. "It's a . . . what in blazes is it?"

Eutychus smiled. "*I'm* a Time Server," he said. "We are named as such because we serve your kind in seconds of time on the clock. Time. Servers."

"A Unicorn! Look! A Unicorn!" Hannalee squealed as she bounded across the street pulling her own unicorn doll out of her pack.

"Look, Unie! It is your brother!" she held the knitted doll to the living unicorn's face for an introduction.

"Be careful," Eutychus called. "Unicorns aren't the type to be friendly."

Hannalee stood next to the muscular beast as it turned its head upward as if Hannalee stunk. Jairus jogged over to stand by her, as though ready to be her shield.

"Don't you want to meet your friend?" Hannalee asked imploringly.

The Unicorn moved so Hannalee was talking to its rump.

"Huh!" Hannalee said in shock. "You need a time out!" She stomped away, leaving Jairus to stare eye-to-eye with the creature. The beast stood powerful, not moving an inch.

Jairus glared at it. "You know, I have no problem making a Unicorn coat."

The Unicorn whinnied and sidestepped until its lead was taut while Jairus stood his ground.

"What the—?" Liora yelled as a Fairy dressed in a business suit flew by her, barely missing the tip of her nose.

"Those Fairies are fast, they are!" Eutychus nodded to two

more flying the other way. "They sure are great at finding and replacing lost things."

Haven remembered the Fairy placing money for her at the small crack at the base of her hiding tree. As she looked around, her heart felt full of excitement. A few minutes ago, they were fighting for their lives, and now it seemed as if the play button had been pressed on a totally different movie. One that included Fairies. Which was kind of weird but still pretty amazing.

"Are they good?" Aiden asked. "Do they give wishes?"

Eutychus roared with laughter. "Oh, my dear boy, your innocence makes me think of my youngest. No wishes from Fairies; that is just a story that has caught on over the years. Actually, they wouldn't be called good or bad, you would call them—fair. Watch the Giant!"

An extremely tall person with orange hair and leather pants skated through the crowd on a board supported by bubbles. He almost ran over the twins, but Jairus pulled them both out of the way.

"Always in a hurry to get someplace on those newfangled inventions. Bubble boards, they call them. My son has one of those," said Eutychus.

"So, uh, how much is he looking to get for it?" Finn asked, craning his neck to look.

A corner flower shop with buckets of pansies and peonies had passersby stopping to trade their items for bunches of their choosing. Watching a trade that involved a pair of shoes but no money, Haven continued to walk and almost ran into the back of a Time Server that had gathered in a crowd. At the center, a nine-foot-tall man made of pure crystal whose face was streaked with yellow and black rifled through a coat, pulling out gadgets and crushing them with his massive foot.

"Stay here," Eutychus whispered, as he set Aiden down and pushed through the crowd. "Edmundo!" he called to the Time

Server whose coat looked like it was being shredded by the crystal bully. "What happened?"

"This," the man said, waving his arms wildly, "ruffian *Sentinel* states that I am smuggling Otherworld artifacts!"

"Nonsense!" Eutychus said through gritted teeth. "He would never do such a thing. Why are you terrorizing us, Schorl?"

"Not your business, tiny man," Schorl said in a gravelly voice. He threw the coat down in tatters and pushed Eutychus and Edmundo to the side, crushing a pair of flamingo sunglasses under his foot. The crowd parted immediately for the crystal man, whose sharp, ebony elbow shards stuck out every which way as he strode down the street towards another Time Server.

Eutychus dusted off the tattered coat, Edmundo picked up his glasses which were mere slivers of pink plastic, and the crowd dispersed.

"The Head R&M Sentinel, Schorl," whispered Eutychus, gesturing to the children to keep walking. "He likes to rough up Time Servers. Their leader, the Magma King, lives beyond those mountains. Has a nasty temper but a heart of gold, if you can believe it!"

"R&M?" Haven asked, her heart pounding. The crystal man and his sudden burst of violence scared her to death. It was all way too similar to their encounter with kidnappers only an hour ago.

"Rock and Mineral. The Clock Watcher uses them in Time Server City for protection. More than we like, I will say."

"Who is the Clock Watcher and why would he need protection?" Jairus asked suspiciously.

Eutychus glanced at Haven's ring and then cleared his throat. "Erm . . . there was a war several years ago. He wants to make sure everyone is safe."

"Huh," Jairus huffed. He looked at Haven pointedly as if saying, *I told you this place wasn't safe*, and then moved past her.

"Scary bullies," Aiden muttered as Eutychus picked him back up.

Haven agreed and looked back in the direction of the Sentinel when someone else caught her eye. A girl, no more than fourteen, yet taller than an average man, stared at Haven. Her green hair spiked in all directions, and her nose piercing danced in rhythm when her deep purple lips moved as she chewed her gum. Haven returned the stare, the girl popped her bubble, brought the gum back into her mouth and allowed a crooked smile to grow. The way the smile continued, Haven thought she looked like a cat that swallowed a mouse. She turned away and shuddered.

"What's wrong with you?" Liora asked.

"It's just that girl back there. The one with the green hair."

Liora glanced back, "What girl?"

Haven looked in the direction of where the girl had stood moments before. But the girl was gone.

* * *

"We are now entering my village," Eutychus announced as they stood under an entrance with intricate lettering labeled, 'North America East.'

"This is where my family lives. He pointed to another large entrance to the left, "That is the North America West Village."

Peering through the ornate entrance that had fragrant honeysuckle growing along its sides, Haven could see that the buildings in North America West were a conglomerate of warm wooden cabins, adobe covered houses with rock gardens, and surf shacks painted bright blues and pinks. This was a stark contrast to the English cottages with flower box windows and houses with rocking-chair porches of the East Village.

They passed through the entrance of the East Village which

was framed in two oak trees draped in Spanish moss, and walked a short way. At the end of the farthest dusty road lay the Hubble house. Eutychus stomped to the door, slapped his hand on a worn sign that read, 'Hubble House — All Welcome!' and smiled. He disappeared into the house only to return a moment later. Every child, including Aiden, who had slid out of Eutychus' arms, paused outside.

"Come in, then. No one is going to hurt you!"

"That's just it, sir, none of us have been in a *house* for a long time. Last time most of us were in a house —" Haven broke off looking at the others who glanced down. "Let's just say whatever happened caused us to leave it."

Tears welled up in the man's eyes and he took out a silver sparkled handkerchief and blew his nose with a loud honk. He paused a moment to think. "Hmmm. How about a picnic outside? I'll get my —"

"Ahem," someone from the front gate cleared their throat. Haven turned around to see an older boy in a midnight blue trench coat leaning against the post with a bright green bubble board underneath his arm. "I see you picked up a few things before coming home."

"Asher!" Eutychus' broad smile filled his face as he turned to Haven and the group. "This is my oldest son, he is in training to be a Time Server."

The boy grinned. "Hey."

Haven blushed as the two locked eyes, his brown ones sparkling with mischief. She felt oddly aware of herself—and of his broad shoulders and tight curly hair. But as he took two steps toward her, a large tearing of fabric sounded, and Asher halted.

"Your coat again?" Eutychus asked.

Asher sighed. "Yeah."

Jairus snorted and shifted his pack.

Eutychus laughed. "I'll sew it up. Three times he's done this. Always with his coat!"

"At least I can be predictable," Asher winked at Haven as he passed her, a piece of his coattail hanging to the side. Meanwhile, Haven was trying not to sweat through the armpits of her shirt.

"Did you finish with Ottokar's Viewing room?" Eutychus asked.

"Yes, sir. It's clean and ready to go," Asher said.

"You and Levi didn't take it for a spin, did you?"

"Uh . . ." Asher paused. "Define spin."

"Ah, my son, you are becoming more like me every day."

A woman wearing a full skirt covered in tiny embroidered carrots came from the back of the house with her arms full of pansies, humming to herself. A small boy munching on berries clung to the hem of her skirt.

"Merry, dear—"

"Oh, Eutychus!" she started, accidentally throwing the flowers in the air. They landed everywhere as if she were in a parade. A few stuck to her platinum-plaited hair at odd angles. "I wasn't expecting you until the sun passed the ridge!" She paused and stared at the children as if seeing them for the first time. "Otherworlds?"

"Visitors in my viewing room. Mind if we host them for a picnic?"

"I—" she said, looking flabbergasted. "Of—of course! Let me get our best place settings!" She picked up the toddler and rushed inside.

"Uh oh, now we've done it!" Asher said, leaning his board against the house. "She is going to bring out the swan plates."

"Swan plates?" Liora asked.

"Fancy plates that have been passed down from her family for years," Eutychus chuckled.

Asher whispered to Haven and Liora, "Really large and really gaudy."

* * *

THE PLATES WERE heavy and cream-colored, with ornate carvings of large swans circling the edge. They weren't just gaudy; they were hideous. And they were placed in the center of their blanket on the downy grass.

As the group sat in a wide circle watching Merry fuss over each child's place setting, Haven wondered who was doing the cooking. Not once did Merry bring out food. She was more concerned with each child getting the very best of her family's plates. After polishing the beak of Aiden's dinner plate, the hostess sat down and looked at each child expectantly.

"Um," Liora said as she shifted her legs and glanced at Haven.

"We don't have any food," Haven exchanged looks with Jairus.

"I'll go into those woods and hunt some," he said, grabbing his pack. Asher laughed at this as Jairus scowled.

Eutychus held up his hands with a twinkle in his eye. "Just wait, it's coming." He nodded to the sky.

They glanced up as if waiting for rain. Instead, a large picnic basket fell at lightning speed. It slowed at roof level of the Hubble's house and floated down to the doorstep, landing with a quiet thud.

"Dinner is here!" Eutychus announced, clapping with glee as he watched each child's mouth open to the size of a large lollipop. "Come now! Don't tell me you haven't had food delivered like that?"

Platters of fried chicken, two large serving bowls of piping hot mashed potatoes, and rolls loaded with butter were passed around. Every kind of food the children asked for was packed neatly inside: chocolate cake for Aiden, a large platter of lumpia. The twins cried with relief as they grabbed lumpia and shoved it in their mouths, the crispy roll wrappers flaking off on their chins.

"Look, Haven, no bugs!" Aiden mumbled as he crammed a fistful of cake into his mouth.

"Unie, you eat too!" Hannalee said, as she fed her stuffed Unicorn a strawberry.

"Guys!" Haven's cheeks turned red as she glanced at the Hubbles and their empty plates. Suddenly she realized they hadn't served themselves yet because everyone else was taking all the food. "Everyone needs to have their food before you ravage your own!"

Fletcher plopped his head in his hand while Finn stuffed a lumpia in his mouth. The Hubbles filled their plates quickly as Aiden continued to lick his fingers.

"Let us give a moment of thanks for our food," Eutychus said. The Hubbles all began to sing a sweet song that, as Haven listened, reminded her of Christmas—something she wished she could have back.

After the song ended, the Hubbles settled in and stared at the children with smiles.

"Now?" Fletcher said impatiently.

"Alr—"

But it was too late. The twins, Aiden, Hannalee, and Liora dove into the food as if eating for the first time.

"Want the potatoes?" Asher asked as he handed them to Finn. "Whoops!"

He accidentally dropped the bowl so half of the mashed potatoes ended up on Fletcher.

"Bonus snack!" he yelled as Finn began to scoop some off of his brother's knee.

"They're hungry, mama!" The toddler whispered to Merry.

"It's okay, J.J.," she whispered back.

"It's been awhile since we've seen this much food at once," Haven explained as she gingerly picked up a roll on her plate.

"In that case, I would eat as much as I could too," Eutychus agreed. He took a piece of fried chicken from the platter, and bit into it, letting the crumbles of the crust fall to his beard.

Jairus dug in but kept an eye on Asher, who kept giving the twins whatever food they pointed to.

After Haven saw everyone was eating, she allowed herself to relax. The salt of the butter mixed with the soft texture of the warm roll was a delicacy she couldn't remember eating. By the time she had opened her eyes upon finishing, two more were on her plate. Merry smiled at her.

"Thank you," Haven said with the second roll in her mouth.

"You looked like you wanted more." Merry said, patting her hand.

As the children filled their bellies, Eutychus sang songs about dragons who happily found their roller-skates, Fairies who traded their hats for treasure, and shoelaces that wouldn't stay tied.

When the feeding frenzy died down, Aiden rested his head on Haven's lap as Merry and Asher brought the dishes inside. J.J. stretched out on his father's great belly, with his little arms and legs hanging on each side as the man gently rubbed the boy's back.

"You say this little one found the ring at the landfill?" Eutychus asked after Haven told their story, ignoring the warning look Jairus gave her. Asher plopped down on the grass, and Jairus moved a few feet away from him, spitting at the ground.

"Aiden is always giving me gifts," Haven answered.

"A sweet-natured boy I can see."

Aiden answered with a soft snore.

"Eutychus, dear," Merry's voice called from the house. "Charity sent word that the council would like to see the children tomorrow at ten after changeover."

Jairus, Haven, and Liora glanced at each other in alarm. Eutychus assured them, "I know you three are used to running, but this is not a place to run from. The Council of World Servers is made up of wise Time Servers that lead our villages and will make sure your group is protected."

Haven nervously looked down at the ring she wore. "What about this?" She asked. "No one seems to want to get near me when they realize I have it on."

He patted her shoulder. "Once they see how fiercely loyal you are to helping people, their fears will disappear," he said. The man sighed and looked up at the sky, which now was turning a fiery orange and red. "Changeover is soon, a new day begins," he added, absentmindedly.

"That's my cue." Asher stood and kicked up his bubble board. "Gotta join Levi at the clocktower. It's our night to complete Seminar CW."

"Don't give that Clockwatcher too many compliments!" Eutychus chuckled.

"We have to appease his huge ego, Dad. How else will I learn how the clocktower works if he doesn't think we truly are interested in his magnanimous presence?"

Eutychus chuckled at this.

"What a kiss up—" Jairus mumbled as Haven elbowed him.

"Alright, son, see you tomorrow and don't let Levi talk you into jumping off the clock tower again. You nearly sent your mother to the Star People!"

Asher laughed, nodded to the new guests, and said gazing up at the sky, "Don't miss your first changeover. The colors are brilliant." He shoved his hands in his deep blue trench coat, the back flap still hanging haphazardly, hopped on his bubble board, and glided down the lane.

Everyone followed his gaze and looked at the sky, which changed from a deep orange with views of pink clouds to a midnight blue almost hidden by the mass of brilliant stars.

A moment later, Merry carried a toppling pile of blankets and pillows from the house.

"Who are these for?" Liora asked.

"Merry is worried we might be cold." Eutychus said as he looked at his wife knowingly.

"Oh, but we can take care—"

"I can see that you are self-sufficient but you are our guests and if you are staying out here, so are we. Besides, it has been a bit since I actually slept outside under the starry sky. Maybe I will get to talk to one of the Star People!"

Eutychus chuckled and whispered to Haven as Merry fussed with her own blankets. "She is not much of an outdoor camper."

Haven let out a sleepy giggle and watched as Merry, who muttered something to herself about bean bag chairs and hammocks, flattened six blankets, one on top of the other until she was satisfied that her pallet was comfortable enough. It was odd to see an adult wanting to sleep around them, usually no one wanted to even be near. Haven figured it was because of the stench.

Jairus sat against his pack, his arms rested on his knees.

"You staying up?" Haven asked him quietly.

"We don't know if it is safe."

Haven paused and took in the scene. Lanterns glowed a warm light where Merry laid them. Eutychus and J.J. were snuggled together. The twins, Hannalee, and Aiden were piled together like bears hibernating for the winter, and Liora was already sleep-fighting to her right. She felt safe here, not like

Haven's Place. There was something inside of her saying it was okay.

"I trust them," Haven whispered. She slipped into her sleeping space. The beautiful ring glinted in the moonlight. It had grown another row of petals on the dahlia that held the indigo stone at its center. Before Haven could form the thought of surprise, her eyelids fluttered closed.

"You trust too much, Haven," Jairus whispered back.

"YOU ARE NOT IN TROUBLE," said Eutychus. "You have done nothing wrong, and The Council of World Servers should not accuse you of anything. Morning, Cricket!"

A man with a crooked flower pot for a hat nodded towards the group. They were moving swiftly through the center of Time Server City amidst the crowds who were shopping in the main center.

Any sleepiness Haven had felt upon waking up outdoors had disappeared as she listened to Eutychus with wide eyes. *Accuse them of what?*

"But just in case someone does try to accuse you," Eutychus hesitated as they entered a building. "I would not worry. There is nothing hidden that will not be made known."

"What does that mean?" Liora asked, looking at Jairus who rolled his eyes.

"It means we better have our guard up," Jairus muttered to Liora.

They strode through a mahogany-paneled hallway that

opened to an arena about three stories high. *An appropriate place to be devoured by lions*, Haven thought.

A grandfather of a man with gray hair, a thick handlebar mustache that outgrew his face, and a plaid overcoat with golden ropes like a military general met them at the entrance and took Eutychus' hand.

"Eutychus! Bringing us the surprise of the day, I think!"

"Otokar, my old mentor." The men embraced and slapped each other on the back. "These are the children that arrived in my workroom."

"Dobré ráno," Otokar spoke in a thick Czech accent, and shook their hands.

Hannalee giggled.

"Let me introduce," Otokar said as he moved deeper into the room. The children followed.

"Council member in charge," he said as he bowed with respect towards a woman barely visible behind four stacks of paper that almost reached the ceiling.

"Joyceline," she said. The council member held out her hand as she made her way to the center of the floor. Her black high heeled shoes clicked with each step. "But people call me Joy. Nice to meet all of you."

"Can we have a lollipop?" asked Finn. He had wandered over to a large glass fishbowl filled with a rainbow of lollipops. An elderly man hobbled towards Finn and tapped the boy's feet with his cane. "Those are mine, youngin'."

Joy laughed. "Vidor, you can share." She turned back to the children. "All of you may have as many as you would like. Don't mind Vidor; he is the retired council leader. He likes to fill his time *trying* to keep the rest of us in order." Vidor shot Joy a glowering look and crossed his arms like he was two years old.

Joy leaned in and whispered to Haven and Liora, "The

lollipops are actually very healthy for you. An innovation of the Giants. They are geniuses!"

"Of course they are," Liora said dryly and reached into the massive lollipop bowl while Vidor fought with Finn and Fletcher over who was first in line.

Haven tried not to sweat out of nervousness, but her brow glistened. She glanced around the room and saw three other council members sitting in the far reaches of the seats. One wore furry headphones and knitted a pattern of llamas on a hat with flaps. Yards of yarn wrapped around her as if in a cocoon. Two others were involved in a board game upon a leather pad with a circle of shells and coins. All looked like they could be her grandparents.

"Haven, I know we look intimidating." Joy put a warm hand on Haven's shoulder as she gestured to the other council members. "However, we are here to help. Will you do us the honor of telling your story?"

Haven tried to keep herself together even if she felt shaky. "Sure? I mean . . . sure," she replied.

"COUNCIL MEETING IN SESSION!" Joy bellowed.

Vidor stopped mid-wrangle with the twins and hobbled to the nearest chair, grumbling about lollipops. The knitting lady took off her headphones and laid down her knitting needles. The game playing pair glanced up, set down the die they were rolling, and focused on Haven.

"Make yourself at home on the couch, dears," Joy said as she made her way back to her desk, her heels clicking on the floor.

Otokar gave a curt nod. "The truth is always best."

Haven wondered why he may have thought lying was an option for her.

As they settled on a deep red leather couch with ornate legs, the couch rotated towards the direction of Joy's seat. Silence filled the room.

"Now, then," Joy said in a soothing tone. "Before you begin, we want to impress upon you seven how welcome you are in Time Server City. It isn't a normal occurrence to have visitors such as yourselves, but as it is the fabric of our society to serve, we feel it is best to serve you by allowing you to stay if you wish."

"Get to the good part, lady!" Vidor yelled, waving his lollipopped fist in the air.

Joy folded her hands and leaned forward. "We are most intrigued by your appearance, and would love to hear more of how you acquired—" she looked down at Haven's ring, "—such a rare thing from our world."

Haven motioned toward the Youngers. "We didn't steal it."

"No, no! I wouldn't think you did!" Joy smiled reassuringly.

"She might have." Vidor narrowed his eyes at Haven. "Those Otherworlds can be tricky tricksters if you don't watch 'em!"

As the younger children were happily sucking on their lollipops, Liora looked up at the ceiling, and Jairus leaned back on the couch. Haven took a deep breath and launched into the story. In the end, silence filled the room again.

She glanced at Eutychus who cleared his throat. He nodded his head and his full cheeks puffed out even more in a fatherly smile. A faint slurping of the lollipops was the only evidence of someone moving.

Finally, a voice broke the silence. "Carolina, representative of the Americas' South Villages," the woman introduced herself.

Immediately the couch rotated to face her. The twins, Aiden, and Hannalee let out a squeal of delight, while Liora held her stomach and moaned.

"The Indigo was found in the trash?" she asked.

Haven merely nodded, then added, "Um, yes Miss Carolina, Aiden found it. He gave it to me."

"It was her prize," Aiden added, licking sticky goodness off his fist.

"No one gives these to anyone," Vidor growled as he held up his hand and showed his own ring. "These are passed down from family."

"Yes," Otokar said. Liora heaved and covered her mouth as the couch rotated again. "However, there was none of this passing down; it was lost."

"Lost things come back to their owners," a round-faced man said quietly as he took a couple of coins and turned them slowly on the table.

Then his playing partner, a woman who wore a dhuku knotted in a flower at the top, nudged him. "Oh yes, Yeshe, representative for Villages of Asia Province." He bowed.

"Yes, true. However, as we know from the Fairies, some lost things choose to stay lost," Joy said.

Yeshe's playing partner spoke up. "Asha, representative of Villages of Africa." She looked gently at Haven to study her reaction. "Are *you* lost, Haven?" She asked her as she smiled. Asha's smile made Haven feel like she was wrapped in a warm hug by a grandmother to her long-lost grand-daughter.

"I . . . no, my parents left me at the landfill. They told me not to come back. That I was too much."

Asha furrowed her brow.

"Haven, may I inspect the Indigo about which we are speaking?" Joy asked.

Haven nodded, standing up to take it off but Joy jumped up, knocking off a precarious pile of papers that had taken residence on her desk. "No, dear! I am not asking for it!"

Haven exchanged looks with Jairus.

Joy sidestepped the other two desks that held the unending paperwork and reached the marble steps taking each one as her heels would allow.

"Let me see, dear." Joy took Haven's hand gently and peered

through a monocle for a closer look. Haven noticed another row of petals had grown around the base of the dahlia.

"Hmm," Joy uttered, tapping her finger to her lips. "The Indigo has grown quite attached to you. And that dahlia! Intricate and filled with beauty." She looked up and smiled. "This shows that there are many good things about you, Haven."

"So, the jewelry is like a fortune teller?" Liora snorted.

"Each grows on its owner," Joy said, ignoring Liora's snark and smiling at her instead. "What is produced on the ring, as you call it, is the fruit of the person's life thus far. Look at my Emerald, sweet dears, and tell me what you see." Joy moved closer.

They gathered around her delicate hand and saw that Joy had a rose gold ring with an emerald green stone and hydrangeas on one side with bunny rabbits around the band.

"Now look at Eutychus' Sapphire."

Obediently, Eutychus stuck out his trunk of a hand and they saw a bright blue sapphire stone. The thick platinum band was decorated with an oak tree whose roots wrapped around it.

"The ring shows the fruit of a person's life so far. Oak trees, animals, flowers, these are all beautiful things that symbolize a person's personality. And each family has their own stone color." Joy looked back down at Haven's ring. "Indigo. That is a color Time Servers do not see anymore."

Looking around the room at the other elders, Joy sighed. "Children, we must have total honesty between us, and we believe you have fulfilled this. In turn, we should tell you the history of the Indigo and why . . ." Joy paused before going on. ". . . no one wants it."

"Many years ago, there was a powerful Time Server whose vision for time serving became twisted. Seeing how our lives were dictated by serving a race that didn't know our presence made him angry, selfish, and joyless.

"The Indigo was matchless in power and since he had it, he

planned to destroy all life in your world to free us from this so-called slavery. Anyone who got in his way disappeared, including his own family. Fortunately, he was captured before he fully succeeded but not before many Time Servers, Fairies, and Giants were killed."

Asha spoke up in a deep timbre. "His family and their Indigos were desecrated at his own hands and there were none left. All except for his. When he was captured, he didn't have it on. Using the best innovations from the Giants, for *years* we searched, yet we couldn't find it."

"How it has found and grown on you, an Otherworld, we do not understand," Yeshe said before moving a few of the shells in front of him.

"It has been linked to much evil and is dangerous to have—as you learned from the miscreant kidnappers," Otokar said, smoothing his mustache.

"Diaper eaters," Aiden whispered, licking his sticky hands.

"Diaper eaters!" Finn and Fletcher howled. "Good one, little Aide!"

Haven stood up, wiping the sweat from her hands. "I—I can give it to someone." She looked around with hope in her eyes. "Is there anyone that would keep it?"

Carolina gasped and dropped her skein of yarn to the floor and Joy gently covered Haven's hand with her own. "No Time Server would ever willingly take the Indigo, sweet girl. Because of its power, the Indigo can bring danger to the one who wears it. The wrong people could murder you and your friends for it, or worse." Carolina looked at Asha and Yeshe who nodded. "You could be put in Magma Prison."

"I think murder is pretty final though," Liora massaged her forehead as Haven clutched her own stomach. She felt like she was going to puke from nervousness.

"Yes, many people want this ring for its powers," Carolina

added, "and it is said that the person who wears it can be . . . cursed."

"Cursed?" Jairus stood up. "What the . . . ? Haven, I knew—"

"Hold on, Jairus! Here. You guys can have it so it can be destroyed. Problem solved." She tried to take the ring off, but it wouldn't budge. "Huh. I can't."

Joy nodded, "Once it grows on you, it can never be taken off unless you have passed it on to a willing person that will carry the burden, have gone to be with the Star People—which means you have left this world—or . . . you are frozen alive in Magma Prison and it slips off of your finger."

"Cool!" Finn said.

"Not cool!" Liora said. "That's not cool at all. Where was the warning on that thing?"

"It would seem," Yeshe said as he rubbed his hands together in thought, "that the Indigo is a burden *Haven* must bear."

Haven's stomach turned and her heart pounded, "There has to be another way. I didn't know when I put it on that I would be cursed. That someone would murder me or my friends for it. That I could be frozen forever. Who does that to someone?"

"If no one finds out about Haven wearing it, can't we go back to the woods? I've lived there for years; no one would find us." Jairus said.

"Anyone in our world can slip into a second of your time and find you," Joy said. "The word has already spread that the Indigo is here."

"Now your enemies will be more than those three scoundrels," Otokar scowled.

"Why?" Haven asked. "Why would my enemies be more than those three guys?"

No one in the room said a word. Even the twins paused crunching on their lollipops.

Joy sighed. "The Indigo's original wearer—we don't believe

that all of his followers have been captured. Even though we have devoted a task force to find them, there might be some in hiding. And when they hear that Haven is wearing it, her life—all of your lives—will most certainly be in danger."

"Wait," Haven said. "When those men came after us, the Indigo protected us. I mean, kind of. Wouldn't it protect us if someone else meant us—or it—harm?"

"Yeah, that one dude turned into a purple frozen goo monster!" Finn said in between licks of his third lollipop.

Eutychus shook his head and clenched his fists. "Those men didn't know about the Indigo's powers. Nincompoops."

Asha spoke up again, her voice soothing the room like a lullaby. "Yes, Haven. Those that truly understand its powers understand the rules of garnering the Indigo. A willing burden-carrier, death, or Magma Prison."

All of the adult Time Servers shuddered at the mention of Magma Prison, which freaked Haven out. *Wouldn't death be worse?*

"Wait a second. Are you saying then Haven can't leave?" Jairus stood up quickly.

"Oh, my little papito! We don't want you to leave, we love having you children with us! But more than this, if the Indigo falls into the wrong hands—" Carolina's voice trailed off as she clasped her own hands, as if to hide the shaking.

"Great," Liora grumbled. "Another protect-us-or-we'll-die story. I've heard enough of those to last forever. And can we get this couch to stop moving every time someone speaks?"

"So, she can't take this ring off—"

"The Indigo," interrupted Carolina. "We call these by their rightful name, the stone that gives them the power."

Jairus rolled his eyes. "The Indigo. Fine. Whatever. She can't take it off or give it away . . . "

"Okay, what *are* my options?" Haven asked, trying to calm herself and Jairus down. If she got him to think of solutions, hopefully that would change his focus. Because he looked like he was going to pummel the candy bowl as he began to pace back and forth.

"This is a quandary," Otokar agreed.

"The girl should be offered training to learn how to use it," Carolina found her voice.

"Wait, what?" Haven said.

"She has shown great traits. Selfless. Loyal. Brave. This may be a symbol of a new season," Asha said.

"New season? I don't know—" Haven tried to get their attention.

"Perhaps," Yeshe suggested, "she should shadow Eutychus, as an apprentice. She did enter this world through his viewing room. That is a sign."

"Whatcha mean?" said the unruly wrinkled man in the front. "You mean just let an Otherworld follow Euty— Euty—," he started a coughing fit that ended with his right leg stiff in the air. "—Eutychus around, traipsing all over the world and let her in on our secrets?"

Otokar looked over. "Vidor, you know this is her duty."

"Ah, these crazy youngins think they know more than me! When I was Lead Council member—" but the group didn't find out what happened when he was the lead council member, for a hacking fit took over the man, complete with fists waving. "Lollipop. I need a lollipop!" he gasped.

Sighing, Joy stood, went to the lollipop bowl which was close enough that Vidor could have reached it himself, and handed him a green one.

"Blue. I said blue, woman!"

She gently dropped the green one and replaced it with a blue one.

"Ahhh, pure Happiness!"

Joy shook her head and smiled, then turned to the rest of the council members. "So, are we agreed then? Haven will be offered training with Eutychus to learn our ways so she learns to use the Indigo's power safely."

"I agree," Yeshe said.

"I, too." Asha stood.

"Três." Carolina stood.

Otokar stood alongside Asha and nodded. "She will be safe."

"This is a great honor to bestow on an Otherworld," Joy warned. "As much as we serve your race, we have never had one train with us. If you decide to do this, realize you are the first."

The weight of those words sat on Haven's chest.

Jairus had been bent over studying the ground in thought. "What happened to the guy who went homicidal? Is he alive?"

Joy glared at Jairus, as though annoyed. "He resides frozen in a prison guarded by the Magma King's R&M Sentinels, a fate worse than death. There, you are ever seeing, ever hearing, but unable to move, eat, or talk. The suffering is great, and you are always alone."

Haven took a deep breath to steady herself. As much as she loved adventures, having the Indigo was more than she asked for and she felt like she may jump out of her skin. She had been in tough spots before, but every time she tried to give herself a pep talk, she felt like she wanted to shrivel in a corner like a withered plant.

"If I train to use the Indigo, will we be safe in Time Server City?"

"Wait a minute. We didn't say we would stay—" Jairus said as he stood up.

"What choice do I have, Jairus?" Haven shot back. "Think about it. I have to learn to use this thing or else we're toast. It's the only solution right now."

He sat back down and ran his hand over his face.

Eutychus spoke softly. "Merry and I have agreed to host you as long as you want to remain here."

"Haven is right," Liora sighed. "Until she can learn to use the *Indigo*," she said sarcastically, "let's just stay."

"We're family, Jairus," Hannalee said. "we have to—"

"—stick together," the twins and Aiden chimed in.

Joy concluded, "Okay! That is it then. I'll report everything we discussed to the Choice Maker. Including the diaper eaters." This made the boys laugh even harder.

"The C.O.W.S. meeting is concluded!" Joy said as the twins snickered.

"Cows, get it?" asked Finn to Hannalee and Aiden. The four began to giggle as they made small mooing sounds.

Otokar stood up and grinned. "It will be my duty to show the Museum of Time to these tiny Otherworlds. They should know about our history."

"More secrets! You're letting them know more secrets, you crazy mustachioed man!" Vidor waved his half-eaten lollipop at Otokar.

"Si, that is a grand idea," Carolina agreed. "The Museum of Time."

"You have time to decide if you would like to train, Haven," Asha said. "But know wearing the Indigo can be a great . . . " she glanced at Yeshe, "blessing."

Joy added with a genuine smile towards the children. "In the meantime, let's show our guests what a haven really means."

HAVEN FELT SICK. Not the kind of sick that got you out of class early but the kind that bubbles up from your stomach to your throat in one-point-five-seconds. She looked down at the Indigo on her finger. Two intertwined stems wrapped around her finger and another row of petals encircled the stone.

Joy's words came to her mind, *". . . when they hear that Haven is wearing it, her life—all of your lives—will most certainly be in danger."*

"So, you afraid yet?"

Haven jumped as Asher appeared beside her, gliding along on his neon green bubble board.

"Nah, she looks like the brave type," a teenage boy behind him chimed in as he made a wide circle in front of them on his board, which was painted in blue and purple stripes. The new boy's hair covered his eyes like a sheepdog and he wore an impish grin. "I'm Levi," he called.

"Haven," she said, and nodded as Asher cruised on his board beside her quick steps. Every part of her skin seemed to tingle while he was inches from her.

"They didn't scare you with the *the Indigo-is-dangerous-and-*

will-destroy-the-world talk, did they?" Asher laughed as they continued their trek to the museum. Everyone else walked ahead to give Haven some space. Haven thought they must know she felt ready to throw up.

"They did tell me the story of the crazy guy who had it before." She tried to act as if it didn't bother her, even though it very much did.

"The council just does that so you don't do anything dumb," Asher said, reassuringly. "With everything I heard you went through, you're not the dumb type."

Haven blushed. Why did her face keep heating up this way? It was as if Asher had the power to make her act like a total noob. *Keep it together, Haven!*

"Yeah, besides," Levi added, as he did a loop with a trail of bubbles following behind him, "you're the one wearing the Indigo, and since you're smart, using its power would be super gnarly."

"Aren't you supposed to be off cleaning something?" Jairus asked as he stopped walking and stood in between Haven and Asher.

"Levi wanted to meet you guys," Asher said, flipping his board up. Unfortunately, he kicked it too hard and it bumped him in the nose.

Jairus rolled his eyes. "What a—" he muttered.

"Yeah, I didn't believe Otherworlds were actually here." Levi popped his board up, caught it perfectly, and mumbled, "Plus, it was only training discussion with Mr. Furgert. Boring stuff."

"Levi! Asher!" Otokar bellowed as he turned around. "You two should be in discussion class."

"Uh, we came to help out, Uncle Otokar!" Levi said, flashing a smile as they neared Otokar.

"This is good thinking!" Otokar slapped Levi on the back.

"My grand nephew! It is an honor for him to be thinking right things!"

"As long as they weren't trying to find out what the council decided," Eutychus winked at the two boys, who both looked at the ground.

Otokar cleared his throat. "Listen, tiny Otherworlds." He paused in front of a magnificent curved building inlaid with stone carvings of Giants, Mermaids, Time Servers, and Fairies. "Museum of Time will answer all questions about our world. You must promise not to do this revealing to anyone."

Liora muttered, "No one would believe us anyway."

"Good," Otokar spoke curtly. "Follow."

Haven began to make her way up the stone steps when Asher stopped her. "Come on, Haven! Enter from the fun entrance on the side."

Haven giggled.

Why am I acting like I'm ten? She tried to keep her cool, but it was like some force had taken over her body in these moments.

A large granite wall, etched with the words 'Entrance of Entertainment,' stood before them. Otokar lay his hand upon it and spoke, "Otokar, Village: Europe, Central." He paused and turned back quickly as if remembering. "Guests included."

Immediately, the bottom of the wall lifted like a curtain and revealed a smooth silver-toned roller coaster.

"Holy Moly!" Finn gasped.

"Back is the best on a roller coaster, little bro. Go there!" Fletcher called.

Asher grabbed Haven's hand. "Come on, powerful Indigo wearer," he grinned. "You and I are here!"

It was like she was hyperventilating and giggling at the same time. Haven had never held a boy's hand before—at least not a boy older than eight. She looked down at Asher's thick fingers, almost like a younger version of Eutychus' hand. His grip was soft and warm and she wanted to hold his hand forever. Only it would probably get awkward when she would have to eat and stuff.

"Ladies first," he said to her as she slid in the coaster car. Much to Haven's disappointment, he let go of her hand as soon as she sat down.

"Jairus, sit with Unie and me," Hannalee said as she dragged him to the center of the coaster. Jairus went, while he eyed Asher and Haven.

"Get ready to go!" Eutychus sang to Aiden who snuggled in next to him.

"Wait! Where are the safety belts?" Liora asked, searching frantically for anything to hold onto as the car started to move.

Eutychus turned around from his seat, "No need for those! This is hardened neodymium. It is a magnet that will hold you tight!"

"And boy does it!" yelled Levi who was standing on the front of the car, surfer-style, much to the awe of the twins whose rapt attention made it clear they had found a new hero.

The coaster entered a dark globe bigger than a dome football stadium. Twinkling lights dotted the walls and made Haven feel like she was soaring in space. She swore she could see planets as they zoomed past them. Haven wanted to reach out her hand. They were so close, she could almost touch the colorful globes.

The coaster picked up speed and leaned slightly to the left, the force causing Haven to grab onto Asher's shirt.

"Are you worried, Haven?" Asher said. "'Cause you shouldn't be! No one is trying to kill you—yet." He squeezed her hand. "Have fun and raise your hands, like this!"

Haven nodded, took a deep breath, slowly released Asher's shirt, and lifted her hands. A wild yell from the twins echoed through the dark cavern of the coaster house. They rose to the height of the ceiling, then dropped, causing their hair to fly up.

A smile crept across Haven's face as she leaned towards Asher. She felt exhilarated, and a laugh escaped her lips. A warm feeling of happiness filled her chest as the coaster twirled and looped. For a moment she had no worries of getting food, being kidnapped, and weird ring curses. In that coaster with her hair flying up on end, and her body feeling like it was floating in space, she felt what she had longed for many times. A chance to be a kid.

With a final whoosh, their roller coaster stopped in an entrance hall large enough to stack twenty school buses end to end. Beige marble columns which framed each museum section —three in total— with dark tan streaks rose to the ceiling. A circular desk stood at the center under large dinosaur bones hanging precariously overhead.

"Well now, we must go here more often!" said Eutychus patting down his beard. "This coaster ride changes every time."

"Atta girl," Asher said in Haven's ear as he stepped out of the car.

Haven tried to hide her smile, but it was too late as it had already spread across her face. Asher looked back at her. Unfortunately, the coaster line barrier was right in front of him and he tripped and fell, face-first, into part of the dinosaur bones.

"Oh!" Haven reached out as if to catch him. Asher stood up, dusted his board off and smiled sheepishly.

The twins jumped out of the coaster whooping, "One more time!"

"No way, you two!" Liora said, still holding on to the car she had just gotten out of.

"Greatest ride ever, Bestie! Did you like it?" Aiden grinned. Then, lowering his voice he whispered, "I think Liora was scared, her screams were too loud." Haven muffled a laugh.

"A Time Server's History," Otokar said as he motioned for the group to follow him. "This will prove helpful."

"Boys, boards up," Eutychus whispered. "Last time it took weeks to clean the ruckus you two caused."

Asher shrugged his shoulders and grinned at Levi while they propped their boards against the entrance wall.

"Hey, look at the threads on this old lady!" Finn called, pointing to a stone statue.

The statue turned toward Finn and in a haughty voice, she said, "Young man, it would be to your benefit to educate yourself in the art of manners!" She glided away as if her stone skirt had wheels on it.

Eutychus returned a nod as she passed him, hers more formal than his, and chuckled. He said under his breath to Finn: "Museum Curator. She has surprised me like that once."

"What a wet rag," Fletcher said, shaking his head.

They walked into a small theatre. The smell of oil lamps greeted them and Otokar motioned for them to sit on the cushioned chairs of all different shapes and sizes spread throughout the space. Each chair faced the enormous movie screen at the front of the room.

"If only we had some popcorn," Haven joked to Liora. At that, silver bowls of popcorn dropped from the ceiling onto each person's lap. Drinks flew up from the arms of each chair, and a candy stand appeared from behind a wall.

"Cool, Haven! Now ask for a billion dollars!" said Finn.

Eutychus whispered to Otokar. They both eyed Haven.

"The Indigo does have unusual powers, no?" Otokar said as he smoothed his mustache.

As everyone munched on their movie treats, the room darkened, and the movie screen flickered until the clicks of the reel-to-reel movie projector found its rhythm. A deep voice boomed from every corner of the theater. "The history of the Time Server is as old as time itself. An advanced race that was here since the beginning of time learned that serving others selflessly gave them purpose. But serving their own was not enough. They began to look for other races to help. Enter the Otherworlds."

A man on a black and white screen reached into his pouch to retrieve a sling bullet and found it empty. A bear drew near to swipe at him, and in an instant, a perfect stone appeared in his sling. The man grasped and threw it, knocking the bear between the eyes.

"They devised a way in which they could enter the Otherworld at a specific second to change outcomes."

Another scene flashed on the screen. Time Servers entered a frozen city from a viewing room. "It has helped millions of Otherworlds in their lives, contributing to the well-being of their existence, and our own."

Liora snorted and Otokar hushed her. "Sor—ry," she muttered sarcastically.

"The Fearless Fairies. Merry Merpeople and Genius Giants, who were saved from extinction in the other world by the Time Servers, willingly joined their ranks to serve. The Fairies with their knack of finding lost things—" A Fairy placed a watch on a bedside table. "Giants whose genius surpasses any creature in the world—" A large lab filled with lanky Giants in black lab coats worked on complicated contraptions "—and Merpeople who help us in our oceanic division," A merman and a Time Server high-fived each other, "—have helped the operation immensely. It has now grown more streamlined than ever."

"Oh man, this is ridiculous," Jairus muttered. Asher narrowed his eyes at him.

"The Time Servers have had a rich history with Otherworlds. It has been our pleasure to serve them since time began."

The film went dark and the lights rose. Aiden clapped and the twins whistled and threw popcorn in the air as everyone stood and filed out of the theater.

"Imma meet the Fairies!" Hannalee jumped off the chair. "Jairus, you gonna come with me?"

"Uh." He rubbed the back of his neck.

"I bet Charity can introduce you," said Asher. Hannalee grabbed his knees and hugged him as he almost toppled over.

"This seems like creepy propaganda to me," Liora whispered to Haven as the theater doors closed behind them. "Serve the Otherworlds? Like we are some alien race."

"Well, it does seem different," Haven said slowly.

"Different doesn't cut it," Jairus whispered. "They help us so they can get joy? While what—stealing our stuff? What are they *really* getting from this? Nobody does something for nothing."

Haven looked at Liora and Jairus. While they both tended to see the negative in any situation, each did have a point. What were the Time Servers' real reason for helping? It was true that when she helped others it made her feel good, but to give your whole life to people that didn't even know you were out there? That definitely was weird.

She paused as she took in the walls that led out of the history section. Each one had an entire photo plastered on the wall from ceiling to floor, depicting massive destruction of buildings and people rioting. A grandfatherly Time Server leading the charge caught her eye. He wore a black overcoat and had his fist in the air. She could see the Indigo—the one she was wearing now—on his finger. The only difference was instead of a dahlia on the indigo, a weeping willow tree surrounded the stone and something like a tiny bird nestled at the base.

Fletcher read out loud from the plaque beside the photo: "—Nahum the Time Server used the Indigo to start a war which would span not only Time Server City but the Otherworld. It is known that he was responsible for hundreds of disappearances, using the Indigo as the source of his power."

All the children looked at Haven, then at the Indigo.

"You're not gonna disappear us with that are you?" Hannalee asked, wide-eyed.

"'Cause if you do, send us to Tahiti!" Finn added.

"Yeah, make sure you send us to a gig where we can eat whatever and don't have to take baths," Fletcher added.

Haven knelt down to Hannalee. "I'm not gonna do anything like this crazy guy did. Remember, I'm always looking out for you."

"Yeah, Haven is our superhero!" Aiden swung on Haven's neck and then toppled to the ground.

Hannalee nodded and wiped her nose. "Unie and I don't want to be scared of you, Haven. We like you."

Haven smiled and hugged her, hoping to soothe Hannalee. But if she were honest, she felt scared herself. Seeing the reaction of the Youngers toward her was the opposite of what she was used to. Haven didn't want to be the bad guy. She was the good one. She helped those kids find a home, she scrounged for food for each of them while many times she went without. Haven looked down at the ring that made her grimy finger look more feminine and wondered if the Indigo somehow made her into some evil person. *That older Time Server looked like he was kind. Maybe it took over your brain somehow.*

"Let us travel to Fairy exhibit." Otokar directed the group across the hall. The boys groaned and Hannalee squealed with delight.

"Ooooo, look at the giant trees!" She exclaimed as the others followed her into a forest. There were banyan trees with roots that made wooden waves on the ground, oaks trees with Spanish moss that draped like an old woman's fancy nightgown, prickly palms that leaned to accommodate the ceiling, redwoods whose trunks were wider than a house, and one lonely weeping willow at the center that had cushions underneath.

Haven stayed behind and squinted at the picture of Nahum

and his followers. Nahum had a white beard, pointed nose, and chubby cheeks like a cheery elf. *He didn't look too scary. Why did he do such terrible things?*

Eutychus stepped behind her and laid a gentle hand on Haven's shoulder. "You are not the same as this man."

She turned around and looked at him. "What—what do you mean?"

"I mean that every person is different. Don't let the past of the Indigo define you."

Haven smiled weakly and tried not to look behind her, for she felt like the picture of Nahum was staring at her as she walked out of the room. It was as if he were begging for her to come back so he could tell her the dark secrets he knew.

"I'm keys! I'm keys!" Finn shouted as he climbed the ladder to the topmost oversized mail slot that mimicked the ones in the viewing rooms.

"Go ape! I'll be glasses," Fletcher said as he climbed the opposite side.

They both nestled into their spots and looked around expectantly, perched just like lost items Time Servers dealt with every day.

"Aw man, it's all show and no go!"

"Use your voice!" Levi laughed and then spoke to the wall. "Fast ride to the first."

Both boys disappeared as chutes opened beneath them. Haven could hear their screams of delight echo through the whole museum as they slid four stories to the Giant's exhibit. She peeked her head over the balcony rail to be sure they were safe. Finn tried to stand up but couldn't get his balance, and Fletcher's hair had static cling that caused it to stand straight up.

"Do we have to go down those things?" Liora asked. "Aren't there stairs?"

"You scared of a little thrill?" Levi poked fun towards Liora.

"You have no idea what fear is," she pushed him aside.

"Sassy," he said to Asher. "I like it." He winked at his friend, jumped over the railing, landed on a dinosaur's head, and climbed down the spine until he reached the first floor.

"Does he always do crazy stuff?" asked Haven.

"Always," laughed Asher. "Come on, try a slot. It isn't bad."

"Maybe she shouldn't," Jairus said, stepping in front of Haven.

"It's safe . . . enough," Asher said grinning at Haven.

"We're not interested in 'safe enough'," Jairus spat. "Why don't you run along to those chutes, and help Daddy with the others?"

Asher stood his ground, his cheeks flushed, "Nah, I think I'll stay with Haven for a while. It looks like she needs a friend who doesn't attack her every time she makes a decision."

Jairus threw down his pack while Asher clenched his fists. Haven pushed both of them away from each other, "I'm going down one of the chutes."

Haven cautiously slipped into a bottom oversized slot labeled Homework. "How about something light and easy for the ride?"

Instantly the chute opened, and Haven twirled like a falling leaf. Liora must have forgotten to tell the chute to go easy because when she emerged from the bottom, her hair looked like scrunchies were stuck inside. Haven raised her eyebrows and Liora answered, "Gotta be specific. I asked for stairs and I guess it sounded like hair. I went through a beauty salon."

The girls turned and bright pink goo hit Liora in the face, knocking her down. Haven turned her head and ducked as another shot of pink goo came full force at her. Fletcher's mad laughter and Finn's whooping gave Haven an idea of who was behind it.

"Run, Lior!" Haven yelled.

Liora took a handful of pink goo, threw it at the twins and

hit one of them in the eye. She then did a dive roll behind a huge rampart made of bamboo.

"I didn't know you could do all that!" Haven said incredulously. "That was so cool!"

"Just watch the goo!" Liora yelled.

In the center was a giant bow and arrow with self-loading arrows. Haven peeked her head around the corner and saw that they had unwittingly stepped into an arena that was divided into four different sections: Giants, Time Servers, Merpeople, and Fairies. Finn and Fletcher were in the section labeled Giant's Pinky Gloop Gun, and from their perch they tried to spray anyone who came into view. Right now, Haven and Liora were their targets.

Haven jumped onto the platform labeled "Fairies." She landed right next to a huge cannon-style gun. Running her hands over the smooth surface, she found the trigger and aimed it at the twins. Huge flowers came out of the end of the gun.

"Really?" Liora asked as she jumped up next to Haven. "Flowers?"

"It was the closest weapon I could find! Maybe if the flowers shot out fast enough—"

Suddenly flowers came out with such force that they piled onto Finn and Fletcher's rampart. Over and over more flowers came out until the boys were overwhelmed and fell off one side of their platform.

"Fairy Flower is the winner!" an announcement could be heard overhead.

"Wait, is that us?" Haven asked looking around.

"Haven! Haven!" Aiden and Hannalee chanted.

"Yeah, how did you get those flowers to come out that fast?" Levi asked. "Everyone knows the Fairy section had the worst shooting range. You must have done something."

"Just pulled the trigger!" Haven said as she tried to get the pink gloop off of her arms. Otokar stared at Haven from the top of the balcony.

Eutychus laughed, "Come, walk through the Insta-Clean to get the pinky gloop off. Boys?"

"Not on your life!" Finn and Fletcher yelled and took off in the exhibit.

Haven laughed. "The twins like their grime."

"Indeed," Eutychus chuckled. "Come you two, just step through and you will be clean in seconds."

They stepped through two silver panels, which instantly cleaned the girls from their years of grime at the dump. Liora's hair shone as if each hair strand was orange and bronze. Haven took a piece of her own hair and felt how soft it was.

"The Giants are great Innovators," Eutychus said as they glanced around the exhibit.

Haven looked around at the hundreds of innovations that lined the walls. She saw Jairus leaning over to study one in particular and walked over.

"Disguise-O-Meter," she read, standing behind him. "That sounds interesting."

Jairus remained silent, studying the description.

"Hey, while we're here maybe you could study some of these. You're the one that comes up with all of our innovations, you can get some ideas."

"All I'm interested in doing is trying to get us outta here. Don't tie me down," said Jairus sharply.

"You don't have to be here," Haven bristled. "I'm the only one that can't take off the Indigo."

"If you had listened to me and hunted in the woods for food, Aiden wouldn't have found that ring in the trash. You don't listen to me."

"Hey, we were surviving just fine before you came along. You complain so much about my decisions, why do you even stay?" Haven shot back.

Jairus looked hard into her eyes, held her gaze, and then walked past her, knocking off the case label for the Disguise-O-Meter.

* * *

LATER THAT EVENING after a full dinner of pot roast, green beans, biscuits, and ice-cream, Jairus stripped large branches near the woods while Liora and Haven busied themselves putting the finishing touches on their shanties. The four youngest of Haven's crew played freeze tag under a sky that was changing from a brilliant yellow to a deep red.

The back door was open and Haven could hear Merry washing the dishes and chatting with Eutychus, who genuinely seemed to enjoy his wife's company. It had taken Merry some time to accept that the children wanted shanties and not to stay inside, but now she sounded relaxed. The dimly lit house and the warm laughter that tinkled through the early evening air gave Haven a fresh hope for what lay ahead.

Haven and Liora patted green foam Eutychus had sprayed on the outside of their shacks to keep the wind out, "Do you think it's weird that I am wearing the Indigo? I mean, I'm wearing something that caused people to disappear—"

"Okay if you are going to an I'm-afraid-of-this-ring spiral, I'm outta here. No piece of jewelry should ever make people that scared; it's a waste of time. Forget about the homicidal maniac who had it before."

The girls fell silent as they stepped back to inspect their work. Merry had given them fresh blankets piled high inside their wooden lean-to; their lavender scent permeated the air. Eutychus had made each of them a sign that swung jauntily side-to-side that had their names engraved on it. Asher tried to nail them in, but he had hit his thumb instead, so Haven finished the work.

Aiden ran to Haven and pressed three more flowers into her palm that he had plucked from the back garden. "It's for you, Bestie! The greatest superhero ever!" He ran to the others and laughed at Finn who was swinging from a tree like an ape.

"You know, this feels like the safest place for us to be right now," Liora said as she opened a door made from half of a hamper Merry gave them. "Away from . . . things," she paused as a dark look came over her face.

Haven knew where Liora's thoughts were going and she had to change the subject fast. "Where else can we live where food falls from the sky?"

Liora glanced up, the shadow changing into normalcy again, "That would have been great if we had that at our old place. Remember the weeks we went having to eat something with mold on it?"

"Yeah, remember the crate we found that was filled with rotting cabbage? We smelled like that for weeks!"

"You said we could try to eat it boiled!" Liora laughed.

"Yeah, that was a mistake!" Haven agreed. "But we were so *hungry*, I thought we could at least *try*."

Both girls laughed and then fell silent.

Haven traced the Indigo in thought. "I am just trying to do what is right for us."

Liora eyed her friend and pursed her lips. "I never found you normal, caring about everyone. Be selfish for a change!"

"It's just the way I'm wired, I guess. You guys are the only family I've got, and I don't want to lose any of you. It's hard to be alone."

Liora rolled her eyes, "Geez, you're so scared about that. You're not gonna lose us. We stick together."

"With the Indigo and training . . . I mean, I know they are strange giving their lives to serve us but, it would be great to learn how they use these."

"After years of surviving with you, I've learned to trust your instinct, Haven. What does your gut tell you?" Liora inquired.

Haven hesitated for a moment and studied Liora in the fading sunset, "I'm supposed to train."

"Then you should—and don't whine about it."

FIRST TRAINING

AFTER CHOOSING the fresh clothes Merry insisted she take, Haven stepped out of her hut wearing embroidered jeans with silver thread, a long shirt that said, 'Smooches Are Special' and a matching purple jacket with pockets on the sleeves.

The yard was in the shadow of early dawn but Haven wiped her sweaty palms on her pants and glanced around for her shoes. "Have you seen my—"

"Your old shoes are gone, Haven." Eutychus said as he beamed brightly and stood next to the lanterns hanging from the oak tree.

"Eutychus traded them for these!" Merry said as she pulled out a pair of sparkly black converse high tops.

Haven's eyes widened.

"It is a present for your first day of training!"

Haven silently moved to the older couple.

Eutychus glanced at Merry and then back at Haven. "Erm . . . You will have a lot of jumping and running to do today."

"Yes, the old shoes you had would have earned sore feet," Merry explained further.

Eutychus shifted his weight. "The shoes will automatically fit anyone; they are a Giant's innovation."

"You look upset dear," Merry cooed. "We could try to get your shoes back . . . "

Haven stood in front of them, blinking back tears. She picked up the sparkly shoes and felt the untouched rubber soles with her palms. *They are perfect.*

"Thank you," she croaked. "I don't remember ever having anything . . . new."

The Hubble parents embraced her with such warmth that Haven felt strong enough to blink away her tears for good. Eutychus began to blubber and Merry blew her nose with a handkerchief.

"Ahem," someone cleared their throat. All looked up and saw Asher leaning against the oak tree. "Now that we have had our warm and fuzzy family moment, are you two ready to go? Charity is waiting for us."

"Listen," Haven said. She gathered her breath as she looked back on the row of shanties glistening in the light of early dawn. "While I am away, I just want to make sure—"

"They will be fine," Merry comforted Haven. "Liora and Jairus seem to have everyone taken care of."

Haven nodded, knowing there was no truer statement.

* * *

"Is this beautiful young lady ready to take on the power of the Indigo?" Edmundo asked as Eutychus, Asher, and Haven met him in front of the Book Exchangery at the City Circle. He twirled Haven and dipped her. His ruffled shirtsleeves and shorty shorts made him look as if he were going to dance in a parade.

"I think she is more than capable, my friend," Eutychus said as Edmundo let Haven go.

"Yes, yes, my dear Edumundie-Pooh," Charity, who dressed in a sharp business suit, giggled. "Haven is a sweetie; the Indigo will be super safe with her. We'll teach her how to use it and—"

Schorl, the R&M Sentinel, stepped in front of them, causing Charity to fall backward as Edmundo caught her. The Sentinel grunted and peered down at the group, his eyes squinting into tiny slits when he saw Haven.

"Otherworld with The Indigo." His glossy black eyes traveled up and down Haven as he crossed his heavy arms. The needle-like canary yellow and black crystals stuck out at odd angles from his forearms like a hybrid cactus-wasp. Even though this guy was terrifying, Haven stood her ground and smiled sweetly. She still felt strong from earlier that day and wasn't going to let Schorl ruin it. Maybe it was the shoes.

"Leave her alone, Rock Man," Asher said, pushing past him and hovering above the sidewalk on his bubble board.

"Get off, tiny boy." Schorl raised his massive, spiked crystal hand, stabbing at the air around Asher's face. A few swipes and he pushed him back. Asher fell to the ground, his board flipping up and landing on his lap.

Eutychus jumped in front of Schorl, and tried to punch the creature, but came up with bruised knuckles instead. "I should sic my mini Gloopie Gun on you!"

Schorl shot his massive hand out to stop Eutychus, who was still trying to punch every part of Schorl. The crystal man leaned down to the Time Server's face. The movement made the needle crystals on him rub against each other, generating a light tinkling sound. "Your time is coming, old man."

"Old man?!" Eutychus flung his fists even more wildly as Edmundo and Charity pushed him back. Schorl sneered but

stood aside as the group moved down the street. Eutychus sputtered and spat until he could take a couple breaths.

"Don't let this barbarian ruin your joy!" Edmundo smoothed
down a ruffle on his left arm. "These creatures think they are better
than you, but in truth, it is you, my friend, who is better than him!"

"Horrific, horrid, Rock Brain! Up, up, up, Asher!" Charity
said, pulling the boy up by his elbows.

"Geez, Dad, you going to fight all of the R&M Sentinels?
You pick a fight with one, and the rest come after you."

"I am not afraid of these Sentinels," Eutychus replied. "I
could fight a hundred, especially if they pick on my friend here."
He patted Haven's shoulder and she smiled.

Haven knew that anyone who had the courage to stand up to
a creature double their height is a person worth learning from.

* * *

THE WATER ENCASED orb at the center of viewing room 450A68
glowed as Asher fiddled with the switches beneath.

Eutychus pulled a notation book out of his jacket, lay his
hand upon it, and recited, "Today's a good day to serve." He then
opened the book and thumbed through the pages with Charity
looking over his shoulder.

"Gigglety Gypers, it looks like a busy day," she said excitedly.
"Two weddings, that will be fun. I need to grab the lost ring
from the grate . . . oh and look, a dog will be returned home."
Charity sighed. "I really enjoy this job."

Noticing Haven staring at them, Eutychus cleared his throat,
"The Sapphire helps us to see the list we must accomplish for
today. Without these," he held his hand up and wriggled his
ringed finger. "We wouldn't know what to do. Try it and see."

Haven lay her hand on the notation book and recited as

Eutychus did, "Today's a good day to serve." Instantly, coordinates appeared on the pages as if an invisible hand was writing them down:

(37.208279, -77.399621) 03:47:36 Put the dog in his kennel

(36.924062, -76.007581) 14:23:59 Buckle right shoe of Wedding attendant in bright pink dress, smooth bride's hair with Insta-stick, fasten rings to the pillow. (Bride's ring is in the grate below ring bearer.)

As Haven read each item on the list, a picture of what needed to be done appeared on the pages, as if someone had hand-drawn each one. She saw a shaggy dog hiding behind the garbage cans, shivering from a night out of his kennel. She saw the bridesmaid's unbuckled shoe that would cause her to trip and knock the entire wedding party over, and the ring that was caught in the slots of the grate.

Eutychus leaned over and sucked in a breath. "My, Haven, I have never seen that before! Usually, the description is enough, but you talked the book into giving pictures down to the detail! Well done!" Eutychus handed the book to Asher. "Here, son, let's start with this. The coordinates, if you please."

Asher glanced down at the book, raised his eyebrows, glanced at Haven, and shook his head as he hid a half smile. He slowly slid his finger over the water of the orb, causing the room to glide as if on the water itself. As the room moved, the numbers above the large circular crystal pieces on the wall clicked along while the circles rotated as if joining the game. He kept his eyes on them, steering.

"Wall of Direction," Eutychus said, patting the wall next to the crystal display. "Each one of these crystal circles helps us to find exact spots on the earth. Almost exact." He whispered to her with a grin, "Helps us not stop right in the middle of an ocean."

"I did it once, and he never lets me forget!" Asher rolled his eyes as Eutychus chuckled.

"Son—?" Eutychus said, pointing to the screen.

Haven glanced over and saw they were in a snowy mountain range.

"Oh, er, right," Asher laughed. "I mixed the two and the four. Whoops. Let me fix that."

He slid his hand over to the right and they moved quickly over the deep of the ocean. Suddenly, the land was encased in a deep blue with the city lights twinkling as they slipped silently through city streets.

"Cool, isn't it?" said Asher. "This entire world, full of people, full of possibilities?"

Haven continued to stare at the large movie screen as they moved at lightning speed, making it seem like they were surfing through tiny stars. "I wish I knew of all the possibilities when I lived at Haven's Place."

"There's no looking back, Haven. You're here now," Asher said, smiling at her.

"Watch your steering!" Eutychus said. "Son, am I going to have to put blinders on you so you won't keep glancing at Haven?"

"Sorry, Dad," Asher said, as he tried to suppress his smile.

Haven was doing the same. It was nice to think about something other than foraging for food.

"We're here." Asher pulled a lever down to bring the viewing room to a halt and then he double checked the Wall of Direction.

They were in an amusement park that had a giant pirate ship on its side and toy airplanes that went in a circle. It was still twilight. The rides stood silently, like dinosaur bones in a deserted museum.

Eutychus looked in his book and ran his finger down the

page. "Let's see, what time do we need to land on? Ah! Hour fourteen, forty-seventh minute, thirty-third second," Eutychus called out to Asher.

Asher rotated the inner wooden rim surrounding the water orb fourteen clicks to the left. Then the center rim several clicks to the right and an outer rim about halfway around. The screen turned from a deep blue to a blazing white. The mid-afternoon sun surprised Haven's eyes and she squinted as they adjusted to the bright rays.

"The Clock Watcher makes sure we arrive at the right moment in every assignment," Charity spoke as she handed Asher a flower encased in a tiny sphere. The sphere was no bigger than a piece of bubble gum.

"I already encoded it to the right memory branch, so be careful!" she warned Asher.

Haven watched as Asher put it in his multi-pocketed jacket and then checked his others. Eutychus did the same thing as Charity handed him several other contraptions, including what looked like a remote control with different kinds of buttons that he stowed in his own coat. Haven looked around, wondering if she needed to bring anything.

"I would love to prep you with help, but nothing for you yet," Charity giggled. "You are a Firstie; just stick with old Eutychus."

"Alright you two, we must do the list together. Asher, you have four more festivals until it is your time to bid for a Time Server position on Testing Day, so you must stay with me."

Asher held up his hands that had no ring on them." Not official yet," he said.

"So, that means that since Haven hasn't done this and you don't have a Sapphire, I am the lead! Got it?"

"Yes, sir," said Haven.

"And no bubble board this time, Asher!" Charity called.

"Yes, ma'am," Asher laughed.

Eutychus pressed the palm of his hand on the screen and said, "Time To Serve."

* * *

"How am I not supposed to touch anyone?" Haven looked at the sea of frozen people in front of her.

Asher laughed, "Gotta be nimble!" He hurdled a food cart, turned, and smiled at Haven, but hooked his foot on a couple holding hands and knocked both of them over. Haven laughed as he righted them and continued.

The crowded amusement park made Haven understand why new shoes would come in handy. She cleared a bush to avoid a forty-person pileup.

"Oh, so you think you are so smart, jumping over stuff, huh?" Asher had a twinkle in his eyes.

"I know things," Haven shot back, hiding her own smile.

"Okay, smart girl, the first person to that food shack over there wins!"

But Haven had already taken off at the word 'shack,' and Asher, laughing, took off after her. They dodged three women pushing strollers, rounded a bush in the shape of a frog wearing a bowler hat, and leaped over a fence to fall face first into a pond. Haven bounced on the surface, completely dry.

"Hey!" she called out, glancing at her arms with wide eyes. "How come—"

"Time is frozen," Eutychus answered, walking up to where Asher and Haven had ended up. "The water won't separate like it normally does. Come, the child is right around the corner."

Asher helped Haven up as they walked on the surface of water that resembled Jell-o. Eutychus strode confidently around the scene, skillfully avoiding any disaster, and glanced down at his notation book. He paused, made a quarter turn to the right, and kept walking as he hummed to himself.

"Does that book give you some sort of idea of where you are going?" Haven jogged next to Asher.

"It gives you directions depending on what you are doing. Right now, it will tell him where to go based on his location."

"How does it know?"

"The Sapphire helps us with the book," Asher said.

Eutychus was now on his hands and knees rummaging through the bushes. "A little help, you two! Sneaking Skreechers, my knees aren't what they used to be."

Haven and Asher knelt next to their mentor and moved aside the thicket. Huddled in the center was a little boy no more than three years old, tears frozen on his cherub face.

"The lost boy," Haven breathed.

Haven watched Eutychus, who stood up again, scanning the crowd.

"Ah! The mother." He pointed to a frantic woman who was speaking to two security guards. "Did Charity give you the F.I.I.?" Eutychus asked Asher.

Asher nodded in response and cupped the sphere the Fairy had given him earlier. Eutychus took out the calculator that Charity gave him with great care, held it in front of the tiny boy and whispered, "Memorize," so softly that Haven could barely hear the word.

Blue light scanned the boy, the bushes, and the ground around him. He then held the orb up to the calculator and the light changed the flower color from white to pink.

"Now, for the mother," he said, reverently. Eutychus moved swiftly to the woman and just as softly told the orb, "Fairy Induced Idea, please."

He squeezed the orb over the mother, and pink dust then shot over her, falling over her hair, eyes, and shoulders.

"So, what's going to happen?" Haven asked looking back to the child.

"Simply put, an idea will fall into her head that the boy may be in these bushes, and she will find him."

"Huh," Haven said, in awe.

Eutychus handed the sphere back to Asher who pocketed it with great care. Then he clapped his hands, rubbed them together, and grinned. "Feels good, doesn't it? Helping people, I mean?"

"Give Haven time to soak it all in, Dad, before you start in with your selfless-giving-is-what-life-is-about speech."

Eutychus chortled and glanced back at his book. "Asher, put Slippy Sludge underneath that no good scoundrel over there."

Haven watched as Asher took a miniature bucket and tilted out about two gallons of bright blue gel underneath a man who was pulling the wallet out of an unsuspecting victim's coat.

"Slipperiest stuff in the world," Asher winked.

"You could pretty much do anything to anybody out here," Haven noted. Then she realized how embarrassing that could be.

"Oh, sweet Haven, we recite the Time Servers Promises before becoming a Server. We respect the Otherworlds' privacy or we must retire," Eutychus called.

"Plus, what would be the good in dishonoring the very people that bring us joy in serving?" Asher said as he leaned on the fence but then stepped on a corner of the sludge and slipped into Haven. "Oh, I uh . . . Sorry."

Haven blushed as she grabbed his elbow to steady him. Why did he smell so darn good?

"Tighten safety belt in moving car A," Eutychus read and then glanced up at a set of coaster cars that were currently upside-down in a loop.

"How are we going to get up there?" Haven asked, shielding her eyes against the sun's rays.

Eutychus dug in four of his jacket pockets before pulling out a spray can. He sprayed it in a wide circle around the pair. White foam bubbled up from the ground and like a spoon coming up from the bottom of a soup bowl and the pair were lifted into the air with their feet on foam.

Haven laughed as they rose higher and higher. It was as if she were in a ceiling-less helicopter.

"Floatie Free," Eutychus said as he chuckled.

From above the crowd, she could see thousands of people frozen in their afternoon of fun, unaware that the three of them were working in one second of their lives.

"Lean a little to the left," Eutychus instructed.

"Wait, what?"

But as Eutychus moved his upper half towards the left, the foam cloud followed suit. Haven fell to her knees as her balance wavered.

"You okay there, Haven?" Asher's head immediately became visible as he rose on his own foam cloud, which moved quite a bit faster than the one she was on.

She half smiled at Asher and tried to stand up, her legs wobbly. "Seat belts," she muttered. "These things need seat belts."

"Tell the Giants that. They love to discuss how to better their innovations," Asher laughed. "As a matter of fact, Scientist Irving will talk to you for *days* about them, right, Dad?"

"Two weeks to be exact," Eutychus acknowledged. "The most famous Scientist in Giant Metropolis yet he prefers to stay in Time Server City."

"It's gotta be the food," Haven jested.

The Hubbles laughed as they reached the coaster.

Haven watched as Eutychus glanced down at his book and maneuvered the cloud towards the front. Each person's expression frozen in time was so abnormal, Haven couldn't help but giggle. The speed mixed with emotions of excitement, shock, and a little fear would have made for a great picture if she could have taken one.

"Son, do you have an extender?"

"Got it." Asher sidled next to his dad as they worked. Haven moved to the shade of the coaster to get a better look. She saw that the over-the-shoulder restraint had become loose and its occupant was about to slip out; he would have fallen, for sure. The woman sitting next to him held his hand tightly.

Suddenly, Haven wasn't next to Asher or in the amusement park. Between one blink of her eyes and the next, she was transported into a sterile white room, surrounded by lengths of see-through white fabric stretched from ceiling to floor. A movie reel of the woman she had just seen at the amusement park played upon one of the pieces of fabric. The woman was still holding the hand of the boy, but in the movie, her pair of sunglasses fell from her head down onto a person's nachos, thirty feet below. The splattering nachos caused three people to topple over. Haven felt drawn towards that particular screen—as if she had to step in and help. She moved forward, reaching out to touch the fabric.

"Tighten that bolt."

Haven startled and glanced around. She was back to where she had previously stood, watching Eutychus and Asher work on the loose restraint. *That was weird.*

"Hey, uh, Eutychus? Do you guys ever, um, see a room of sorts with a bunch of screens when you're out here doing this work?"

Eutychus paused and looked at Haven. "What was on the screens?"

"Just different . . . stuff that would happen. I thought that I should help this woman with her sunglasses."

Asher glanced at Eutychus. Eutychus stared at Haven. Haven wondered if she had said the wrong thing.

"Maybe you should help her," Eutychus finally said.

"Okay, I need something that makes things stick."

Asher handed Haven what looked like a pack of gum. "Pull only one sheet at a time. You have five seconds to stick it where you want. When time restarts, it will hold things in place for a few minutes."

Haven nodded, moved to the woman, and did what Asher directed. The sunglasses stuck fast to the woman's head, and no loop would shake them loose. However, three more Sticky Sticks slipped out of the pack and Haven's hand stuck to her shirt as she tried to wiggle it free. Asher suppressed a smile as he came beside her and took a small device shaped like a toothpick and disintegrated each sheet.

"That was interesting," Eutychus said. "Watch the edge!"

Haven shuddered at the thought of falling forty feet and glanced below. Among the sea of people, one of them moved.

"Has someone ever become unfrozen?"

"No, sweet Haven. No one is able to move within a second of time unless it was another Time Server."

Haven squinted harder in the afternoon sun. There it was again. A flap of a red coattail on a jacket moved. "Do other Time Servers bump into each other during their work?"

"Not usually. We are assigned our own territory. None of us should overlap."

"Huh," she said as she leaned over to get a better look. She wasn't entirely sure something moved under the shade of the carousel below. *Maybe I'm seeing things?* As she squinted, Haven leaned too far, and she fell.

It was an odd sensation of falling in frozen time. There was no wind. The temperature wasn't even cool. Nobody was there to spot her and yell for the thousands of people to help. It was just her and the fall.

"Gotcha," Asher said as his foam cloud scooped her up amidst the blue sky. But before his hand grasped her waist, she slipped through again and continued her fall, this time Asher with her.

Haven closed her eyes, willing this not to be the end of her life . . . or Asher's. She thought of the floatie free coming underneath them. Just as the thought formed in her mind, the floatie free zoomed beneath them and they landed with perfect precision in a mass of fluffy foam.

Breathless, Asher stood up. "How did you do that?"

"What?"

"You saved us. You . . . the floatie free just . . . it came from forty feet above instantly with no one driving it . . . and caught us," he said incredulously.

"I don't know. I just wanted us to live."

08:23:00

THE JOYLESS HOSPITAL

THRONGS OF TIME Servers filled the city hub, their unique coats making the small space look like a fashion show. One man wore a high collared red coat with ribbons attached to the back. Another had neon messages flashing along his coattails. A third Server strutted about in a coat whose arms looked like the rainbow scales of a fish. Looking closer, Haven saw that when the sunlight reflected on the scales, they didn't just turn color; the fabric transformed from rainbow silk to blue velvet.

It was Haven's first day off from training and she sat with her friends under the bright white and red striped umbrellas. People around them sipped their drinks as if they were at a European street cafe. Above the building, a sign that read 'Scoffee: WAKE UP!' creaked in the breeze as it swung side to side.

"Jairus said he was going where?" Asher asked as he fiddled with his bubble board.

"I don't question him," Haven said. "He wants to explore."

"But doesn't he know he is an Otherworld? He is supposed to stay with us!"

"Jairus never follows the rules, Bucko," Liora interjected. "Give it up."

"Want anything today, Asher?" A girl Haven's age clomped to the table in thick-soled leather boots with chains whose links resembled hearts. Her lavender hair was wild but tamed by a single kitty cat clip that meowed every time she turned her head quickly.

"Eight please, Esther," Asher said.

The girl stared at Haven, smacking her gum in the process. "Who is the girl?"

"My, we are friendly, aren't we?" Liora said snarkily. Esther remained unfazed.

"This is Haven. She is training with my dad."

"Huh," Esther continued to stare and let her eyes travel to the Indigo. Haven smiled at her, but the girl continued to stare. *Does she think I'm going to do a magic trick?*

"What happened to the chair?" Esther asked as her purple lipstick-tinted lips turned downward into a frown.

The chair that Haven sat upon had grown a few dahlias around the legs and had sprouted three extra cushions so Haven's chair looked more regal than everyone else's sturdy wooden seats.

"We're thinking it's the Indigo," Asher whispered.

Haven appreciated Asher trying to keep it quiet, but everyone was staring at her chair anyhow.

"Asher! Third time this week! Esther was beginning to think you were going to ask her to Giving Day!" a woman called from the kitchen. "Esther, stop staring and get our customers their scoffees."

Esther reluctantly turned, the meows of her cat clip fading as she let the swinging kitchen doors slap closed behind her. As she did so, a tiny woman popped out of the kitchen.

Asher laughed and spoke to the woman. "No dates to Giving Day just yet, Harmony. Concentrating on hosting our new friends."

"I see that," Harmony smiled. "I am so glad you can show these Otherworlds what true kindness is. You Hubbles are good at that." The woman looked directly at Haven. "We are glad you are here, sweet dear."

"I—thank you," Haven said, squirming slightly as more customers began to stare at her. One whispered to their friend and she was quite sure the words "indigo" and "disappearances" were used.

Esther sauntered back to the table with an oversized tray filled with mugs of steaming cocoa-colored liquid. By the time Haven had a chance to look them over, Esther had slid the drinks to the twins and Liora, who took them instantly.

"Tell me what this stuff is called again?" Liora gripped the cup, her nose still halfway in as she eagerly took her second sip.

"Scoffee," Asher smiled. "Strong-Coffee."

"Boy is it!" Fletcher said, his eyes wider than usual.

Haven tilted the mug to her lips and let the syrupy liquid fill her mouth. When she swallowed, a deep warmth began in her belly and spread. The weight of her arms vanished, and her eyes, which had trouble remaining open due to the lack of sleep last night because of her reliving the fall, lifted to their rightful place, refreshed.

"You know what people are saying about her, right?" Esther said before she popped her gum several times.

Haven felt heat rising to her cheeks and wasn't sure if it was the scoffee. "What are they saying?"

"Nothing," Asher said, suddenly standing up and grabbing the extra scoffee to go.

"They say she is causing the dis—"

"Stop it, Esther!" Asher cut her off.

"Whatever," Esther said as she grabbed Haven's cup and eyed her up and down. Haven didn't move but made sure she smiled to let her know she wasn't afraid. Esther loaded the rest of the empty cups on her tray, and holding Haven's gaze, she slowly turned and sauntered away, her cat clip hissing in the process.

Liora and the rest of the friends stood up and trailed behind Asher. His long strides were fast enough to cause him to spill his drink, as his bubble board was tucked tightly under his arm. The crowd gave the group a wide berth as they followed Asher down the street.

At first, Haven thought she was being paranoid, but she noticed the crowds seemed to avoid her. Her suspicions were confirmed when a Time Server in a green and pink striped coat fell over onto the sidewalk and crashed into the door of a lampshade shop while trying to avoid going anywhere near the Indigo on Haven's hand.

"No one messes with us 'cause Haven has the Indigo," Fletcher said as he and Finn bounced off the sidewalk and onto the cobblestone street. "Hey Asher, can I ride your board?"

"Sure." Asher handed it to him.

Fletcher hopped on and zoomed around shopping Time Servers, almost knocking a few off their feet. *Well, at least no-one avoids Fletcher.*

"I got next!" Finn yelled after his brother. "Nabbit! I want one!"

Hannalee skipped with Unie at her side, weaving through a group that looked on as a seamstress made a new coat. She sang her own made-up song as she went, "Dresses, flowers, and fairy wings!" Haven noticed several Time Servers made no effort to avoid Hannalee either. However, a Time Server in an electric blue top hat squeaked and jumped out of Haven's way.

"Asher, what rumors are there about me?" Haven pressed as they walked down the street, Aiden holding her hand.

"It's nothing. Sometimes people are too scared, that's all." Asher looked at anything but Haven.

"You know something. And you won't tell me."

"It isn't a good idea to repeat any of the rumors. Not here in the street, and not in front of you. It's just dumb stuff people say."

"—another missing building on my list," a graying Time Server said urgently to the Time Server beside him.

"And what of the Otherworlds inside?" his companion asked.

"I don't know what happened. I was too gobbildy gooked to find out."

They both noticed Haven, stopped talking abruptly, and stared. Asher took Haven's arm and willed her forward while the two Time Servers whispered to each other. Now Haven was officially freaking out.

Haven turned back to Asher. "Missing buildings and Otherworlds? Are they blaming that on *me*?" she asked him, a tone of urgency in her voice.

Asher rubbed the back of his neck.

"If Haven can disappear stuff, then she better disappear all the broccoli in the world, 'cause that stuff is disgusting," Finn said with a grimace.

"Why are they scaredy of my Bestie?" Aiden looked back.

"Because they don't understand that misplaced fear can cause panic," Asher said. "Let's just drop off Mom's scoffee at the Joyless Hospital. She is working double shifts and needs an extra pick-me-up."

They walked further in silence and halted in front of a glass-domed building with a big sign in front of it: 'Joyless Hospital: We'll Get Your Joy Back: Together.'

"Okay, now this is creepy," Liora glanced at Haven.

Haven noticed that the building was made entirely of glass with painted flowers, clowns, and candy on the side. "We'll Get Your Joy Back: Together," was in neon lettering in an arc above the double door entrance, and a statue of a dog and a cat on either side looked like they were cartoon characters trying to get a laugh out of the entrants.

"Like a giant upside-down fishbowl," Fletcher said as he stood breathless, still holding the bubble board.

As they entered the building, an enticing smell that was unlike any other wafted through the air. Haven took a breath and a smile erupted from her lips. Liora's expression matched Haven's. By the look on Liora's face, she was smelling the same.

"Coconut?" she asked.

Haven shook her head, "Vanilla. Huh. It must change depending on what you like!"

"Cinnamon cookies." Aiden sprinted to the bakery cart.

"Bouncy Area!" Finn grabbed the bubble board and headed for the right, Fletcher following after.

"Fairy garden!" Hannalee skipped ahead.

"Um—" Haven paused.

Haven watched as Aiden received a large cookie from a rotund caregiver who allowed him to sit in her baker's chair as she readied another batch for him to sample.

"Don't worry, MaryAnna used to watch me when I wandered in here. Aiden is completely safe," Asher patted Haven's shoulder. She wanted Asher to stay close to her without her even knowing why.

Rainbow-robed patients and caregivers wearing all shades of yellow roamed the hospital's pathways as the bright sun shone through the ceiling of the dome. The light gave the place an outdoor feel.

"They like everything to feel like an open space," Asher

explained. "It was proven that people got their joy back outside more easily—rather than being stuck inside under fluorescent lights and in small rooms."

A flagstone path wound around pruned potted trees in the shape of socks, hats, and sunglasses and led Liora, Haven, and Asher over an inky pond. Blue, purple, gold, and white koi fish the size of canoes slid silently beneath.

"They don't, um, eat—" Haven asked.

"People?" Asher laughed. He leaned closer to Haven brushing her cheek as he whispered, "Only on Tuesdays."

Haven blushed and glanced at Liora who mouthed, *You've got a boyfriend!* Then proceeded to make kissy faces behind Asher's back.

Haven opened her eyes wide to get her to stop. Asher kept his pace on the pathway until he reached the information desk in the center of the koi pond.

"Levi?" Liora asked incredulously.

The teenager was sorting through a stack of books while on his bubble board. Speakers blasted classical music in the background.

"Huh? Oh hey!" he yelled. Asher took his bubble board and let it glide to the power button to shut the music off. Levi floated on his bubble board towards them, coming out from behind the desk. "What's up?"

Haven was shocked, "Aren't you training to be a Time Server? Why are you working *here?*"

Asher grinned and looked at Levi pointedly. Levi leaned in close and motioned the girls to do the same. *At least he's not afraid to get near me*, Haven thought. "It's because I am a spy. My Uncle Otokar sent me here looking for members of the evil Indigo wearer's army."

Asher and Levi laughed as Liora and Haven stared at them.

"Okay, I see we have now entered the land of Humorless Chicks," Levi said.

Asher nudged Haven, "He's joking, there isn't really an army. Not that we know of."

"You two are weirder than weird," Liora rolled her eyes.

"Do you like weird?" Levi lit up.

"No."

Levi made a mock showing of a heart attack, fell backward, and knocked over the books he was stacking. "How about now?"

"Less of a no."

"Hey, while you are still trying to impress Liora, can you tell me where my mom is?"

"Doctor Hubble is in the rock garden," Levi said as he picked up a few books. "Brought scoffee again for her?"

Asher held the scoffee up. "Trying to get bonus points so I can be the favorite son."

"J.J. still wins according to all the womenfolk around here. It's his cheeks."

"Yeah, whatever," Asher laughed and motioned the girls to follow. "See ya."

A large bronze statue of a woman with a flowing dress and a book in her hand loomed at the center of the garden. She looked stoic, her gaze to the sky, wisps of her hair breaking free from the bun tied at the nape of her neck. The plaque underneath read: "Mrs. Violet Krankerton: Dedicated her life to serving others without expecting notice."

"Will you make a huge statue of me like that when I am gone?" Liora asked Haven. "Let it read, Liora: Snarky, Smart, and Sassy."

Haven laughed out loud and startled a cat that was lounging in the crook of the statue's skirt. Haven noticed there were many animals about; a dog was being petted by a smiling patient, another cat wove itself between the legs of a caregiver who looked like they were trying to keep their balance.

"We have animals here because it helps bring joy to the patients. They were once lost animals in your world, but we bring them here to live out their days in luxury." Asher glanced at the cat who now jumped on the shoulders of a patient and started to lick its paws.

"Asher! Girls!" Merry called from the depths of a garden made entirely of stone. "It is so good to see you."

Merry hugged the girls tightly and Haven let herself relax around someone else who didn't seem afraid of her.

"Scoffee?" Asher held up the cup.

"What would I do without your thoughtfulness?" The doctor beamed at her son.

"Go to sleep in the bean bag section," Asher smiled.

Merry sipped the strong liquid and took a deep breath. "Now that you are here, let me give you a tour of the place—" she looked around them. "Are the others at home?"

Haven glanced around. "Nope, wandering around somewhere."

Merry smiled. "It is just as well; I couldn't get Asher to stay in one spot here until he was eleven. Come on, then, I will take you two around." Merry picked up the hem of her full skirt—one with a pattern of tiny suns peeking over the horizon on it—and motioned for them to come with her.

"The Joyless Hospital was built years ago to house Time Servers who lost their joy," Merry said as she turned back to Asher, Loira, and Haven and smiled. "It is pretty simple for us. As Time Servers, our main purpose is to serve others in various forms." Merry ushered the group through an area where patients lounged on bean bags the size of school buses. "Sometimes, it is helping Otherworlds solve problems, avoid disasters, that sort of thing. Sometimes it is serving others here in our world."

"You gotta take care of yourself at some point," Liora chimed in.

"Yes, true. But it is our job to bring back into balance the desire to help others. Taking care of yourself isn't usually the problem. Being selfish is."

"What do you mean?" Haven asked.

"Selfishness is to only think of yourself all the time. There is no room for the desire to help others. Over time, it will cause a Time Server to degrade. To live in fear, feeling alone, angry, and anxious. That is why we are here to help."

"Why would you help someone that sounds like they just need to get over it?" Liora asked as she eyed Merry. Haven could see who Merry described was way too similar to Liora herself and it rattled her friend.

"Oh, Liora dear, when you focus on helping others, you create a balance. It's life-giving to everyone around you, including yourself."

"Not everyone may want your help," Liora muttered.

A female caregiver rushed past the foursome, speaking into her collar. "Got a pink alert in the bounce area. I repeat: a pink alert in the bounce area."

"Finn and Fletcher?" Liora looked at Haven and rolled her eyes. "I'm not claiming responsibility. After what they did in the museum, I'm done."

"I'll go," Haven offered.

"Don't worry, Haven," Merry said. "They won't harm the boys, but we definitely should check on them. This way."

Haven paused as Liora, Asher, and Merry walked ahead. Suddenly, the Joyless Hospital, the garden, and even the ground she walked on vanished. She was standing in the sterile room again, just like when she had been transported out of the amusement park, but this time there were more movies playing on the fabric. Like before, she could see choices to help the people around her. Merry's shoelace was untied, and would cause her to trip, a man twenty feet away needed a boost onto the highest beanbag, Finn and Fletcher now had ahold of the air blower to one of the bounce houses, and the nurses needed help.

In a second, the room vanished and she was back in the Joyless Hospital.

Haven felt dizzy. She moved to the large statue of the woman whose hair permanently blew in the silent wind. She leaned against the flat, cold bronze and slid down to cradle her head in her hands. *Am I going crazy?*

Sitting against the statue, her breaths went in and out, settling her each time they did. Haven opened her eyes and noticed a small etching in the bottom right corner of the statue's pedestal. She moved closer, her cheek roughly brushing the statue. In the corner of the pedestal a pair of gears were carved, embedded in wings with an hourglass at the center. It was so small and hidden, most people wouldn't notice it.

"Excuse me, miss," a pale Time Server who looked thinner than a Pixie Stick pushed a bucket and a mop towards her. "Are you lost?"

"Me?" Haven stood up anxiously, "Oh, um, no sir. I was . . ." she glanced down at the symbol, but the Time Server's mop bucket now blocked her view. To Haven, it seemed like the man was blocking her view of the etching on purpose. "Doing nothing. Just wandering around." She willed the corners of her mouth to turn upwards to a smile.

"Seeley! Thank you so much for finding her!" Merry called across the garden. "Haven, come dear, and stick with us!"

"Coming, Miss Merry." Haven glanced back at the man; his watery black eyes followed her.

"The bouncy house area will need cleanup, Seeley," Merry called.

"Yes, Doctor," Seeley answered, still watching Haven.

"Miss Merry, who was that?"

"Seeley? He works here. Was a patient for years, and after he found his joy, he decided the best way to serve was to keep up the very place that helped him. Isn't that nice?"

Haven nodded but had an uneasy feeling about him. *Why didn't he want her to look closely at the symbol?*

"Why would anyone throw potato salad at our huts?" asked Liora as she scrubbed bits of pickles off the outer wall of her shed.

It looked like someone took a family picnic and used the makeshift huts and the Hubbles' house as target practice. An explosion of ketchup, mustard, potato and pasta salads, and collard greens with bits of bacon left greasy blobs that slid down the walls and door frames. Over three dozen biscuits littered the yard.

"That's commitment," Fletcher said, clearing bits of bacon off their doorway.

"Redecorating your new huts with condiments?" Cricket called from the other side of the fence.

"What? Oh! Hello, Cricket." Eutychus glanced up. "Yes, well people can be a bit opinionated when the Indigo reappears."

"Indeed, they can," Cricket said, watching Eutychus as he finished painting over the words 'Where are the Otherworlds?' that had been scrawled over the Hubble's front door.

"Still being accused of the disappearances, I see," Cricket noted, drumming his fingers on the fence.

Eutychus shook his head as he bent down to drop the paintbrush in the bucket. "Yes, she is."

"Alrighty, I'll let you get on with your cleaning. I am headed for the Fairy Market to prepare for Giving Day. I have a feeling this one will be a smash."

"Good day, Cricket," Eutychus called. "He has certainly taken an interest in our house. I caught him passing by four times this week."

"Haven causing Otherworlds to disappear! I can't understand why people actually believe it!" Merry handed Eutychus another pot of paint. "Look at Haven, how do they think she could cause whole buildings to disappear? She is only fourteen!"

The lump in Haven's throat felt permanent. "I'm sorr—"

"Don't you worry about it, dear Haven," Merry said as she began to wash out the old paint pot. "We are grateful you children are here with us."

Eutychus agreed. "The Council is aware of what happened here. They will find out who pulled this prank." He sighed, wiped his hands on his pants, and looked at his watch. "Gheepie Jeepers, our morning has surpassed us, Merry. We need to head to the Fairy Market if we are going to get our trades for Giving Day."

"What *is* Giving Day?" asked Liora.

Merry shooed J.J. into the house and turned around, waving her hands and sending drops from her wet hands flying. "Giving Day is a great time to give gifts to the other people in our city. We'll go to the market to trade something for the gift that we think will best serve someone."

"I don't have anything to trade," Aiden wailed.

"It doesn't have to be something expensive or even new,

sweet boy." Merry leaned close to Aiden. "I know Fairies would love a button from your collection."

Aiden clapped his hands and raced to his pack, which laid in the middle of the yard.

Haven grabbed her bag to look for something to trade. Next to it, Jairus tinkered with a contraption he had built.

"You going?" she asked and tossed him a screwdriver.

He took it and grunted.

Haven sighed, threw her bag back to the ground, sat on it and rested her chin on her fists. "What?"

Jairus continued to fiddle with a screw as Haven watched him, her lips pursed. After a moment he tossed the tool aside in frustration.

"You know, after exploring the city, the heat is on you with this ring. People are talking about deportation to some desert. You still want to stay here and give them a chance?"

Haven picked up the screwdriver and fixed the screw Jairus hadn't been able to get. "Yeah, Jairus. I do. The council has our backs and it's not like I have a lot of choice. I mean, what else are we gonna do?"

"We could leave."

"Where would I go? I've seen what these rings can do! If someone wants to take me, I would be helpless and all of you could be hurt."

"Just give it to whoever wanted it. Then we would be out of danger and the Hubbles wouldn't have to clean their front porch. It would be someone else's problem." Jairus shrugged.

Haven paused. *But what kind of person would really want the Indigo?* She looked around. *And what would they do to this world and people like the Hubbles?*

* * *

A SHORT TIME LATER, they wove through the village streets following Eutychus, who sang a song about wrinkled warthogs.

"Your bell? You finally gonna trade that away?" Fletcher asked his brother.

"It has pictures of flames on it!" Finn exclaimed. "Ful-am-es, bro! It's my best trade."

"Okay," Fletcher said reluctantly, "but remember when we almost got nicked because you forgot it at the old place?" The boys snickered while Finn stuffed the bell into his pack.

"Pick what you like!" Eutychus motioned to a large field with rows and rows of bicycles.

J.J. had toddled over to his older brother and jumped up and down until Asher propped him up to sit on a seat that rested on the handlebars of a bike. The bike was low to the ground and had a crimson stripe down its side like a racing car.

Aiden yelled, "Cool! Come on, Haven! You and me, Bestie!" He picked a bright blue bicycle with stars and sat in the front seat that was mounted on the handlebars.

Finn began to spin the pedals with his feet as fast as he could, but the bike remained still, making it look like he was on a workout bike at the gym. "Aw, man! it's all show and no go!"

Merry and Eutychus had hopped on their own bicycle—one made out of wicker and looking like something out of the 1800s. "Now, you have to tell the bicycle where you want to go. Use your words. Like this." Eutychus spoke in a genteel tone, "If you could be ever so kind, would you take us to the Fairy Market, please?"

They began to pedal and the large tandem bike rose in the air and drifted above Time Server City. Every single person from Haven's Place stared unblinkingly.

"I'm not getting on one of those!" Liora said. "What if I fall off?"

"You won't fall off," Asher said. "The bikes won't let you."

"Ugh, why is everything in this place a million feet off the ground, moving on its own, and made to kill us?" Liora grumbled.

"Come on, Lior. Just pedal slow, you'll be fine," Haven coaxed. "What do you say again?"

Jairus snorted. "Just tell the dumb bike, the 'Fairy Market.'"

No sooner did the sound of his voice hit his arrow-shaped bicycle than it shot up in the air forty feet and then dipped low almost hitting the ground. It swerved to the left and right as if on an autobahn course trying to knock Jairus off.

"You have to say please!" shouted Eutychus after Jairus. "They like manners!"

Jairus nodded his head, swallowed his pride and shouted, "PLEASE?" Immediately the bike leveled out and began to gently follow Eutychus' own bicycle.

"Jairus can't control his bikey!" whispered Aiden as he muffled his giggle.

"Don'tcha be mean to Jairus," Hannalee scolded.

Noting Jairus's tone, Haven did the exact opposite and spoke as politely as she could as she climbed onto the bike Aiden had already perched on. "Hello, incredibly smart and lovely bike. I would like to go to the Fairy Market. Would you be able to get me there, please?"

Her bicycle rose gently off the ground as if she were on a paper airplane alighting in the wind. In no time she was pedaling with the rest of the pack in midair, above Time Server City. One by one, everyone in the group climbed on their own bikes and took off. Liora had chosen an oversized tricycle that had a basket and foot boards and had said "please" to it about six times. Her bike wobbled along as the last in the group, going slower than a turtle.

"A ginormous snowflake!" Aiden squealed, leaning over to get a better look.

Haven looked down and saw that he was right. Each village, twelve in all, made up a tip of the snowflake arm as offshoots of what looked like fern leaves joined together to make a massive flower. To the left, Haven could see a vast body of water with a mountainous island. Ahead was a forest of trees.

Hannalee had her unicorn in her front basket, its woven hair flopping in the wind. She looked down. "There's Oak, and Ash, and Maple, and Banyan! I know those trees!" she announced with glee.

Haven forced a smile. She could hear Eutychus's baritone voice start in with a song about the tickling tree.

"Not feeling up to anything today, huh?" Asher pedaled next to her.

Finding the right words were useless, especially because of what had been written on the front of the Hubble's house.

"You know, my dad would say, 'Enjoy the day that was given to you.'"

Haven continued to pedal slowly. Not only had she put her friends in a tight spot, but now the Hubbles were being targeted, too. Her stomach hurt. *Don't puke, it might land on the villages of South America.*

Asher pedaled closer to Haven and nudged her elbow. "This slow pace is nice, but it is more fun if you race."

Haven half grinned at Asher and he bent down to the handlebars of his bike. "Go faster, please." Instantly his bicycle surged ahead.

"We're not going to let him beat us, are we, Bestie?" Aiden looked back at Haven.

"I'm not much in the mood to race right now, Aiden."

The tiny boy gave her his best puppy-dog eyed look. "Pul-lease?"

"You got that from Hannalee, didn't you?"

"Yup, and gonna keep doin' it like she does."

Defeated, Haven bent down to the handlebars and gently asked, "Pardon me, would you mind ever so much as to pick up speed, please?"

The bicycle reared on its hind tire and zoomed past Asher and J.J. with no problem. Haven had to weave in and out between Fletcher and Finn. She heard them yell "Hey!" in unison somewhere behind her. Liora and Jairus, who had been in deep conversation, had to move out of Haven's way in order to stay on their bikes. Pretty soon there was nobody in front of her.

The feeling of the air was exhilarating. Aiden yelled in delight and Haven closed her eyes, letting the rush of wind spread over her face and through her hair. The whole land was before her and she was a bird passing by. It felt so good to Haven to be free.

"Fairy Market entrance up ahead," Eutychus called.

Haven opened her eyes as her bicycle slowed, and as if on a feather, floated towards a lake that looked like it held golden-pink water. Surrounding the lake were jagged ebony rocks pointing in all directions, forming their own circle.

There's no way I'm landing on that, Haven thought. *These bikes don't float!*

But the bike headed straight toward it. Haven panicked and looked around. She hadn't been swimming in a long time, and didn't even know if Aiden *could* swim.

"Ooooo! Look, Bestie! Just like the stream in the woods— lots of water!"

Haven tried to remain calm, but the closer they got, the more she prepared herself to save Aiden. "Hang on, Aides," Haven called to him. "I am going to hold on to you and we can have a fun time." She wrapped her arm around Aiden's chest and waited for the bike to splash in the water. She knew not to panic. That was rule number one.

Haven took a deep breath as the bike tire hit the water.

However, just as the front tire touched the lake, the bike became smaller, shrinking ten times its normal size. Then Aiden's little feet shrunk, the handlebars, and Haven's legs.

"It feels funny!" exclaimed a miniature Aiden, as Haven nodded in agreement. Like a thousand soft feathers were tickling her inch by inch. As they broke the surface of the lake, Haven realized, it wasn't a lake but some sort of barrier. She glanced up at the pink film above, fully able to breathe, now knowing she was ten times smaller than she once was. She almost laughed maniacally because she was so relieved.

Aiden jumped off the handlebar seat. "We win! We win!"

She smiled and knelt down to Aiden, tightly squeezing him. She didn't know if it was because she won or if it was because they both were still alive. Perhaps it was both.

Asher and his bike floated down second. "How did you do it?"

"I didn't do anything you didn't do," Haven laughed.

"That bike must like you because I have never seen one go that fast before," Asher said as he helped J.J. climb down from the seat.

"We're tiny like the Fairies!" Hannalee giggled.

"I hope no one squashes us!" Fletcher looked up. Above them was what had looked like a pink lake from the sky. Only from down here, it looked like a pink layer of film they had passed through. All around them was a field of emerald green.

"Fairies prefer even ground when it comes to trading, and most of them do not like to be larger than they usually are," Eutychus said as he motioned the children to follow him. "If we were our true size, it might be a bit dangerous tromping around. Thanks to the Giants and their innovations, we can be the same size as the Fairies to trade evenly."

An arc of white and black stone spanned from one end of the field to the other, creating a large entrance way. Time Servers and Giants alike, all the same size now, filed towards it like ants in a line. Above the arc was cursive writing 'Fairy Market: Come With Your Best Trade.' Marble gates opened to let the flow of people in and out of the market.

As Haven passed a Fairy who stood on one side, she noticed that at her new shrunken height, the Fairy was two heads taller than her, with fierce brown eyes, and an attitude to match. The Fairy wore armor with spikes topping her wings and shoulders, and had a pair of long wooden sticks tucked in the back of her armored sling.

"Fairy Fighter," Asher whispered. "One of the toughest fighters anywhere. Can slice through three tons of rock by finding the right pressure point."

"Remind me not to get in a fight with one of those."

"Hold on!" said Eutychus who was pushed in every direction by the throngs of people. "Go in the right line, so we can stick together. Once you enter the gates, wait by the first stall. It is bedlam in there."

Haven was tossed about as she forced herself and Aiden through the gate, almost losing him in the process. Once through, everyone immediately started shouting and offering their wares.

Cricket, who had gotten to the market before them, hung onto his flowerpot hat as he yelled to a Fairy in the stall across the way, "I've got two pocketbooks! Two for a Fairy painting!"

The Fairy behind the stall was dressed in a business suit with every hair neatly in place. "Pocketbooks for a Fairy painting? Are you out of your mind?"

"But they have laser engravings from a Giant!" Cricket argued. "It will write for you!"

The two started to argue when a third Fairy wearing a black and white striped suit like a referee with matching pants came in with a stern warning: "Not a fair trade. Not a fair trade."

Haven smiled when she heard the Fairy Referee's response, 'Not a fair trade.' How many times had Twigette said the same to her? She wondered how her own junk dealer was doing. Would she ever get to see her again?

The wide road leading from the arc was lined by stalls. It twisted and turned like a maze. Each stall had different fabric that covered it, making the space look like the Middle Eastern bazaars Haven had seen in the world travel magazines at the gas station. Only, every Fairy looked as if they were lawyers instead of the nature-loving creatures in old books and movies.

Haven passed a stall with paintings as high as a four-story house. One painting was of a red-headed Fairy and a Turquoise R&M person with a white crystal streak in her hair as she worked on something.

Haven blinked and it was as if tiny bits of confetti came from the sides of the panting toward her, then shrunk into dust particles. It surrounded her, comforted her, and made her feel as if she was protected simply by just being still. The sounds of the Fairy Market had gone silent and were replaced by the crackling of the fire and whispers of a language she could not understand. Haven took a step forward.

The Fairy and stone person, still unmoving, huddled around their work in the smoky room. Haven felt the heat from the fire behind them as she moved toward the two creatures. They were forging a ring, the Fairy bending the metal while the R&M creature placed a dark stone at the center.

"Keep going, let's move out of the main street and go to a quiet trading district." Eutychus' voice snatched Haven out of the painting and back on the street again. The loud shouts of the market filled her ears once more, and although she didn't feel cold, she definitely didn't feel comfort like she had mere moments ago.

"Fairy painting," Asher explained behind her. "Takes over one hundred years to paint one and it's so realistic you can step into it. Can get lost in one for hours."

"The fire felt hot. It isn't alive, is it?" Haven rubbed her arms where the heat of the fire made them feel toasty.

"Nah, it's just art, but the Fairies have a knack for painting a moment as if it is really happening."

Merry took J.J. and Aiden by the hands to inspect a booth run by a plump fairy with a pencil skirt and a navy-blue blazer. Her look was akin to a school principal who wouldn't put up with misbehaving children. Aiden happily pulled out his button collection and the Fairy fell backward in surprise, smoothed her hair, and nodded enthusiastically.

"To the scales of Fairness!" Haven heard a shout over the din of traders from two stalls away. A crowd amassed, picking up Finn and carrying him atop their heads. The crowd then headed for a pair of one-hundred-foot-high scales in the center of the market. The bowls on each side could fit a monster truck. A panel of three business suited Fairies sat at a large marble desk in front of the scales. An emblem of scales was emblazoned on the front of the desk and on the front of each of the Fairies's suits.

"Fletcher! What happened?" Haven cried.

He looked flushed and had to gulp down a few breaths to speak. "It's Finn. He wanted to trade a fancy knife for his bike bell. He thought it was worth the trade and argued with a dude in a suit."

Haven looked up and sure enough, Finn clutched the bell in his hand and looked defiantly at a thin Fairy Trader who wore a crisply ironed royal blue suit with diamond buttons. The Fairy placed a dagger at one end of the scale. It slid down to the center of the bowl.

"Why didn't he just walk away?" asked Liora.

"He wanted that blasted knife thingy so badly. He couldn't let the trade go!"

Haven saw Eutychus pushing through the crowd.

"Eutychus! Surely, they wouldn't do anything to a child! He has never traded until now!"

"Fairies are a tough sort. They will decide what is fair, you can be sure of that," he answered with a slight worry in his voice as he glanced at the three Fairy judges.

"What happens if the trade isn't fair?"

"If they think it is done on purpose, then you are sent to the Magma King for a few days to think about what you have done."

"Where does the Magma King live?" asked Liora glancing around.

"Underneath the West Mountains."

An armored Fairy Fighter pushed Finn towards the scales and told him to lay the trade down. Finn did so purposefully, never taking his eyes off the other Fairy with the dagger. The judges at the marble table peered down at the boy, studying him with great interest.

The dagger was on one side of the scales and the bell on the other. The scales started to sway. Beads of sweat appeared on Haven's upper lip. *Please be fair, Please be fair,* she thought.

When the scales stopped she looked up amidst the gasps of surprise all around her. They were even!

"Wha—" Fletcher took the words out of Haven's mouth.

"Hmmm," said Eutychus thoughtfully scratching his beard. "It would seem that the Fairies look at all aspects of the trade, not just the physical value of the object."

He looked at Haven and Fletcher with a smile at the corners of his eyes, "That object meant a great deal to your brother," he spoke to Fletcher. "So, its value was of greater worth."

Haven looked at the Fairy judges and silently thanked them. The center Fairy looked right at her and nodded. *Do they know I am thanking them?*

A flash of a red coat appeared in the surrounding crowd.

Someone had turned to leave, wearing a dark hooded coat with red coattails. Haven paused. *Was that the same coat I saw when I was training with Eutychus at the amusement park? How many red coats could there be?* She stepped toward the crowd to follow.

"What's up, Eutychus?" a lanky Giant called from his booth. "Getting ready for Giving Day tomorrow?"

Haven looked back to where she last saw the person with the red coat and decided it was too late to follow, anyway.

"Scientist Irving!" Eutychus walked the few feet to the Giant's booth and gave him a high five, grinning broadly. He turned toward the rest of the children, "I'm introducing our new guests to The Fairy Market!"

"Hey man, Scientist Irving," the Giant said as he held up his hand for a high-five to Jairus. The boy didn't move so Irving high-fived Jairus's closed hand hanging by his side instead.

He then stepped out of his booth, wild white hair moving every which way. His dark lab coat and striped converse shoes made him look more like a skater than a scientist. "The holder of the dreaded Indigo!" Scientist Irving smiled at Haven. "You have to know that your presence here has given me much to meditate about."

Haven looked down.

"No worries, though," Scientist Irving straightened a gadget on his shelf, "The odds of you causing the same destruction the previous ring owner created is about nine trillion, two hundred forty-six million, eight-hundred thousand and eighty to one."

"Which means it's not gonna happen," Liora whispered to Haven as she moved to the next booth.

"What's this?" Finn asked as he poked his finger to move a rotating ball on top of a track.

"Oh that," Scientist Irving hopped to the booth and clapped his hands, "is a Determinator. If it spits out red slime here," he pointed to a pair of tiny doors, "it means you are not telling the truth."

"Does it work?" Fletcher asked, squinting at the doors.

"It did," Scientist Irving said as he fiddled with the track. "Until I totally dropped it this morning, and now can't get the rotator to move with the track. No red goo until that is fixed."

Haven noticed the entire booth had gadgets and contraptions of all sorts. "Did you invent these?" She asked him.

"Yup," he said, fiddling with the tiny doors of the contraption, "every one."

"Scientist Irving won't tell you this, but most of the innovations we use for Time Serving are from him." Eutychus said proudly as he slapped the scientist on his back.

The scientist half grunted and continued with his work. Jairus watched intently.

Haven moved through the booth of innovations, recognizing some of the ones Eutychus had already used while time-serving during her training. Hair Rearranger, Laundry Folder, Room Cleaner. She picked up the Taste Bud Eradicator and it stuck to her finger. She shook it off but knocked over a few innovations in the process.

"Sorry!" she said as she tried to place them back the best she could. A dusty wooden box flipped over. On its side was an etching of an hourglass with clock gears embedded on the wings. The same emblem on the statue in the Joyless Hospital.

"Scientist Irving," she called, gingerly picking up the box. "Where did you get this?"

The scientist moved to the back of the booth as Jairus knelt to look at the Determinator.

"The box with the Freedom symbol?" he took the box in his hand and turned it over in his hands slowly. He sighed. "Just a silly gift from one of my students."

And instantly, red goo shot out of the Determinator.

THE RED COAT

"SCISSORS!" Eutychus called, holding his hand up.

"Got 'em!" Finn grabbed the flower-handled scissors that had impaled the dirt mound Aiden and J.J. dug in. As soon as Finn had them, he ran over to the porch where Eutychus sat.

"Finn," Merry said as she pinned the bottom of Haven's dress, "Running with scissors—"

"—is dangerous," Fletcher finished for her as Finn slowed to a snail's pace. "It's hard to get that in his noggin, Miss Merry. He'll get it."

"Thank you, Finn." Eutychus winked at the boy who moved in sloth-like fashion and handed the pointed scissors over. "Oh, and can you hand me the measuring tape that rolled under the table? I don't have time to lose that again!" Eutychus moved back to his sewing machine, silken fabric flying everywhere.

It was late afternoon and the Hubble household was preparing for Giving Day. Eutychus tasked himself with sewing dresses for the girls while Merry did the precision cuts and hems.

Haven stood as the model in the midday sun, draped in

swathes of champagne-colored silk while Liora held pins for Merry.

"You don't have to make dresses for us," Haven said, her muffled voice audible from under the mountain of fabric.

"Oh, ho! Of course, we do! Everyone attends Giving Day wearing their very best."

"Yes, dears," Merry agreed. Then, with added determination, she jabbed a pin in the hem. "There is no way, in this world or yours, that we are going to let our guests attend in everyday clothing!"

"Ow!" Haven gasped. It was the third time that morning that Merry stabbed her accidentally with a pin.

"Glad it's you and not me," Liora whispered to Haven.

Asher furrowed his brow. "Uh, Mom? Are you still frustrated with Doctor Habberty?"

Merry let out a frustrated grunt. "Every year she tells me we should have our best on for Giving Day, but who can sew thirty lengths of embroidered silk for a six-year-old?"

"Oh, dear wife, she is just jealous because you cracked the case at the hospital helping to heal Burt," Eutychus called over his shoulder as more fabric flowed around him. "You are the best doctor there!"

"Mr. Eutychus, Mr. Eutychus!" Hannalee ran from the back of the house looking wild with excitement. "It was in the woods! Come, see!" She grabbed his oversized hand in her petite one and pulled him out of his chair with surprising strength.

The wooden chairs scraped the floor as the entire group shuffled off the porch. Haven skillfully squirmed out of the fabric, shaking the last bit from her shoulders. It was like freeing herself from the coils of a snake.

Hannalee dragged Eutychus around the back, pointing and chattering the whole length of the house. There, munching on Merry's bright yellow daffodils, was a majestic, white beast.

"A unicorn—" Merry drew in a sharp breath as she adjusted J.J. on her hip.

It raised its head when the crowd rounded the corner. Hannalee softly stepped to the edge of the forest. It turned its eye quickly on her and froze as she spoke reassuring words. Haven recognized the words instantly; they were the same words she herself had said to Hannalee the day Hannalee showed up at the dump.

"Come here. It's okay. You're safe."

Asher moved to stop Hananlee but Eutychus swiftly grabbed his son's arm and gently held him back without saying a word.

Unwavering, Hannalee came close enough to share the same air as the unicorn and stood still, holding out African violets that had seen better days. The warm afternoon sun shone down on the pair, a waif of a girl and a shimmering mythical creature, illuminating the outline of each. After what seemed like a day, the unicorn nuzzled the violets in Hannalee's palm, gathering them into its mouth, and then sauntered into the forest as if it were telling everyone they may be dismissed from its presence.

Asher let out a low whistle. "I have never seen someone get that close to a wild unicorn."

Eutychus shook his head. "Hannalee, you have a way with that creature. Not many people come close to them. Snobbish, they are. Very snobbish."

"I'm gonna to call him Unie Junior," Hannalee beamed as she watched the last of its tail disappear behind the trees.

Haven leaned against the house as she watched the Hubbles disperse—Eutychus to his sewing, Merry to pinning the rest of the dress that Haven had made sure to neatly lay on the ground, and Asher to sorting out the gifts for Giving Day. The boys played freeze tag in the yard as Hannalee jumped on the low branch of an oak tree and climbed atop to see if she could spot her new friend. All of Haven's friends looked healthier since they had arrived in Time Server City. They were fed whenever they were hungry, and slept peacefully under the stars with the sweet smell of Merry's garden wafting in the air. Haven took a deep breath. This place felt like home.

"You've got your thinking face on, genius," Liora said. She leaned against the wall next to Haven, chewing on a piece of sour grass. She gave a handful to Haven.

"Yeah, just thinking how happy I am right now." Haven bit into a blade, letting the sour juice pucker her face.

"You know, this place isn't half bad." Liora looked around. "I mean, there are some angry Time Servers who like to throw condiments at our stuff, but who cares? We get free food when we want it and Asher's parents are okay. Weird, but okay."

Haven turned towards Liora, putting her hand on the wall of the house. "Whoa there, softy! Saying something nice about a place and two adults? It sounds like you like it here. Maybe even feel . . . safe," Haven teased.

Liora looked down at her hands and said, "I've been in worse places than this, so yeah, I do. At least those three crazies can't find us."

Haven shuddered at the thought of the three men who had tried to kidnap them. It seemed so long ago. But Liora was right. Even though she felt terrible about bringing the responsibility of the Indigo on her friends and the Hubbles, everyone seemed to be genuinely happy here. Except for Jairus, who sat under the willow tree, his favorite spot, looking out into the woods. If Haven was honest with herself, seeing Jairus apart and silent, staring off into space, made her feel sick to her stomach. She didn't want to lose any of her friends. She didn't want to lose anyone close to her, not like she had lost her parents. She had to remind herself that not everyone would leave her.

Haven pulled herself out of her worry, took a breath, and looked up thoughtfully. "As nice as this house looks," she added,

"I'm not sure this house could fit all of us, though. I mean not that we would go in, but I often wonder what it would be like to sleep in a real bed."

At that moment, a low rumbling came from the house. Haven quickly pulled her hand off the house and glanced up. Part of the upper wall started to expand as if a mushroom the size of a football stadium was growing out of the top. Liora and Haven both dashed to the yard, grabbing Aiden and J.J. in the process. They stood at the edge of the forest, staring.

The roof shook as dust flew out from the eaves.

"No one went inside, right?" Haven yelled desperately. "Should we go in and look?"

"They're all on the porch. Stay back," Liora hollered over what sounded like twenty construction sites.

The house grew, like a blooming flower, adding three different balconies, a second story observatory, and a slide that came from a new dinosaur-shaped window at the top of the house. The slide unrolled towards the ground like an elephant trunk. As soon as it touched the ground, the house became silent again.

Eutychus dashed around the back with Merry at his heels. "What happened?" He glanced up, shading his eyes from the sun.

"Our house!" Merry exclaimed as her eyes widened.

"I—don't know what exactly happened." Haven felt heat rise to her face and her stomach cramp, like she was in trouble. "We were talking about sleeping in a real bed. You know, *inside.*"

Everyone stared at the new second story above them.

"It had to be the Indigo," Asher said in awe.

"So, you guys can grow your own houses if you want?" Haven asked, looking from Eutychus to Asher. *Please, please say this is a normal feature of Time Server houses,* she thought.

"Actually, that is not a skill we normally see, dear." Merry's voice was kind. She exchanged looks with Eutychus.

Asher laughed. "Like, never. Mom, you can't go all Doctor Hubble on her. Tell her the truth."

"How can I be able to grow houses when you guys can't?"

Eutychus gently stepped towards Haven and patted her on the shoulder. "If it was as you said, and you were only thinking of more room, maybe the house grew because you wanted it to."

Haven glanced down at the Indigo, looking delicate as ever, the dahlia which had now lifted the stone higher because of the extra petals, surrounded the deep bluish-purple stone. She loved wearing the ring, but the stuff that was happening to her because of it made her feel the same way she felt when she first saw time freeze and unfreeze: worried that something was wrong with her.

"I'm checking to see if I got a room!" Fletcher said as he made a beeline for the slide to try to climb up. Finn was right behind him.

"Me too!" Aiden said as he ran after the boys.

"Come on, Miss Merry! Let's see if we get to stay!" Hannalee skipped towards the back door.

"Wait!" Haven yelled. "You mean after staying outside for weeks you want to go in the house *now*?"

Everyone paused. The Youngers looked at Merry and Eutychus, who beamed at them.

Hannalee silently tiptoed to Merry and slipped her miniature hand in the woman's round one.

"Yeah, I do," Fletcher said.

Finn pumped his fists as he slid down a few feet, "Dino Slide! Dino Slide!"

Aiden and Hannalee joined in as their chorus continued through the back door.

Liora glanced at Haven. "Might as well. I'm tired of smelling nasty."

Haven laughed to herself as Liora went into the house. It was the first time she saw Liora enter a house without visibly shaking, and the smile on her face brought a lightness to her chest that hadn't been there before.

She glanced around the yard and took in a deep breath.

It was a new season for all at Haven's Place.

As she crossed the yard, she saw a person across the street who was as tall as the eaves. The man or woman was obviously staring at her from the shadows but what really got her attention was that they were wearing a hooded red overcoat, like the one she saw during training, and at the Fairy Market. Haven moved towards the person and just caught a red coattail disappearing behind the house.

She had to know who was watching her.

"Hey!" she said as she ran towards the front of the house, following the billowing tails of the red coat.

"What are you doing?" Jairus appeared out of nowhere and followed swiftly behind her.

Haven didn't answer. Instead, she trailed the person who made a sharp left behind a flower garden, then scaled the fence onto another street. It was easy for her to keep up after weeks of jumping and running in her training.

Their red coat tails flapped around every turn as they avoided a collision with Cricket, who was taking a stroll down the street. Haven matched pace with the mystery person as Cricket stared after them, in awe.

Haven continued her pursuit, but suddenly she was in the white room again and almost ran into a thirty-foot high piece of fabric playing an option to serve. Dozens of screens flickered on different fabrics, and she knew that the neighbor to the left of the Hubbles should put more seasoning in their soup, and the neighbor across the street needed to oil their bicycle. A young Time Server who hung upside down from a tree needed rescuing, as the branches that held him cracked precariously. She could see the outcomes of each situation stretch miles long, like dominoes knocking into one another as one decision affected so many others. But the one with the boy drew her attention. She could see stretching beside his image rows of possibilities. In at least two, he lay unmoving on the ground, with either his back or neck broken.

Within a second, she was back on the Time Server Streets, chasing the person in the red coat. She staggered one step as she made the adjustment between the white room and this world. Rounding the corner of a house, she could hear a child crying in the front yard. Haven glanced to see him dangling from a tree branch. It was the same boy she had seen a moment ago.

Haven knew she could catch the red-coated person and find out who they were. She could see who had been following her all this time and find out what they wanted. But something inside her told her to stop. The child needed help and she couldn't be selfish. If she chose what she wanted, it wouldn't sit right with her.

Groaning in frustration, Haven stopped, watching the red coattails round the corner, slapping the side of the house. She hopped over the white picket fence and spoke softly to the boy in the tree. "It's okay. You're safe. We'll get you down."

Jairus caught up to Haven and gasped. "You let them get away! How could you do that?"

"This kid's safety is more important," she said glancing around the yard looking for something to stand on as the tree branch began to splinter.

Jairus shook his head. "I just don't get you, Haven. You were right there."

"I know!" Haven found a wooden chair on the porch and dragged it to the boy. "But I just couldn't let this kid fall."

Jairus looked up at the tree. "He could have held on for a bit longer."

Haven paused, looked at Jairus and said, "No, he wouldn't have made it."

"How do you know?"

"I just knew." Haven avoided Jairus's piercing eyes as she held onto the boy's shoulders.

"How?" Jairus said moving closer to Haven, not letting her look anywhere else.

"It's just . . . " She stood on the chair trying to untangle the boy from the branch. "Will you give me a little help?"

Jairus jumped onto the chair, pulled his hunting knife out of his boot and in one motion cut the boy free, which allowed Haven to catch him as he dropped from the tree. The boy sniffed, wiped his eyes, and ran inside without saying a word.

Jairus looked back at Haven, inches from her face, both of them atop the chair. "How?"

Haven held his gaze. His azure eyes had an intensity that many others did not. It had been a while since Jairus stood close to her and she didn't know if she should hug him because she missed him, or knock him off the chair since he had been acting meaner than a feral cat.

Deciding to do neither because she was just thankful he wasn't spitting insults at her, she sighed and rubbed her forehead, "It's strange. I keep getting these visions of a white room with screens showing me choices I can make. I just knew this boy would have broken his neck if I passed him. He needed me."

Jairus stared at Haven for a moment. Then with an air of concern, he replied, "Yeah, that *is* strange."

"Anarchy! Kidnappers! We want a free state! No baths for all!"

Finn and Fletcher writhed in the grip of Haven, Liora, Merry, and Asher. A mass of tangled shirts, boots flung off high into the air, and a pair of incredibly pungent boys struggled in the middle of the chaos—boys who had not dipped their toe in any type of bath for months.

"Now, dears," Merry tried to console them, "It is Giving Day—" she dodged Finn's left elbow, "—you must be clean."

"Ow! Hey! Fletcher, you bite me again and I'll bite you back," Liora growled at the boy.

"I'm not smelling like a girl!" he yelled.

The group reached the top of the stairs of the Hubble house, and Asher kicked the bathroom door open. The circular soaking tub was waiting for them, filled with steaming warm water and bubbles piled high.

"On three," Haven commanded.

"One, Two, Three!"

Both boys were tossed into the large tub howling, "Unfairness all around! I'll give you a knuckle sandwich—"

A mass of bubbles, water and dirt sloshed out of the tub. After a few seconds, the twins popped their soapy heads above the bubbles and grinned from ear to ear.

"Hey, this isn't so bad!" Fletcher spat water from his mouth.

"A bubble pool!" Finn agreed.

The Hubbles, Liora, and Haven laughed at the twins who were now taking turns pretending to do the backstroke.

"All right," Fletcher said. "We can't take a full bath with you staring at us like that."

"Yeah, split!" Finn splashed water their way, causing everyone to back up a few more feet.

"Don't be too long now!" Merry called over her shoulder, "I have sugar pastries waiting for you when you are out of the tub!"

"How about sugar pastries *in* the tub?" Finn asked.

"Don't count on it, dears."

Haven bounded down the stairs and saw Jairus sitting at the table, already helping himself to a bevy of pastries and muffins from the buffet Merry set up for them earlier this morning. She plopped next to him and began to select a few for her own plate.

"What, you couldn't help us?" she asked.

Jairus glanced up. "I don't blame them. I wouldn't want to take a bath either."

"Yeah, you'd rather wash with rainwater outside." Liora nudged Jairus as she slipped into the seat next to him.

"Better than being tied to a house for what you need," he grumbled. "Besides," Jairus eyed Asher, who was sitting on Aiden and tickling him. "It looks like you had plenty of help." With that, he picked up three pastries, rose from the table, and walked outside.

Haven sighed and watched him as he made his way around the house to the willow tree. There was no making him happy here.

Liora picked a blueberry from her muffin. "You know it is driving him crazy not being able to do anything in this place."

"How do you know?"

"While you are off training, we have a ton of time hanging out. I mean, Merry likes to keep us busy, and we explore the village when we can get away, but honestly, we have lots of free time since we don't have to scrounge for food."

"I told him he doesn't have to stay," Haven said as she watched Liora take a giant bite out of her muffin. "This is my thing, not his."

"You know, for a person who can figure things out, you can be so thick sometimes." Liora rolled her eyes. "Jairus doesn't leave because—" she paused as Asher walked to the sink and Haven's eyes flitted to the boy as he winked at both of them.

"Because of what?" Haven asked, trying to hide a small smile forming on her lips.

Liora shook her head, "Never mind."

* * *

"THIS IS TAKING FOREVER!" groaned Finn, his hair slicked to the side.

"Girls take so long!" Added an exasperated Fletcher as he hung over the armrest of the chair, dangling his arms back and forth in a steady rhythm.

The boys donned nice black slacks and button-up shirts with new shoes to match. In fact, almost every male had dressed in their new clothes, looking ready for an elegant affair. Jairus, however, remained in his jeans and camouflage jacket that had the words Fearless embroidered on the back.

"Girls take a while 'cause they're prettier than boys." Hannalee bounced down the steps in a buttercup yellow silk dress with miniature pink flowers embroidered on the hem of the knee-length skirt.

"Nah, the skirts take longer 'cause they think too much." Fletcher poked the side of the armchair where a bit of stuffing had fallen out.

Haven made her way down the stairs in a floor-length champagne pink silk dress and matching elbow length gloves. Her sandy blonde hair had been swept up in a sea of tiny white dahlias, with escaped strands falling around her bare shoulders.

"Wow," Asher said, stunned.

"Ew!" Finn said looking from Asher to Haven. "I think Asher likes you, Haven!"

Eutychus chortled and said, "What's not to like? Look at this beautiful girl! I do have an eye for dress sizes!" He met Haven at the bottom of the stairs and hugged her tight.

"You look beautiful, my dear." Eutychus winked.

"Liora!" Finn jumped up. "You look—you look—"

Liora marched down in a seafoam green dress much like Haven's but hers had a high halter neck with embroidered daisies adorning the collar. Her fiery red hair was arranged in an upswept 'do, dotted with daisies.

"—like a girl!" Fletcher said, finishing what his brother could not.

Merry followed, dressed in pale gray with panels of silk draping to each side, making her look like a flower whose layered petals swayed as she walked. Her thick platinum hair had glittering jewels in each plaited braid, making it shine like the nighttime sky.

"My bride is as beautiful as ever." Eutychus said as he gently took Merry's hand.

Merry closed her eyes as Eutychus kissed her on the nose. She took a deep breath. "It is time to go!" Merry looked around the room. "Where is Jairus?"

"Sitting under the willow again. I'll go get him," said Asher.

"Better get your gift, son," said Eutychus, stopping Asher in mid-step. "I'll make sure he is ready." He patted his son on the back.

Haven walked over to the table and found the hourglass she had traded at the Fairy Market a few days ago.

"Is that what you are giving?" Asher asked her. His deep clean scent of soap surrounded her.

Haven nodded. "Apparently, it keeps track of whatever you want it to. What about you?"

"Multi-hammer." Asher laughed at Haven's look of confusion. "It is very handy when you are building things. Watch," he said as he lifted the hammer clear of everyone and flicked his wrist as if he were hammering an invisible nail. Immediately, out of every end of the hammer a different tool came out—a screwdriver, drill, saw, and even a router.

"That is handy," said Haven as Asher flicked his wrist the opposite way to bring the tools back in place.

Liora stood beside Haven with a large coat rack over her shoulder. "Don't ask," she said dryly.

* * *

"Now, remember," Merry said, holding J.J.'s hand tightly, as they all ambled to the center of the city. "Your gift will tell you who it belongs to. No giving it to just anyone."

"How are we going to know?" asked Liora, fidgeting with the ornate coat rack she carried.

"The gifts tell you," said J.J. with his thumb in his mouth as he stumbled alongside his mother's skirt.

Eutychus sang about giving scoffee to billy goats as the street became crowded with Time Server families representing every Otherworld culture and nation, dressed in flowing silks and sharp suits according to their tribe. Jairus was the only male whose clothes looked like they needed a wash.

"Wished you changed before we left, huh?" Liora ribbed Jairus.

"Shut it!" he said, turning red.

The city hub loomed into view. The din of the crowd slowly became a roar as thousands of Time Servers intermingled with each other. Children wove in and out of the gathering crowd. A towering oak tree, large enough for hundreds to sit under, festooned with thick wooden vines entwined with flowers, sat as the centerpiece of the city. To the right, a 24-hour clock tower rose over the scene. Each of the twenty-four circles on the clock face was painted with a scene. One o'clock in the morning showed a grassy hill under a clear starry sky. In the circle representing six o'clock in the evening, a painting showed a family of Time Servers at dinner. In the center of the clock face were four mini-clocks, each keeping a different time.

Under the clock, R&M Sentinels roamed about the city, watching each Time Server as they passed. One Sentinel with deep green streaks of malachite that looked like they had bubbled up from his chest and froze, commanded to see inside a package, ripped it open and stepped on the delicate wrapping as he did so.

"What's with all the meanie stone guys?" Aiden asked.

Asher shrugged. "Don't know," he replied. "Hey, Dad, why are all the Sentinels here? There usually aren't this many around."

"Because of the reports of some disappearing buildings and the appearance of the . . . " He cleared his throat. "Of certain things, some Time Servers felt it safe to have them around."

"Because of me." Haven looked down. "It's because of me bringing the Indigo back here."

Eutychus patted her shoulder, "I wouldn't worry about it

much," he comforted her. "Things have a way of working themselves out better than we could imagine. Now come, the heads of council are already gathered. We should be starting soon."

A stage sat underneath the clock tower, with the six heads of council mingling amongst each other. Haven spotted Joy, who wore a high-collared red taffeta gown, chatting with Carolina.

An extremely tall and lanky Giant, who wore blue converse shoes and dark pinstriped coat with long coattails, bounded up the stage. "Welcome, fellow Time Servers, to this wonderful day: Giving Day!" The crowd cheered and hats were tossed into the air, blocking out the blue sky above.

"In thirty-seconds, the clock will strike seventeen, I am sure of it—" The crowd tittered with laughter. "—and you will begin your gift giving. Remember." He pointed his long finger as if scolding young children. "Give only one gift!"

When he stepped back from the platform, the clock face opened up and a mechanical warrior Fairy, a wildly-clothed Time Server, and a Giant wearing neon pink Converse slid out on a track. The Fairy's scales swayed to the left and then to the right until they showed even. The Time Server's hourglass flipped, causing the sand to go to the bottom, and the Giant turned a crank, which shot candy from the top of the entire clock.

A deafening cheer rose from the crowd and inspired people to mill about, looking for the owner of their gifts.

Liora was the first. She was looking around when her coat rack jumped and squirmed out of her hands and into a gentleman's grasp.

"Thank you!" he said with a broad grin. "I have been hoping for one of these!" He shook her hand wildly as Liora tried to pull her hand away in horror. She never allowed anyone to even high five her much less shake her hand.

"Go on!" encouraged Asher to Haven. "Try to find the owner."

Excited, Haven marched to Merry and held out the hour-glass, "Here! I have been wanting to give—"

Merry turned around with a pot of daffodils; someone had given her a present already.

"No, sweet Haven, that lovely gift is not for me," Merry said, shaking her head. "Remember: the gift will tell you for whom it is meant, not the other way around."

Haven sighed, disappointed. She had wanted to give Merry the hourglass she traded a couple days ago. Looking around, she decided to wander around the square. A teapot whistled when a man passed a woman, signaling that she was its owner. A telescope swiveled to point towards the young man to her right, much to his delight.

Distracted, Haven looked up at the beautiful sky. She saw baskets fall throughout the boughs of the tree to the people gathered on the grass below as they readied themselves for a picnic. People would be eating soon.

Haven looked at the hourglass. "Who do you belong to?"

The hourglass shivered in reply. Looking at it curiously, she turned left, and the shivering stopped abruptly. She turned right, and the shivering became shaking. The more steps she walked, the more violent the shaking until it was like trying to hold a cat on a leash. Haven wrestled with the hourglass, like trying to contain a rambunctious toddler, but it jumped out of her hands.

She dove after it.

A pair of leather boots stepped in front of her. She looked up to see none other than Vidor, the ornery council member. He held out his hands to receive the gift.

"For you," Haven said as she stood and gingerly laid the calmed hourglass in his gnarled hands.

"Thank you for the gift," he mumbled.

An awkward silence spanned the distance between them.

Vidor pointed his cane at Haven. "You may have the Indigo

to join us Time Servers, but that don't mean you can get away with tomfoolery or tricks!" He squinted his eyes at her, bringing his face within an inch of hers. She could see every detail of his creviced skin.

"Watch your step." Then he nodded curtly and hobbled off, clutching the hourglass.

"Did Mr. Vidor just say tomfoolery or tricks?" Asher laughed as he walked up to Haven.

She smiled and glanced down as she smoothed her dress. "Yeah, I seem to have to watch my step."

The sound of a flapping overcoat came nearer to the pair. Joyceline was barely able to control it the closer she got to Haven.

"Sweet dear, it would seem that my gift is for you." She held out the dark grey coat, which by now was flapping so wildly that it looked as if an invisible person were dancing a jig.

"Thank you, Miss Joy. I really appreciate your gift." Haven said as she took the coat. It settled down immediately as a baby would to its mother.

"Put it on!" Joy urged.

Haven laughed with uncertainty as she slipped her arms into the luxurious fabric. It was soft and warm, and the high collar, along with the downy feel of the coat, was like being wrapped in a snuggly blanket after dipping in a cool pool.

The coat changed from a charcoal gray to a purple-blue indigo. Silver thread wound around the cuffs, creating embroidered dahlias. Buttons with the letter 'H" in the decorated center popped on the collar. People around stopped to stare in awe.

"One of a kind," Joy marveled.

"The coat or Haven?" Asher laughed.

"Both," Joy answered with a knowing smile.

A pounding drum wove its way through the air from an

orchestra of instruments. The power of the notes brought smiles to everyone's already stretched faces.

"The Welcome Dance!" a little girl pushed past the trio.

Couples rose to their feet to gather on the circular dance floors that rose to its own platform. All manner of best dress from every Otherworld continent on earth was represented in this moment. Saris inlaid with beads of silver, ball gowns with trails of organza, layered skirts with alternating colors, and thin dresses that flared at the bottom with intricate circles and triangles. Time Servers changed their direction by the hints the drums offered. Shouts of joy rang through the crowd as not one language but hundreds, all sounding in harmony with each other. They jumped, twirled, and hopped depending on the change of the notes. It was joyous and powerful. The setting sun turned the city center from a golden yellow to a deep rose.

"I guess you want me to ask you to the welcome dance," Asher asked Haven, as he ran his hand through his hair.

"I'm—" she couldn't find the words, "—not sure I know how," she answered truthfully.

"Well, that's good because I'm a terrible dancer. How about we swing instead?"

Joyceline stepped back. "It isn't every day you are asked to swing on Lover's Tree by a handsome young Time Server." She smiled knowingly and kept her eyes on Haven as she turned to float away on a red sea of taffeta and chiffon, looking like the dress was carrying her instead of the other way around.

Haven took a deep breath and let her shaky hand slip into Asher's strong one. *Lover's Tree?* she thought as she tried not to read too much into it. She also wished she hadn't eaten that onion bagel earlier.

Asher led her through a group of Time Servers who gave them a wide berth, passing Esther and Harmony who were handing out scoffees in a makeshift cart. Esther narrowed her eyes when she saw Haven and shoved a scoffee into a poor elderly Time Server's hand, accidentally burning them in the process.

With Asher's hand in hers, she ignored the unwelcome stares the others gave her. Asher stopped at a giant Magnolia tree with dozens of wide swings hanging from the branches. He picked a small one high in the back—one decorated with hearts.

"This one will give us the best viewpoint," he said.

The couple climbed onto the swing and began to pump their legs. As they did, cushions seemed to grow under them on the seat and magnolias with strands of soft light wove up the ropes all the way to the branches.

"Whoa," Asher said as he glanced upward.

"What?"

"That isn't normal, Haven. Things keep growing for you. Did you do this on purpose?"

Haven glanced up as they continued to swing. Other people stopped and stared at the tiny swing up in the branches. *Great, I didn't want everyone in the city to notice my most awkward moment— my first swing with a boy.*

"Um, no. But it is nice," she said as she did her best to focus on the Indigo to hide her cheeks flushing with embarrassment.

Asher laughed. "Yeah, nice isn't a word I would have used. *Freaky cool* would be."

Haven half-smiled, her blush easing up and making her cheeks a light pink now as she felt more at ease. She chose to accept the word cool. Because accepting the word freak meant that he would think of her like a science experiment. They looked out over the dance floor as the music changed to a softer tune. Hundreds of couples settled into each other, twirling and swaying to the lilting music like flower petals against a pond. She noticed Edmundo spinning Charity, who giggled with glee. Next to them, Scientist Irving and a Ukrainian Time Server danced the Charleston, heads pressed together and smiles plastered on their faces. Seeley pushed against Vidor, trying to dodge them. Vidor scowled at Seeley, who looked as afraid as if he were being chased by a lion.

"You able to enjoy yourself today?" Asher asked as they continued to swing higher into the boughs.

"Yeah," she said, unable to look in his eyes and just now realizing how close she was sitting next to him. It made her unusually aware of herself again. *Come on, Haven! Don't act dumb!*

"You know, Haven, I'm glad you guys showed up when you did." Asher grinned.

"Why is that?" Haven tried to focus on the couples dancing but she could feel her skin tingling. Or was that the wind? Either way it was uncomfortably electric.

"Because—" He paused, searching for the right words. "You —I mean all of you, bring life into our world." He squeezed her hand and searched her eyes.

"That's nice," the words sort of stumbled out of Haven's mouth as an uncontrolled smile spread across her face. "It's nice to be wanted."

She willed herself to look at him even though part of her wanted to keep her gaze to her dress. There were happy crinkles at the corner of his eyes as he smiled at her and leaned closer. *Wait, was he going to kiss—*

A scream pierced through the moment and the music stopped. It was like everyone had been frozen in time. Then a second ripped through the crowd. It came from under the large oak tree on the opposite end of the city circle. Another yell, this time a man's voice. Haven recognized the voice. *Eutychus.*

"Down!" She told the swing which obediently and gently let the pair down to the soft grass. Asher tumbled over his feet, and Haven pulled him up. Both of them moved with the crowd. For once, Haven was grateful Timer Servers avoided her because it meant they leapt out of the way, leaving a clear path for her and Asher.

When they reached the clearing, Merry was on her knees, sobbing and trying to pick up the broken pieces of her hideous family plates. Their whole picnic—pies, roasted meat, rolls, all manner of fruit and drink, along with every piece of Merry's valuable family plates—were smashed and torn to bits. Painted on the mess was the same phrase that had been written on their house: Where are the Otherworlds?

"WHO DID THIS?" Eutychus bellowed. He stood next to Merry who was still on the ground, sobbing. "Somebody must have seen something!"

All Time Servers fell silent and shook their heads.

"What is this loudness?" Otokar pushed through the crowd.

"It was you, wasn't it, Sanjay?" Eutychus threw his coat to the ground, rolled up his sleeves and was preparing to fight a middle-aged Time Server. "I saw you over here talking to Seeley a moment ago! I'm gonna give you the worst black eye . . . "

"No, Eutychus, you must not throw your wild monkey fists!" Otokar wrapped his thick arms around Eutychus as Eutychus swung his fists into the air.

Edmundo and Charity gasped as they took in the scene. Charity ran to help Otokar, whose grip was slipping so he was holding Eutychus by his pants. Charity sprayed Freezish Spray on Eutychus's feet so all he could do was stay in one spot and wave his fists, hitting no one.

"Great Goody Glipsies, you stay put until we know who actually did this!" Charity cried.

Asher knelt next to his mother and spoke reassuring words to her as she continued to pick up the pieces of the feast. As Haven stepped from the crowd to help, everyone changed their focus from the Hubbles to her.

"It's her," one woman whispered.

"She is the one that brought this on the Hubbles," a man said across the way.

"No, dear," another said. "It is the Indigo she wears. They say she has been using it to make the Otherworlds disappear."

"Where are the Sentinels?" one called.

"Yes! They will handle this!" another agreed.

Murmurs rose from the crowd. Haven felt hot with the eyes of so many Time Servers on her. Her heart raced and her palms began to sweat. She was so angry. She just wanted to blend in and be happy with her family, yet the Time Servers wouldn't leave her alone. She felt angrier than Liora when Jairus stole her helping of an old sandwich at the Landfill.

"I did not cause those disappearances!" she shouted. "You are all crazy for thinking I would do that. All I have done is train to *help* serve and you are blaming me for taking us humans? And what, waving a wand over them and making them disappear? Hiding them in a closet somewhere? I am innocent, you blazing dolts!" *Blazing dolts?* In her effort to sound angry she was beginning to sound like the twins.

Haven glanced around; her fists balled and ready to fight. Esther smirked, her arms folded and the cat clip in her hair alternating between a meow and a hiss. Jairus shook his head and looked to the ground. Haven knew he was trying not to shout "I told you so!" above the crowd. Most everyone else stood there with their mouths open, not quite knowing what to do.

So, she turned and ran. The crowd parted for her as she raced through the myriad of gift givers still reveling in the center circle. Everyone paused to watch Haven as she dashed, her full champagne skirt flowing and the tails of her indigo coat whipping behind her.

She cut down a side street. A sign overhead—'The Book Exchangery'—caught her eye. She slammed her palms into double glass doors underneath the sign and they easily opened. The place was closed, most of the lights turned off, but she didn't care. As long as there was no one there to stare, accuse, or be afraid of her.

Rows upon teetering rows of books filled every corner with neon signs labeling each aisle. There was a strong smell of paper and scoffee as she moved through the maze. Each row spanned no wider than three feet and her skirt brushed against the sides of the books as she made several turns, haphazardly aiming for the back of the building. There, she reached a clearing with small chairs in a semi-circle and a frosted arc window along one wall.

Underneath the window was a nook and Haven squirmed her way in, with only her shoes peeking out.

Crying felt only natural, and that is what she did. She let out the frustration she felt over things that happened without her control. She was tired of trying to remain positive and smile through it all. She knew the Indigo had indeed brought suspicion on all of them, especially her.

"That is a waste of time, dear," a tiny voice came from the corner of the room.

Haven paused mid-sob, the shock of finding she wasn't alone replacing her frustration with curiosity.

"Is all of this worth the Indigo? Is it worth getting your friends involved in a place that doesn't welcome them?"

Haven crept out of her nook and slowly stood up in the center of the children's reading area. A stuffed dinosaur as tall as the ceiling leaned against a book rack in the corner. A mobile of paper Fairies hung from the center of the room, fluttering in a circle. Hobbling toward her was a sphere of a woman. She looked to be over one hundred years old and her round face filled out the wrinkles that tried to take over. Her eyes were as beady as a lizard's.

Haven's stomach dropped to her knees. *Should she run?* She wasn't sure if this librarian was for her or against. Haven glanced toward where she came, past the woman who was advancing on her slowly. Her frame filling the entire row. She was trapped.

"That is nice of you to care, ma'am." She found her voice. "I'm not sure if that is entirely true though. People care about us."

"They don't, actually. At least, not about you." The old woman continued to step forward, inching her way toward where Haven stood. Shuffle, shuffle, step. "If they had any sense, they would have found someone to take the Indigo for you. I mean, honestly, a child! With the most *dangerous* ring! Preposterous."

Haven glanced at the ring, whose petals had grown three more bands around her finger. "Who says I don't want it?"

"Oh dear one . . . Haven, is it? " The use of her name gave Haven the shivers. "I know you don't want to be a burden to the Hubbles. I know what has been happening to them. Time Servers talk. Many aren't happy it is back."

"Who would want it then? If it is so cursed, who would take it?"

"I will, dear girl."

Haven paused. This was the first time, other than the leathered man at Twigette's store, someone had offered to take the Indigo. For all the times she had felt cursed, something about the offer gave her the chills.

"W-Why? No one here wants it. Why do you?"

The woman was now no more than an arm's length away. Her breath smelled of sardines, and her flowered muumuu dress swayed when she paused. "Because it contains a power that I want."

Haven paused. Did she know about her visions? Was that the power from the ring?

The woman laughed and waved her hand, an ebony stone ring on her middle finger looking oddly out of place on her wrinkled small hands. "Oh, you have been experiencing some of those powers already, have you? I'm not surprised—it did grow on you."

"What powers are you talking about?" Haven tried to remain firm-footed, but her knees weakened as the woman came closer.

"Child." The crone put the hand with the heavy ring on Haven's shoulder. "The Indigo can do things others can't. It collects powers from each of its previous owners. One of the owners had the ability to visit the Star People. That is what I desire."

Haven screwed up her face. She remembered the Council mentioning the Star People but the overwhelming smell of sardines made it hard for her to think. "The Star People are—"

"People that have passed on. Yes, girl, get it together."

"So, you want this to go visit dead people?" Haven couldn't help herself. The woman looked like she was going to join the Star People herself at any moment! "Why now?"

She gripped Haven's shoulder unusually tightly for such a small woman. "You are a nosy thing, aren't you?"

Haven crossed her arms and stepped backwards. "If I am going to give you the Indigo, I should at least know how you are going to use it."

The woman's dark eyes glowered. Haven didn't breathe. At least, it felt like she didn't.

"Someone I loved. I want to talk to them again," she said, her voice wavering. "They were taken too early."

Haven softened. "Oh, I'm so sorry."

The woman straightened as if brushing off Haven's pity. "You know about wanting to be around the people you love, don't you?"

A stab hit Haven in the heart. *Of course that was true.*

"You don't need the trouble of the Indigo weighing on your friends, weighing on those Hubbles. You give it to me, and you won't have to worry about it hurting them anymore."

Aiden, Liora, Jairus, the Twins, Hannalee, the Hubbles. They all trusted her and now they were in danger.

The woman whispered, "What did you think you were going to prove by wearing the Indigo? Do you think you are so special that only you can use its power?"

She looked down at the Indigo again. *This is the thing that everyone was afraid of. The evil Time Server saw to that.*

Suddenly the front door—which had seemed miles away—made a tinkling sound as it opened. Someone entered the store.

"Think about it, Haven." The woman stepped forward as she whispered with urgency, "You can go wherever you want with your friends. I'll see to it. The Indigo is too much of a burden on you."

Haven traced the Indigo with her fingers. Should she really give it to her? It would certainly free the Hubbles from being ousted. It would pull her friends out from danger.

The woman held out her gnarled hand, cupping it to receive the Indigo. Haven saw more detail of the ring the woman wore. Besides the inky black stone, there were a pair of wings with gears embedded in them and an hourglass at the center.

"Freedom," she said under her breath.

"What did you say?" The woman snapped her hand away quickly.

"Haven?" a voice called from the other side of the store.

Haven knew that symbol was a warning and it creeped her out. It was the same symbol at the bottom of the statue. The same one on the contraption in Scientist Irving's stall at the Fairy market. And now on this old woman's ring—the one person who, oddly enough, was the only one willing to take the Indigo.

Haven eyed her; she couldn't give her the Indigo. But they couldn't stay in Time Server City anymore and put the Hubbles in danger. They had to leave.

"Over here," Haven called as she stepped back from the woman, who was now glancing nervously toward the aisle. "I'm sorry, but I can't give this to you."

The woman narrowed her eyes as footsteps came closer from the other side of the store.

"Found her! I win!" Aiden reached Haven first and ran straight into her full skirt, wrapping his arms around her legs. "You gonna leave us?"

She knelt and hugged her little friend tight, feeling the warmth of his body against hers. "I'm not gonna leave you, Bestie," she said.

"Who were you talking to?" Jairus came out from a different row, glancing around.

"Just—" she glanced to where the old woman had been standing, but she was gone. Haven exhaled before finishing her sentence, "—having a conversation with myself." She smiled at Aiden. "It doesn't matter. We are leaving this place."

"What? No, Haven!" Aiden whined. "I like it here."

Haven stood up, "I know, Aiden. But the Indigo has put all of us, including the Hubbles, in danger and we have to leave."

"It's about time you saw it my way," Jairus said. He looked a little *too* giddy.

"Yeah, yeah." Haven moved to the front of the store, with the two following behind her, "We need to get our stuff and get out of—"

She stopped abruptly. Blocking the entrance of the Book

Exchangery was a figure—one whose head almost touched the top of the door. They wore a hooded red overcoat, so Haven could not see their face.

"The Choice Maker would like a word with you," she said in a hushed tone.

EUTYCHUS, who had a black eye and a ripped shirt sleeve, sat in the Choice Maker's waiting room subdued by the day's events. The youngers, all gathered as well, leaned or lay on the other chairs while Jairus and Liora whispered to each other, conversing —or planning—Haven wasn't sure which.

Did the Choice Maker have the person in the red coat follow her? If so, why? Did he not trust her?

Haven had her head in her hands while the thoughts swirled around like one of Twigette's old record players in her shop. The hour was late and the clock ticked pointedly as if it were reminding Haven how little time she had left in Time Server City. She took a deep breath and then let out the air, hoping the questions and problems she faced would be solved with it.

No matter what, as long as we stay together, we'll be okay.

"Did you win?" Finn whispered to Eutychus.

The Time Server smiled, causing the swollen cheek to raise past the slit of his eye. "Took three of them to pull me off the scoundrel."

Finn's jaw went slack then the corners of his mouth turned upward.

"Aw, Finny Pooh found a new hero," Liora teased.

Finn crossed his arms and scowled at Liora, "Not like you've ever fought three people at once."

She rolled her eyes and grimaced. "Whatever."

Haven glanced at the doorway where the person in the hooded red coat had gone twenty minutes ago. With the exception of the quiet phrase, "Trust me," she quietly led everybody up the flights of steps hewn from the same stone as the viewing rooms. Her fingers with fingernails painted in cranberry tones wrapped around a Bo staff.

Why would she need a weapon? Is it because of me?

She took another breath as the worry of the danger she had put everyone through overtook her thoughts. She tried to focus on the door to the Choice Maker's office.

A sign above the curved entryway was painted with the words "Sandwiches Welcome" with a stick figure drawing of a gnome eating a sandwich. Two other doorways flanked the first. One, a tall, thin steel door that looked like it belonged in a bank vault with a clock gear emblazoned over the top. The other, a black marble door engraved with white scales and a tree at the center.

She tried to will the center wooden door to open and slightly jumped when the door did just that. The Clock Watcher's spindly legs in their striped pants slipped through first. The rest of him followed, black lab coat complete with a gear encircling a CW embroidered on the pocket. He ducked underneath the shortened archway.

"The Choice Maker is ready to begin our discussion," he said, motioning the group in.

Everyone hesitated. "Come on, man, he won't hurt Other-world children," the Clock Watcher said as he laughed.

He smiled down at them as they filed past. Haven felt his eyes boring into her skull like heat rays. She forgot about him as she stepped into a large, circular, roofless room that smelled of sandalwood and revealed the brilliant night sky. Half the office was lined with windows that looked out over the world below. The other half of the office was lined with bookcases whose tops blended with the sky. A fat, miniature dachshund lay in her bed, snoring loudly.

"Eutychus!" A stout man with dark bushy eyebrows, spectacles hanging off his hooked nose, and tawny complexion hopped off his work stool to shake Eutychus's hand. As he did so, part of his shirt sleeve ripped. He was a full two inches shorter than Eutychus but his presence filled the room with life.

"Ezra!" Eutychus shook the man's hand wildly, "Been practicing with more innovations?"

"Yes, yes," The man chuckled. "Never been good with those. I see your eye could do a bit of healing." He motioned to the red hooded figure who sat at a drafting table with a single desk lamp shining on a book that lay open. "List Collaborator, did you garner any--?"

She nodded causing the flaps to sway in front of her face, as if teasing Haven to guess her facial features. *Was she an ogre?* She took flattened leaves from a jar on her desk and moved swiftly to Eutychus, pressing them on Eutychus's black eye. He let his shoulders droop with relief. After a minute, she peeled off the leaf press and the eye looked better than it did before the fight.

"One of the many benefits of having a Fairy Fighter as a List Collaborator," the Choice Maker chuckled.

Well, that explains the weapon, Haven thought.

"Thank you," Eutychus said to the hooded figure, feeling his cheek.

She nodded and returned to her position in the corner of the room, where she sat at the table and wrote furiously in what looked like a worn pocketbook.

The Choice Maker went on. "Oh, macaroni! Look at these children. How wonderful!" He hobbled over to them, put his arm around the twins and laughed while he squeezed their shoulders. Next was Hannalee, whose innocent face he gently held in his hands.

"So precious," he said in awe.

The elderly man winked at Haven as he passed her to stand in front of Jairus peering at him through his glasses.

"You are a very strong young man," he said at last. "I can see you are not to be taken lightly."

Jairus grunted and looked away.

The dachshund awoke and shook as if trying to wake up the rest of her sausage-like body. She stretched her stout legs and yawned loudly enough to catch the twins' attention.

"That is Piggy," said the Choice Maker. "She has given me great company over the years."

The dog ambled to the group and sniffed each child, sounding remarkably like a pig. She stopped at Hannalee, who knelt down to scratch her under the chin, a spot that looked very difficult for the animal to reach due to the lack of lengthy legs.

Eutychus stifled a yawn and Aiden rubbed his eyes.

"Yes, it is such a late hour after the events of Giving Day. Please, rest yourselves over here and have a snack." The Choice Maker gestured to the far end of his office. Everyone paused. "There are latkes and sour cream, crisp borekas filled with cheese, and my favorite." He smiled. "Chocolate cake."

The twins raced to a dark couch that had double stacked cushions and jumped to the top, toppling over half of the cushions onto the floor. Eutychus settled into a heavily cushioned love seat, with Hannalee and Aiden snuggling on both sides.

The Clock Watcher sat on a high backed chair and took a forkful of latke topped with sour cream which plopped off the side.

Haven tried to remain casual but leaned against the door-frame ready to leave Time Server City. She wanted to run so badly, but after looking at Eutychus she knew it would disappoint the Hubbles if they left. Jairus stood by her side, unmoving.

"Haven," the Choice Maker said quietly as Finn and Fletcher grabbed three mini cakes and stuffed them in their pockets. "I understand the choices you have before you and how difficult it must be to feel torn between what is safe and what is right."

Haven looked down, willing a tear to stay put.

"But I have discovered something that you must know. Please, sit, relax, enjoy our company."

Haven glanced at Jairus who remained stony. She took a deep breath and made herself sit on the outermost chair next to the window overlooking the curve of the earth. Jairus followed.

"First off," the Choice Maker hobbled to a worn armchair no higher than four feet. "The Clock Watcher, List Collaborator, and I would like to apologize on behalf of the rest of the Time Servers. Some have treated you terribly. It is not right and we are remedying that."

Jairus snorted. "Are you *remedying* the missing buildings and people? Haven being blamed for something she isn't doing, and angry mobs who deface property don't feel safe to me."

Haven half smiled at Jairus.

"Yes," the Choice Maker said slowly, as the Clock Watcher tapped his long fingers on the arm of his chair in time to his watch. "There has been a discussion about that."

"Discussion?" Haven asked. "Is someone doing something about it?"

The List Collaborator tapped her bo staff against the ground impatiently and Haven shifted in her seat. It was like a school teacher correcting a student.

"We are, sweet Haven," the Choice Maker replied, "but until we can catch the person doing it, we have nothing to go on. We need, what do you call it? Proof."

Jairus grunted as he grabbed a dusty contraption in the corner of the office and began to inspect it. Meanwhile, Piggy continued to circle the table like a shark as Finn and Fletcher threw a boreka to her as bait.

Liora rolled her eyes. "Sounds like a typical answer for someone that has no idea."

The List Collaborator hit her bo on the floor with more force this time and the Choice Maker put his gnarled hand up.

"You are correct, Liora," he answered calmly, "I am unable to track who is doing this. My gift is to see choices, but my gift is limited."

Haven studied the man's deep brown eyes. They were kind, filled with deep affection, and something else. *Worry*.

"What do you mean see choices?" Liora glanced at the Clock Watcher, who had chosen a small cake. She picked one of her own.

"I mean I can see choices of people and how they affect the future."

"Kinda creepy," Finn whispered to Fletcher.

"Oh, children!" The Choice Maker chuckled. "It is not to be used for anything but how to decide to best serve you. This is how I know who to help each day."

Liora's face flushed, "You mean you can choose who to help?"

"It is one of the most difficult parts of my jobs as Choice Maker. We are not allowed to help every Otherworld."

"Allowed?" Liora stood up. "Not every *Otherworld* deserves to die."

"Lior—" Haven grabbed her arm.

"No, Haven, this guy could have done something to save my —!" she stopped and looked around. Every being in the room was looking at her. The Clock Watcher had a bemused expression on his face.

"Liora," the Choice Maker's voice was much softer. "I am sorry."

She looked into his eyes, her face stony. "Yeah, whatever."

The Choice Maker bowed his head and clasped his hands over his mouth staring at the ground. "Most difficult," he whispered.

Suddenly a whirring noise came from the contraption Jairus held.

"My Eggy Squeaker!" The Choice Maker exclaimed. "You've repaired it. I haven't been able to get it to work for over fifty years!"

Jairus shrugged, put the contraption on the table and looked up as if nothing happened.

"Hey! You would be an awesome candidate at the Giant University," the Clock Watcher said. He picked up the Eggy Squeaker and turned it over. "Huh. Bypassed the washer mechanism and rerouted it to the corner sparker. Ingenious."

"More than one of you has great talent," the Choice Maker said. He then looked at Haven. "The List Collaborator has been keeping an eye on you these past few weeks for me. We have noticed that you are able to have a command of things in our world—more than Time Servers themselves." The Choice Maker raised his eyebrows.

Haven glanced around the room. Aiden and Hannalee, exhausted from the party of Giving Day, were sound asleep, leaning on Eutychus who himself was snoring softly. The twins, still feeding Piggy, lounged on the upper cushions. Jairus pretended not to be interested but kept glancing at her sideways.

"I...yes."

"And you are able to . . . see . . . for lack of better words, choices you can make?"

"Yes, sir."

"There is a room, isn't there?" the Choice Maker asked, leaning closer.

Haven nodded.

The dainty teacup rattled as the Clock Watcher set it on the table.

"The Room of Choices," he whispered. "Only Choice Makers have been able to access this room."

Everyone stared at her. She couldn't take the scrutiny, so she glanced upward, trying to trace tiny lines between the stars to make patterns. If she concentrated hard enough, she could make out a house, one with tiny flowers at the door and a window in the center. *Perfect for a safe place.*

"This would make sense though wouldn't it?" The Choice Maker asked the List Collaborator as she nodded, again the flaps covering her face. She looked like she could play the character of Death in a movie. *Maybe she was Death's cousin and she couldn't show her face. All she needed was one of those sharp cutter things at the end of her staff and she would be set.* At that, Haven felt miserable.

"It doesn't matter," Jairus said, breaking the silence. "We need to get out of here."

Haven snapped back to reality, "Jairus is right: we have to leave. I have put too many people in danger by being in Time Server City with the Indigo. Choice Maker, is there a way you can get us out without causing any more disruption?"

He stood and put his hand up, "You can't go."

"Yeah, we can," Jairus stood up. "Watch us."

"What I mean to say is, if you do, four of you will be buried alive."

THE LOST BUILDINGS

"THAT CHOICE MAKER GUY IS CRAZY," Jairus argued, as he, Liora, and Haven sat under the weeping willow behind the Hubble house in the early morning hour. "He is trying to control you, Haven, by playing on your weakness."

"Wanting to keep you guys safe is not a weakness," Haven growled. She was exhausted; her mind ran in all different directions. The safety of her friends and the Hubbles. And then there's the whole dying thing.

"It is when you refuse to leave on the word of the man who thinks he is God," Liora snapped. "Come on, Jairus and I both agree, he is just keeping you here so they can keep that ring here."

"Just give it to the old woman who wants it and get out," Jairus said.

Haven rubbed her bleary eyes. She took a deep breath and clenched her jaw. She wanted to leave, but now, whenever she thought about doing so, she pictured four of her friends underground. Would it be Jairus? Finn? She could picture Fletcher not making another '40s movie reference, laying under a thin layer of dirt, his lips blue. That thought made Haven feel like she had an elephant sitting on her chest.

"Does the white room tell you no?" Jairus spat.

Heat rose within Haven. "Don't be rude. Weird stuff is going on and you aren't helping. And if I leave, *you* could be one to end up underground. Did you think about *that?*"

Jairus scoffed.

"Listen, genius," Liora said, a little softer than before. "I want to be in a safe place, too, but after listening to the Choice Maker," she rolled her eyes, "this isn't a place I want to stay."

Haven glanced over. Liora had dark circles under her eyes and her lips were pursed. She looked like she had aged twenty years. "Look, you had wanted to stay this whole time and now you are switching sides?"

Liora looked down, then out into the forest. She fiddled with a fallen leaf and then crumpled it in her hand. "If what he says is true, then he could have saved my brother. Anyone who would choose to let a kid die isn't worth my time."

Jairus and Haven didn't move. It was the first time Liora had spoken openly about her past.

"I—I am so sorry," Haven moved to console her friend.

"No, Haven," Liora jerked her arm away. "I'm not looking for pity. I want to get out of here. Jairus wants to get out of here. Let's go."

"The youngers want to stay," Haven argued. "They are safe here. The Hubbles care for them and feed them. It's better for them here."

"You mean it's better for *you*. You want to keep everyone by your side so you aren't alone," Jairus spat. Haven's mouth dropped open. "You and your new boyfriend," he said as he threw a rock to the forest.

Haven shook violently; she couldn't control herself. She turned on Jairus, "Dumb, jealous boy. Asher has been nothing but kind to me. Which is more than I can say for you, Jairus. All you seem to do is complain about everything I do. You're not happy about timing the trash. You're not happy we don't hunt in the woods. You're not happy about arriving here. You'll never be happy until you choose to be!"

Jairus stood up and grabbed his pack. "Fine, Haven. I'll be happy when I am outta here, so I'm gone."

* * *

"What is it you Otherworlds say? A penny for your thoughts?" Asher peeked his head into the room where Haven was supposed to be returning a necklace to an elderly woman who had lost it a week ago in the park. Instead, she stood there, staring at the Indigo. It was midnight in a rural Georgia town, time was frozen and Haven was back in training.

She shook her head, hoping that the heaviness she felt would go away. Jairus hadn't come back after stomping off, and Liora wouldn't speak to her this morning. She had sat under the willow tree watching through slitted eyes when Haven walked down the road with Eutychus and Asher to head to the day's training session.

"You know, I can always do Dad's rendition of 'why hair is good for the nostrils'," he said with a wink as he tripped over the elderly woman's bedroom slipper.

Haven couldn't help but crack a small smile as she pulled the necklace from one of the many pockets in her overcoat and placed it on the woman's nightstand. "You remember all seventy-five verses he came up with?"

Asher grinned, "Maybe about thirty-five. I get lost somewhere in the middle."

Haven made her way down the stairs as Asher sang the

second verse in a baritone voice with an operatic flair, "Hair is so soft, it keeps out debriiiiiiis!"

It was hard to keep a somber face, but the more he went on the more ridiculous it sounded. She glanced outside into the inky darkness as a smile formed on her face. The only light came from a fluorescent bulb at the corner of a chicken coop. Her smile froze. Leaning against the haggard coop was a dark figure, and they were not frozen.

Haven paused at the window as the person pulled something from out of their pack. Darkness covered everything and she couldn't make out the features of the person, but she saw a long golden pole glint as it passed through the light of the coop and stuck firmly in the ground.

Before she could turn to Asher, a slow rumble sounded from the earth. The windows rattled, and plates began to crash to the ground along with the elderly woman's knick-knacks of porcelain frogs.

Somewhere from the other side of the house came Eutychus's voice "Get out! Get out--now!"

Haven and Asher glanced at each other as the center of the room began to fold in on itself like a huge accordion. Haven leaped over the growing crevice that had formed in the center of the room and grabbed Asher's hand. Eutychus rounded the corner to the front sitting room. The front door collapsed and dirt rose from the ground, covering the windows. The house was sinking.

"Up, you two!" Eutychus commanded.

Asher pushed Haven up the stairs. He and his father followed close behind as pieces of wood and ceiling fell on top of the trio. Haven saw an open window ahead of them at the landing. Through the window, she could see the grass; the whole second story was now almost ground level. Asher reached in his overcoat and pulled out a tiny box of dental floss. Haven pumped her legs up the stairs as the house continued to sink amidst the loud cracks and crashes of household items.

"Window," she cried above the din as Asher popped the top of the floss and handed it to her.

"Throw it!" he yelled.

Haven tossed the floss toward the window but missed and it retracted back to her. She tried again, but she accidentally let it go and the entire box of floss flew out of her hands through the window.

"Here!" Euthchus said as he threw his own floss and it caught and held tight against the windowsill. "Asher—!"

Both of them lost their footing as the stairs crumpled into the growing abyss. Haven, breathless, had reached the window first, threw it open, and looked back to help the others. They both hung from the floss, the stairs disappearing into the earth below.

"Out!" bellowed Eutychus. If the house they were in hadn't been trying to swallow them up, Haven would have been shocked at his commanding tone. Asher scaled the floss and climbed out next and then Eutychus followed, barely getting his leg out before the window sank to the ground.

They ran to the edge of the property as the house looked like it was in quicksand all the way up to its roof. Haven paused and turned back, a terrible realization coming over her. "The woman! She's still in there!"

Eutychus grabbed her arm and held her back. "It's too late. She won't know anyhow. She is still frozen."

Haven looked back at him, wide-eyed. "We can't just leave her! What about her family?"

"For now, we'll have to let her go, Haven."

Her heart dropped as she looked around, desperately holding her stomach. Within five more seconds the rest of the roof disappeared into the ground. A layer of dirt and grass spread out over the top, looking as though the whole site has been undisturbed for years. It was too late to save her now.

"Look!" Asher said pointing across the lot. On the other side, the figure by the chicken coop pulled the golden staff from the ground. Eutychus made a move at the person, but they clearly expected it and moved swiftly behind the coop. The three dashed across the now grassy lot, reached the coop, and rounded the corner. No one was there.

"Bushy Bobbins, Eutychus, what was that?" Charity stepped out of the gateway and helped them into the viewing room. "I saw you were in trouble and couldn't drop my lost things fast enough!"

"A collapsing house caused by a golden staff," Eutychus coughed and tried to shake the dust from his hair. Beside him, Asher collapsed on the floor in exhaustion.

"A what?" Charity brushed the dust from Haven's hair and deep purple trench coat, accidentally brushing her face.

"We almost got sucked under," Asher gasped from his spot on the floor.

"But how? Who? Why? I mean, there wouldn't ever be anything that would cause this damage. There couldn't be. Are you sure?" Charity now wildly dusted Haven's shoes but missed them completely and swept the floor instead.

Haven felt completely sick to her stomach and sank down on the viewing room couch with her head in her hands. The person who made all of the buildings disappear was now targeting her and her friends. But why?

"We have to tell the Choice Maker immediately," Eutychus stated firmly. "Charity, stay here; Haven and Asher follow me. I want you two close—just in case."

* * *

"What do you mean he is out with the List Collaborator?" Eutychus asked, incredulously.

"I'm sorry, sir," simpered a thin woman who resembled a shriveled raisin. "He left several hours ago, told me to hold all of his appointments today, and didn't say when he would return. Would you like to leave a note?"

"Of all the times . . . " Eutychus ran his hand through his hair. Haven had never seen him this distressed before. To be honest, she felt the same way, as her stomach began to feel shaky. Almost being buried alive did that to her. "Yes," he threw his hand down. "Please tell him we have discovered why the buildings are disappearing."

The woman paused and looked up from her note. Just then, the thin steel door was thrown open and The Clock Watcher poked his head out.

"Dude," he said with an annoyed look on his face. "Why are you causing a ruckus?"

Eutychus stiffened and stared blankly at the Clock Watcher. He then glanced to Blythe, the administrative assistant, who eyed Eutychus with a sour expression on her face. Haven wondered why Blythe seemed to dislike Eutychus so much.

"No reason," Eutychus pushed Haven and Asher out of the office. "Just need to check with the Choice Maker on something. Come on, children."

"Hold your voice next time, man. You're ruining the vibes up here."

"Yes, Clock Watcher." Eutychus cleared his throat and began to move towards the exit. "I'll do that. Thank you, Miss Blythe," Eutychus called over his shoulder to the old woman as he pushed Haven and Asher down the stairs.

"Ow! Hey, Dad, I have a body attached to that arm!" Asher said as they arrived in the viewing room once again, but Eutychus ignored this as he paced from one end of the room to the other.

"Did you see him? What did he say? Was he angry?" Charity floated from Asher to Haven.

"Not there," Asher replied. "He told Miss Blythe to hold all of his appointments."

"Creaking Crockwoods I have never heard of that happening before." Charity flitted to the picture of Edmundo by her workstation and pocketed it. "I'd better keep you here for safe keeping, my little bushykins."

Haven wondered where the Choice Maker could have gone. Hopefully not buried underground as they almost were. Her stomach did another flip and her head began to pound.

"Why didn't you just tell the Clock Watcher?" Asher asked as Haven rubbed her temples.

"To be honest, I think the Clock Watcher would love to be the one to announce this discovery to make himself look better. If he does that without us having evidence who it was," Eutychus said as he patted Haven's shoulder, "there would be no telling who would blame you."

Haven laughed sarcastically. "Everyone already has at this point."

"True, most do think it is you," Eutychus agreed.

Haven squeezed her eyes shut. This was never going to end. Everyone she knew and liked would start disappearing or be buried underground. And what she experienced today, she would not want anyone to go through that. Haven took a deep breath. *Think, Haven. The only way to stop this . . . would be if they caught the person doing this.* "We have to find out who it is," Haven said resolutely. "Until we figure out who is doing this, they won't stop, and everyone will keep thinking it is me."

Eutychus continued to pace and scratch his beard, "I didn't plan on being a detective today, but it does sound like that is our

only option. Okay!" He clapped his hands together. "But where
—" he stopped. "I just realized who we can talk to."

He grabbed a few innovations from the top shelf above
Charity's desk and turned to her. "Will you shut down our room
and send the unfinished assignments to Edmundo? He won't
mind. Just make sure he brings reinforcements in case that staff-
wielding scoundrel comes back."

Charity nodded quickly.

He then looked at Haven and Asher and said pointedly: "You
two coming or am I going to have to use a Ropey Roo on the
both of you?"

Charity flitted to her desk with a determined look as she
prepared to contact Edmundo. "Where should I tell him you've
gone? Eutychus?"

But he had already disappeared up the stairs.

"This house—" Otokar clasped his hands and rested his chin upon them. "Disappeared into the earth?"

Eutychus nodded and scooped a mouthful of warm goulash that Otokar insisted upon serving to the trio. Haven pushed a dumpling around on the side of her plate, not feeling the need to eat.

"And you did not identify the collapser?" Otokar adjusted the plaid handkerchief decorated with goldfish he had around his neck.

Haven glanced around at the cozy room. There was a fresco of fleur-de-lis on the ceiling and a coat of arms on the wall that read 'Mluviti stříbro, mlčeti zlato' with the translation underneath: 'Speaking is Silver, Silence is Gold.' A fire burned in the fireplace and a kettle bubbling with warmed goulash hung over the fire.

As the men talked, she made a mental list of the possible suspects. Who hated her enough to try to bury her? She paused. This could be a long afternoon.

"Hey," Asher whispered. "Got any ideas yet, genius?" At that, Haven felt a pang. Liora. She hoped her friend was okay.

"No ideas, but making a list of who hated me enough to frame me for the disappearances and bury me."

"Okay, that's a good start. But you know, that's like all of Time Server City. Start small."

"Esther?"

"Nah, she is feisty, but not the murdering type."

"You sure? Her cat clip sounded like it wanted to attack me at Giving Day."

Asher laughed. "When I first met Esther, that clip hissed so loudly that Harmony had to serve me scoffee two blocks away. Now who else? Start from when you got here."

"Well, there was this girl Giant when I first stepped out onto the streets. She looked weirdly happy I was here, like she recognized me."

"Do you know her name?"

"No."

"Have you seen her since?"

"No."

"Okay, moving on," Asher said, running his hands through his hair much like Eutychus.

"Vidor isn't too fond of me," Haven offered.

"Eh, he isn't too fond of anyone, but let's put him on the list of suspects."

"What about the three men that tried to kidnap us?"

"How would they get into Time Server City?"

Haven shrugged. "We did."

"Yeah, but they don't have a ring. So, the possibility of them getting in is like zero. Stealing it is one thing, but burying you for it?"

"What about the old lady at the Book Exchangery? She

wanted the Indigo pretty badly and seemed irritated when I didn't give it to her."

"Okay, okay. I mean she is like, what, one hundred and two? But maybe . . . " Asher grinned.

Haven groaned, "I am almost out of options here!"

"Hey! What about Schorl? He is at the top of the 'I Hate Haven' list."

"Haven squinted her eyes to try to remember the person with the staff. They were so far away it could be anyone. Every time a new name was mentioned, she could picture that person being there. It was like the original memory was being erased.

"The golden staff, this is interesting, no?" Otokar interrupted Haven's thought as he closed his eyes. "Where would he procure such a dastardly item?"

"I don't know, but we need to get that scoundrel!" Eutychus waved his spoon, splattering goulash on the wall. "If I get a hold of him first, I'll put him under the thousand finger tickle gun. He won't last two minutes!"

"Do not make a camel out of a mosquito yet, comrade," Otokar patted Eutychus' shoulder then wiped the mess off the wall. "Now, hush so I may obtain this puzzle answer."

Haven continued to stare into her bowl, trying to shut out everything around her. She had to decipher this problem; too many people's lives were in danger. As much as she liked Asher, she wished Jairus were with her. They were able to solve any problem that came their way.

"Haven," a voice quietly spoke.

Haven glanced around the room. An overtly decorated clock and the crackling of the fire popped. Haven rubbed her eyes then stared bleakly into her bowl again.

"Haven," the spoon echoed in her goulash.

She glanced at Asher who furrowed his eyebrows and leaned forward, then sat up as if nothing was going on.

"Talk to the spoon," Asher whispered out of the corner of his mouth.

"The wha—?"

"Trust me."

Haven leaned forward and pretended to take a bite," What?"

"It's Levi," the spoon answered. "Outside. Quiet. Don't tell . . ."

"Haven, are you talking to the goulash?" Eutychus squinted at her.

"It is delicious, yes, but no need for a discussion with your potatoes, eat! Eat!" Otokar spooned more into her already over-flowing bowl.

Haven looked past him as he went back to the fire and saw Levi outside the window on his bubble board, waving his arms wildly.

Haven stood up, causing the bowl of piping hot goulash to slightly spill on her jeans as the spoon clattered to the floor with a quick, "Ouch!"

"I am so sorry, Mr. Otokar, but I need to get a breath of fresh air. Asher, join me?" She pushed Asher out the door as Otokar moved his chair back to the table and smoothed his handlebar mustache, seemingly not really hearing either of them. "This puzzle is challenging for the brain of age."

"Levi? How did you know—" Haven whispered as soon as she got outside. She tried to brush off the remainder of the potato from her pant leg.

"Giants' invention," Levi answered.

"Did you know it was Levi?"

"After I saw it was the spoon talking to you, yeah," Asher nodded. "We used them all the time when we were younger."

"Follow me," Levi answered quietly, weaving his board in and out of a row of bellflowers, moving swiftly as he passed two more houses. Haven and Asher half-jogged to keep up.

"Skipped your training again?" Asher ribbed Levi as they continued their quick pace.

"Shhhhh! If my uncle finds out, I won't get to volunteer at the JH."

"Why is that a big deal?" Haven asked.

"Because," he sighed. "My passion is keeping medical records. Making sure paperwork is organized."

Haven surpassed a laugh. She would have never guessed Levi was an organization lover.

"But my uncle gave my parents his word that I would train to be a Time Server."

"Tell your parents what you want." Haven shrugged her shoulders.

Levi put his foot on the ground to halt his board, rubbed his neck, then kept going. Haven turned around and raised her eyebrows at Asher, who whispered, "He lost them in the war years ago."

Haven felt a pang of loss for Levi. Although her parents rejected her, she knew what it was like to want the comfort of a loving parent.

"So, where are you leading us?" Haven looked at the brightly-colored Ukrainian cottages with thatched roofs along the road they adventured down.

"To see a guy that knows answers," Levi said while he bubble-surfed over the cobblestones. "Thought I would help you out on your quest to find out who this psycho building destroyer is."

"Wait. How do you know about that?" Haven said, coming to a full stop.

Levi shook his head. "Are you kidding me? Receptionists talk. At least three dozen people know by now. I heard one Time Server tell another."

Levi kicked up his board into his hands and led the way up the steps to a toppling house with a deep pink rose roof and light blue trim. The blue and pink made the house's yellow walls stand out. At the top, a large antenna stood out like a humongous T.

"Ukrainian T House," Asher said as he followed Levi through the dainty front door. "Scientist Irving lives here when not inventing in Giant City."

An aroma of orange peel and spice wafted from the front room. Haven glanced around at the wooden cubicles on the wall that held hundreds of types of tea in numbered jars. A uniquely decorated teapot was at the center of each table; one with rabbit playing cards, another a multi-color hummingbird, and one with a sunflower wrapped around the handle.

Time Servers chatted amongst themselves, holding mugs painted with sunflowers. They sipped carefully as steam from their hot tea floated from the mugs and over their faces. Everyone paused when they saw Haven.

"Uh, just passing through," Asher said as they wove their way around the tables. "Mr. Shevchenko, enjoying your tea?"

A bushy man who wore a blue embroidered vyshyvanka, or shirt, gaped at Asher as he pushed Haven through the room and into the kitchen. She wanted to yell, *Hey! I almost got buried underground by the person who is causing the disappearances so, please know it is not me!* But she knew to keep her mouth shut.

Levi had already reached the kitchen by the time Haven and Asher caught up and had just finished explaining the story to Scientist Irving.

"Complex, man," Scientist Irving said to Levi. He was in the middle of stirring a pot of borscht. He wore a tall baker's hat that scraped the ceiling every time he turned his head.

"Yes, but can you solve the problem?" Levi insisted.

Scientist Irving set down the ladle on the crowded countertop. "Hmmm," he said, tapping his index long finger on his flour-dusted forehead." We should research the ICN."

"The what?" Haven couldn't help herself.

"Oh hey, Haven, didn't see you standing over there. Did you chill out after Giving Day? Seemed pretty upset."

Haven felt oddly aware of herself as the whole room paused. "I . . . yeah, maybe. I mean almost being swallowed by a house kinda put things in perspective for me."

Scientist Irving waved his hand. "Don't freak out about stuff like that. If it was an innovation of ours, there's always a reversal switch." He leaned towards her and Asher. "I've needed to use it myself sometimes. Never did find my other astronaut sock though. Complete bummer."

He took off his dough-encrusted apron and wiped his hands on his shirt. Haven noticed it read 'Ukraine: it's awesome here!'

"I have my own private lab upstairs. Come on, we'll search the," he turned back and winked at Haven, "Innovation Compilation Network."

They moved through the kitchen, ducked under teapots and baking racks hanging from the ceiling, and climbed up a narrow flight of stairs.

"Are you boarding the Great Loopy Ramp yet?" Scientist Irving asked Levi, who was clomping up the stairs while munching on a sugared babka.

"Yeah, I'm on level 10 right now. I'll be ready for the Xcellieb Games next season. You?"

Scientist Irving ducked under a row of wires that crossed the hallway. "Dude, I'm ready. Just making a few adjustments on my board, and I'll be able to rip with the best."

Scientist Irving glanced at Haven. "Bubble Board Games. Every season in Giant City we have a huge contest to see who can do the best tricks. Levi can win it if he decides to stay on his board this year."

"If my uncle will let me practice," Levi grumbled.

"True, true. Otokar can be—?"

"—like a general?" Asher offered. Levi grunted.

"Yeah man, he *is* committed to the Time Server's life," Scientist Irving said.

"Way too much," Levi agreed.

They reached a landing where wooden beams stretched high above the Giant's head. Tables overflowed with wires, tools, and parts. In the corner was a neatly made bed with rows of shelves overhead. Miniature innovations filled every spot with the exception of a picture of the scientist and a young giant who was just as tall and lanky.

Scientist Irving sat down at a nearby table and a panel immediately appeared. A wall that glowed blue and was continuously solving a math problem was across from him. Scientist Irving spoke to the wall, "Please rifle through the ICN for staff or cane innovations currently housed in our lockers."

The wall blinked a few times, as if someone pulled the power plug. To Haven it looked like when Hurricane Irma came through and knocked out the power for days.

"Messed up connection, too far from Giant City," Scientist Irving typed furiously on the panel as the wall blinked twice before presenting a running list of names, numbers, and pictures. It sorted through them, glitching every few records.

While Scientist Irving banged on the panel, Haven moved closer to take a look at the picture above his bed. The young giant had the same jaunty smile as Scientist Irving, with wild hair and pointed nose to match. Their arms were linked together and they both held bubble boards at their sides, looking like they just had a laugh at a joke told long ago.

Alongside the picture was the circular box with the symbol of wings with clock gears behind an hourglass—the same box Haven had been curious about at the Fairy Market in Scientist Irving's stall. She felt the engraved symbol on the smooth wood and wondered why it kept showing up. In the Joyless Hospital on the statue, the old woman's ring, and now here again on this box that Scientist Irving said she didn't have to worry about when she was at the Fairy Market.

One blink of her eyes and she was in the white room again, only now there was an overstuffed indigo chair in front of the thirty-foot fabric panels. On one panel, a clip played her handing the box to Scientist Irving and saying two words to him. The aftermath of this choice seemed to stretch for miles as it opened up thousands of possibilities. It was like a bolt of lightning from a hurricane struck her. This is the choice she must make.

Blinking a few times to come back to the loft, she gingerly took the box and brought it to the scientist who was furiously typing. "Tell me," she said, grasping his hand and pulling it open. It was three times the size of hers.

He paused and stared at Haven, as did Levi and Asher. She repeated the words again with more force as she put the wooden box in his palm. "Tell me . . . please."

It lay in his hand as if begging to reveal its secret. He stared at the tiny thing in a trance, as though willing it to be quiet. Finally, he spoke.

"It was Clarence's. He made it for me a long time ago, when wars weren't really wars and Giant City was a peaceful, creative place."

He motioned for Haven to sit next to him as he continued.

"Our mother always said that we were twins separated by eleven years. When he was born I was a kid, but took to him right away, helped take care of him, and when he was old enough, taught him everything I knew about inventing. He was wicked smart—caught onto quarks at age three. He knew every chemical and its makeup before he could ride a board.

"That little dude would follow me into my makeshift lab and we would invent things until it was wave-riding time. Everyone knew he would be a successful inventor, including himself, and I was so stoked to be a part of his life.

"Then the great war came. This symbol cropped up everywhere, man. It was what the Indigo wearer used to send his messages. Super sketchy, and made most of us fearful. Yet, to the young Giants, it meant freedom. Freedom from being forced to invent for the sake of saving Otherworlds from their fate. They wanted to create without the responsibility of having to. But I saw it for what it was. A total trap.

"You see, this symbol meant that any Giant that bought into the lies would eventually be forced to create things for the Indigo wearer's selfish will, not to help others. They would be forced to sit at their lab tables, producing innovations made to kill, maim, and harm. If they didn't, then they would vanish at the hands of the Indigo. It was scary, man. And what is worse, nobody saw what was going on until it was too late. Clarence was one of the Giants that found out the truth pretty early on, and that is when he . . . "

Scientist Irving bowed his head and his shoulders shook as he cried silently. Haven pulled out a checkered handkerchief and handed it to the scientist, then wrapped her small arms halfway around the lanky man and patted his back.

"He was a very brave Giant," she reassured him.

He sniffed, looked at her with bleary eyes and smiled. "You're an awesome encourager, Haven. I didn't think about it that way. Bravery."

"No records as of today, Scientist Irving." The computer's voice echoed throughout the room.

"Whoops. Almost forgot about the staff." He let out a guffaw along with a bout of snot from his cry. He mopped his face, patted Haven's shoulder, and took a deep breath.

"No record at all?" Asher asked as he pulled his eyes from Haven.

Irving put an elongated finger to his lips. "The problem here is that we may not be asking the right question."

Haven glanced at the wall, which showed a zero flashing upon it. She knew she had to find out where the staff was. She tried to will the white room to come up again for an answer by squeezing her eyes shut, but all she got was an eyelid cramp.

"Hmmm, this is a puzzler," Scientist Irving said as Haven rubbed her eyes.

"Yes, a Giant quandary," Levi offered.

The scientist bellowed.

"Funny," Asher said. He then looked at Haven, "You're the smart one. That's why Liora calls you genius." He winked. "Got any ideas?"

She took a deep breath. They were searching for innovations currently housed in their network. But what about the ones that weren't currently there? Then she grinned. "What about any missing innovations?"

Scientist Irving slowly smiled. "Of course! The innovation may have totally been stolen!" Irving turned to the computer. "What Haven said."

The computer filed the records again. "One record belonging to a Clarence Archibald. Innovation Number 1302786Z. Top Secret, Class I."

Immediately, the picture of Scientist Irving's brother popped up with the picture of a golden staff with a round circle at the top and a handle in the center. The scientist turned pale and his smiled faltered.

"Top Secret, Class I?" Haven asked. "Computer, what does that mean?"

"It means, wearer of the Indigo," the computer spoke. "That this innovation was created for your forebearer."

"The previous Indigo owner?" Haven asked.

"Affirmative."

"And what was the staff to be used for?"

"Coupled with the Indigo, it was created to bury Time Server City."

"Great," Haven said.

Scientist Irving took a few deep breaths. "Computer, there's gotta be an image map of the locker where the staff was housed. Will you scan it to see if there is any image of who may have pilfered my brother's innovation?"

The computer looked like it was being unplugged every two seconds as it glitched. Scientist Irving turned to Haven. His pallid complexion told her he was on the verge of passing out.

"We're gonna find this person," Haven assured him.

"It's not that. It's just . . . Clarence. I didn't realize he created such a gnarly thing."

Asher put a hand on Scientist Irving's shoulder as the Lanky Giant sobbed into his handkerchief.

"He was forced to. You have to believe that," Haven assured him.

The glass panel behind Scientist Irving blinked and three black images with green outlines appeared. To Haven, they looked like basic cartoons—like something Hannalee might draw. "I have compiled three scans that will be helpful, Scientist."

Haven squinted at the dark screen. She could see the green outline of the staff housed in a rectangular locker. Then someone's thick hand wrapped around the staff. Then a glimpse of the side of the person's face standing near the locker.

"No!" she said as an angry heat rose to her face.

"Bruh—!" Asher said at the same time.

The spiked hair and stubby beard were unmistakable: it was Sketch, the leader of the three men who tried to kidnap the kids of Haven's Place at the landfill months ago.

THIEVERY AT THE MUSEUM

"SO LET ME GET THIS STRAIGHT," said Liora a few hours later. She stood in the alley beside the Museum of Time with Haven and Levi. "We are going in there to steal a Disguise-O-something, so Asher can pretend to be Eutychus to get into the viewing room, find out where that guy who tried to kidnap us is, and then steal the staff back from him?"

"Disguise O Meter, and yeah," Haven said in the shadow of the alley. One hundred yards away, dozens of Sentinels wove their way through the streets in front of the museum, as though they were already tipped off about their plan.

"How do you know he is even in our world anymore? He could be jumping around in one of those floating rooms trying to find his next victim to bury."

"We have to start somewhere." Haven squinted her eyes to count the Sentinels, timing how many passed and how many seconds they had to enter. "And finding out where he lived in the Otherworld is the best place to start."

"The Otherworld?" Liora asked incredulously. "Are you

listening to yourself?" She threw up her hands, thoroughly annoyed.

"Look, Lior, I know you are mad at me for not leaving because of what the Choice Maker said—"

Liora huffed.

"—but I really need you to make this work. Please?"

Liora eyed Levi, who raised his eyebrows at her and then at Haven. She let out a breath as if solving a problem she had on her mind.

"Fine, I'll help," Liora said, looking directly at her. "But you sure you want to do this? Ever since you grabbed me to go along with your plan, you have been acting crazy-determined. More than usual."

Haven stared at Liora. "This guy tried to kidnap us, he almost buried me underground, and who knows how many others he has hurt? The Choice Maker is gone, and Eutychus or Otokar wouldn't bring us with him if I told them what I wanted to do. We don't have any other options."

"You have a plan once you see him?"

"Yeah, I do," Haven said, resolutely.

"So, what's the plan?" Finn's head popped between Liora and Haven. Haven jumped back, her heart racing.

"Finn!" Haven looked behind her. "Fletcher? Aiden!"

"Hiya, Bestie! We get to be Super Spies!" Aiden's toothless grin filled his face.

"No, no, no!" Haven's voice rose to a shrill. "You guys are not participating! I purposely left you with Merry!"

"C'mon, Haven! We ain't ankle biters!" Fletcher said.

"Yeah, stop babying us like we're six," Finn agreed.

"Hey!" Aiden said, crossing his arms.

Finn patted Aiden's shoulder, "You're the coolest curtain climber I know. That's why we let you hang with us Bad Boys."

Aiden grinned again and stood like Finn, "Yeah, us Bad Boys aren't biter-ankles."

Haven glanced around. "Where is Hannalee?"

"Walking in the woods with that unicorn she found," Finn said, pulling a crispy waffle out of his pocket and munching on it.

"What?!"

"Awwww, she's fine," Fletcher said waving his hand away. "We watched them for a minute before we left them, and they seemed fit to split."

Haven looked at Liora, who shrugged. "She always explored in the woods back home. I wouldn't worry."

"Besides, she's only looking for Jairus," Finn added.

At Jairus's name, Haven's heart hurt. She looked at the boys, her chest feeling tight as she remembered the house collapsing around her, sounds of the wood snapping beneath her feet.

"Guys!" Asher strolled up to the group from the other side of the museum. "Changeover is in three hours. If we are trying to sneak in when everyone is gone, we should hurry." He paused and looked at the boys, then at Haven. "You need backup?"

"Not planned," she said through gritted teeth.

"Haven, listen," Liora said. "They have been through worse. If they want to help, let them. You won't control what they do anyhow."

Haven took a deep breath. Liora was right. They had been through worse and came out okay. "Alright, you three, but if you see a crazy person with a golden staff, run."

The twins saluted.

* * *

CLICKS of heeled shoes on the polished stone floor echoed off the soaring ceiling of the museum. The curator, nowhere in sight, and the patrons, a thinning crowd, did not disturb their plan.

"I'm sneaking upstairs to loosen those dino bones," Levi whispered.

"We're in!" the twins jumped onto Levi's back as they climbed the curved staircase.

"Giant exhibit this way," Asher whispered to Haven and Liora.

They slinked past the Giant's Pinky Gloop Gun—where Finn and Fletcher had picked a fight with Liora and Haven weeks ago —and went deeper into the exhibit.

"It's over here," said Asher, pointing to an ornate display close to the center of the room. It was the case Jairus had knocked off the sign from. Haven wished he could be here helping them steal the Disguise O Meter.

Asher dug through his coat pockets, "Maybe you can use Frictionite to cut the case open?"

"I'll try it, thanks." Haven nodded. She appreciated the help. When she looked around, she saw another doorway to the back, and motioned to Liora. "Doorway."

Liora glanced in that direction. "You going to smash and grab?"

"I can't ask permission to take it, can I?"

"The whole time we lived together you always made me promise not to steal anything," Liora laid her hand on her friend's shoulder. "I'm so proud."

"Hush." Haven tried to suppress a smile. "Let's just get this over with. Aiden, stick with me, okay?"

Aiden grabbed Haven's hand tightly and started to tiptoe.

"That isn't suspicious or anything," Liora muttered as she broke off from the pair and headed for the back doorway.

They reached the display case and glanced at the label: 'Disguise O Meter. Invention for the Evil Indigo Wearer. Could perfectly imitate any being. Confiscated after capture.'

Haven shivered. This was the second time an innovation for the previous Indigo wearer had come back to haunt her. First the staff, now this.

A loud crash rang from the entry hall. Every museum patron that was in the Giant exhibit left hurriedly to see what the commotion was, and Haven found herself alone with Aiden. She placed a square of the frictionite against the glass and pressed hard. Normally it would dissolve the glass neatly for five seconds. But now . . . nothing. Haven sighed. *I guess I'll have to try the Otherworld way.*

"You see a latch?" Haven asked Aiden.

"Nope!" Aiden's muffled voice came from underneath the display case. "But I see a caterpillar. Come on little guy, keep crawling."

Haven let out a breath. There was no latch, no opening.

"Now's the time to smash and grab," Liora hissed from the doorway.

Haven searched for anything to break the glass. Two exhibits away was an enormous pipe. With Liora and Aiden's help, they toted it to the case, heaved it up and let it fall. It landed on the case with a heavy thud, but the glass remained intact.

"Try again," Haven commanded.

The pipe clamored to the floor, but the glass remained unscathed.

"Quick!" Levi's voice could be heard down the hall. "They're coming!"

Haven frantically looked at Aiden and Liora. "You two go, it will look less suspicious."

"Uh uh." Aiden shook his head. "Not leaving without my Bestie."

Haven took a deep breath of frustration and pounded the glass. "Why won't this thing open? Please, just . . . open!"

Like sand, the glass fell in tiny spiked circular shards, first in the center, then outward until an opening large enough for Haven to put her hand through allowed her to grab the innovation. Haven did so quickly, and as if time reversed, the shards lifted back up into their original position as if nothing had been touched.

"That was easy," Liora said, wide-eyed. "I coulda used that ring to get us a ton of food, you know."

"Go!" Asher said as he ran to the girls and Aiden. "The entrance is guarded. To the back!"

A gruff voice echoed just outside the exhibit. "Sentinels! Flank to the halls."

"Schorl," Haven whispered as Liora and Asher dove behind a Giant's shoe on display in the middle of the room. Haven grabbed Aiden to follow but he couldn't keep up and the pair were pinned to the edge of the oversized shoe as Schorl closed in. Haven ducked her head in her own high coat collar, wrapped her arms around Aiden, and turned her back to the approaching Schorl. She didn't think and closed her eyes shut, the way she had when alone in the pitch black at the landfill whenever she'd get scared.

Schorl's heavy steps moved closer and stopped right in front of her, the tinkling of the crystal needles reverberating through her head. Haven waited breathlessly, expecting a heavy hand to fall on her shoulder. Instead, Schorl moved to the entrance resolutely, calling for his subordinates to follow.

After a few minutes, Haven opened her eyes and looked up. He had left! She glanced down and saw that her coat had mimicked the exact pattern of the Giant's shoe behind her. She blended in perfectly.

The group broke into a run. Liora hit the back door first,

slamming it open into the bright afternoon sunshine. Aiden, Haven, and Asher followed and they sprinted to their designated alleyway where Levi and the twins were already waiting.

"Got it?" Levi asked.

Haven held it up.

"I can't believe it," Asher marveled.

"Yeah, the way she got it was even weirder," Liora said dryly.

"Smash the glass?"

"*Asked* the glass was more like it."

Levi, Asher, and the twins stared incredulously at Haven as she cleared her throat, "Alrighty, so, um, let's turn this thing on."

She inspected the Disguise O Meter. The freedom symbol was engraved neatly at the center, a tiny switch on the bottom. Haven flicked it on and nothing happened.

Asher flipped the switch a few times. Nothing. Haven turned it over in her hands. It felt light, almost as if there was nothing to it.

"Lay it on me," Finn said as he grabbed it from Haven.

"Nope!" Fletcher wrestled it out of Finn's hands. It dropped between the two boys and the case split open revealing nothing inside.

Levi picked up the two outer shells, "There is no way this is the Disguise O Meter; it's just the outer shell."

Asher picked up one of the halves, "Maybe it's on loan to someone?"

"Or someone really did nab it before us!" Fletcher piped in.

Liora looked at the boys. "Now what? How are we going to get into the viewing room?"

"It's not like we can just go to a random wall and ask the wall to open to Eutychus's room!" Levi said.

Haven thought of the glass case that opened for her a moment ago and said, "Maybe we can."

UNEXPECTED VISITORS

"Hey, he's sneezing!" Fletcher snickered as he pointed to a man whose half-closed eyelids and unnatural-looking puckered mouth made it obvious the sneeze was not a small one.

"Ooo, can I touch his boogers? Yup! Look, they don't stick on me!" said Finn, and with that, the boys rolled on the ground howling with laughter.

Haven laughed and picked her way through the frozen, crowded city street with Aiden. They passed a woman pointing at her son, her face contorted with rage. The poor boy had tears on his full cheeks and his hands behind his back.

"She is a meanie mama," said Aiden.

"Here," Haven said. "Let's turn her around so when she wakes up she is yelling at herself." She turned the woman to face her own reflection in the store window.

Aiden clapped his hands. "Yay, Bestie!"

Liora dodged a bicycle with the rider unnaturally balancing, and a few passersby. She was stuck in the middle of the sidewalk trying to figure out how to bypass a portly man and his unruly dog when Asher yelled from across the street. "Just move them, Liora. They're very light. Really."

Liora yelled back. "It grosses me out! I can't."

"You lived in a garbage dump for years and *this* grosses you out?" Haven said incredulously. She took the portly man's arm and readied herself to heave him out of the way when he moved —just the slightest pull.

"It is like he is on ice," she marveled. "Try it. It is like they all are squishy pillows on ice."

Liora gave a pained look and moved the dog out of the way with the tip of her toe. It slid to a halt next to the man, looking more obedient than he had before.

"Block your neighbor!" yelled Finn, as he pushed a pedestrian in front of his brother.

Fletcher jumped out of the way and pushed another towards Finn, blocking him. Finn dodged the sliding person and pushed a woman diagonally in front of Fletcher.

Levi shook his head, gliding through the street on his board. "Man, when everyone wakes up, they won't know what happened."

"Yeah, my dad wouldn't like us moving everyone," Asher agreed. "Hey Haven, any idea where the kidnapper is?"

Haven surveyed the stores. They had entered the viewing room with no problem—even though it wasn't Haven, Levi, or Asher's training time—thanks to the Indigo. Since that worked effortlessly, she asked the viewing room to take them to Sketch. The room did, which landed them on this city block.

"There is no way you're gonna find him, genius. Where's Jairus when you need him?" Liora said offhandedly.

Haven was about to retort when she noticed the sign behind Liora's shoulder: 'Sketch's Sycle Shop'

"There!" she cried.

The group gathered around Haven. "I don't know if Sketch is

alone or what, but what I do know is he is danger—Finn! Fletcher! Aiden! Where did you guys get that food?" Finn and Fletcher were both eating french fries and Aiden had an unmelting popsicle in his hand.

"Five finger discount," said Finn.

"Stop stealing stuff," Haven said.

"You nicked the Disguise O Meter," Fletcher shot back.

"Not the same."

"Seems like the same."

Haven groaned, "Okay, whatever, don't steal any *more* stuff, okay?"

"Got it, boss," Finn and Fletcher said in unison and saluted, spilling fries over the hood of a car.

"We have less than one hour before we have to get back to the viewing room." Levi tapped a watch on his wrist.

"Why?" Liora asked. "What happens if we stay an hour and one minute?"

"Nobody knows. We have all been warned not to be on the grid when it happens though," Levi said.

"What do you mean, the 'Grid'?" Liora furrowed her brow.

"The Otherworld," Haven said. "They call it the grid because of the coordinates. But hey, I actually never asked why we had to get off the Grid."

"Well, the Clock Watcher changes the day on the Grid at nineteen strokes our time. We can't go back in time in this Otherworld and can't travel forward any more than the next day after changeover. So, if we are caught . . . " Asher trailed off.

"Wait, you have these cool rings and you can't travel in time? What a rip-off," Fletcher said. Finn nodded.

"Let's just not get caught, okay?" Asher looked at Levi knowingly.

Haven opened the door to the shop. The floor had a layer of greasy grime. Motorcycle parts were haphazardly stacked on shelves and two men were in the shop, working on motorcycles. Haven recognized them as two of the would-be kidnappers.

The heat in Haven grew as she started to shake. She wanted to do something terrible to them at that moment. The terror they gave her and her friends, including little Aiden, who wouldn't hurt a fly.

"Haven?" Asher asked. "You okay?"

"These guys." Haven scowled. "They were the other kidnappers."

Levi rolled up his sleeves. "Come on," he grinned. "Let's do something to them."

Asher laughed. "Hey, do you still have the Glopie Gloop I loaned you?"

Levi threw two eggs to Asher as the twins watched, their mouths hanging open. With a deft hand, Asher cracked one on each man's head and let the transparent goop run from the top of their heads to the bottom of their feet.

"Good stuff," Levi cracked, as he tied their shoelaces together.

Haven moved to the tiny shop office where she found Sketch at his desk, his putrid stench telling her that he was past needing a shower. He was sleeping with his mouth open as if he were snoring. *Probably exhausted after he almost sucked Eutychus, Asher, and me under the earth earlier today.* She searched the cabinets, under his desk, and even the small bathroom. No staff.

"Alright,' Haven said, coming out of the office. "He's here but I can't find the staff. Levi, Lior, take the boys and make sure his cronies can't help, and no one else comes in. Asher, I need your help."

"I'll cover them with Ever Sleep Eyes so they think they're dreaming," Levi said as he pulled two pairs of goggles from his pocket and put them over each man's face. They looked like they wore giant fish eyes.

Liora shut all the windows and locked the front door, and the boys went to work on the two men as Levi showed them how to use the innovations.

"Can we stick him to the ceiling?" Fletcher asked Levi.

"How about we stick everything to the ceiling?" Levi took out an innovation that looked like a Rubix Cube while the Twins and Aiden whooped.

"Oh, man," Asher said as he followed Haven back to the office. "This will be tough to explain to my dad." As he stepped into the room, his hand shot up to his nose as he almost wretched. "Ugh! It smells so bad in here! How are you able to stand it?"

"Years of living in the trash," she said as she shut the office door. "Okay, remember, you go first, and don't let him see me. Not yet."

Asher put a couple of drops of Piper's Peppermint Oil under his nose then visibly smiled as the relief from the smell relaxed him. "I'm in. This'll be the best game of freeze tag I've ever played. You ready?"

"Ready enough," she said.

"I'm with you."

Haven looked down at the Indigo and then rubbed her sweaty palms together. She put her hand out much in the same fashion Eutychus did when unfreezing time and simply said, "Begin."

The tiny office was filled with the loud open-mouthed snoring of Sketch..

Asher poked the man in the side and said in a hushed tone, "Get up!"

Sketch waved his hand in the general direction of the poke but continued his nap.

Haven rolled her eyes and grabbed a half-filled sports drink from his desk. "Stand back," she whispered to Asher as Sketch continued to snore, vibrating the walls. She stood behind him and dumped the drink over the man's head, jolting him upright.

"What the—" Sketch sat up. He spotted Asher across from him. "Did you just pour my drink on me? 'Cause I'll—"

"Tell me where the staff is," Asher replied calmly.

Sketch laughed, electric blue liquid dripping down his pointy nose, making him look like a shark.

"I don't need to answer your question, fruity," he snarled and jumped up.

"Stop," Haven said calmly.

Time froze with Sketch in mid-air like a pouncing lion. Asher turned him around so he was facing the wall.

"The way this guy looks, no wonder everyone was terrified of him," Asher said, wiping his brow.

Haven nodded and breathed to let her stress out. "Begin."

Sketch slammed his face into the wall with full force. Stunned, he lay back on the ground and looked up.

"Ow!" he yelled, feeling his nose. Blood poured from it and he glared at Asher.

"Ready to answer my question?" Asher asked while Haven remained hidden in the corner.

Sketch spat. "I'm not talking to you, crazy! Get out!" He jumped again at Asher.

"Stop."

Time froze with Sketch's arms high above his head in an ape-like position. Asher and Haven moved Sketch to the corner of the room in "time out" like a child.

"Begin," Haven said, and instantly Sketch ran into the wall and lay crumpled there as he tried to figure out where he was.

"How did I—" He turned around and spotted Haven. "Y—You," he sputtered. "What are you doing here? You're not going to blast me and make me talk backwards are you, key stealer?"

"Where is the staff?" Haven said and rose to her full height.

"You don't know who you're messing with, little girl."

"Stop," Haven said, and again, time froze.

Asher stepped aside and allowed Haven to push the large man to the toilet.

"Toilet, huh?" he asked her with a smile. "That's creative."

They lifted Sketch, who, now that time was frozen, was light as a pillow, upside down so his head rested inside the bowl.

"That's gonna hurt," Asher said.

"Not as much as it'll hurt his pride when he's beaten by a *little girl*," Haven said with a smile.

"Begin," she said and leaned against a wall opposite of Sketch.

He fell headfirst into the toilet, pulled himself up with sopping wet toilet paper hanging around his ears, and sputtered the toilet water out of his mouth.

"No, you don't know who you're messing with, Sketch," Haven replied calmly.

"What the—"

"Where is the staff?" Haven stepped forward, growing bolder by the second, which surprised even herself. He lunged at her, and again she froze time.

"Haven, you are a rockstar at this," Asher said.

"He is not wanting to talk yet," she said. "Any innovations we could use?"

"I have an idea," Asher said as he pulled a pen out of his pocket and set it down on the ground of the office. "It's a Scenescape. It changes the scenery of where you are in an instant."

"How are you so good with these innovations?"

"It's a gift," Asher smiled at Haven.

She returned a half-smile. "So where do you think we should take Sketch?"

"I've got a place, but just know we will be in this office, no matter what it looks or feels like around you."

"Got it."

Asher spoke to the pen. "Cliffs of Edoar, Orange region."

The room came to life, and suddenly they were standing on the edge of a high cliff overlooking a valley below. The rocks of the valley gave off an orange glow while the warm wind whipped at their faces.

"Whoa," Haven said. "Do the Giants win awards for these innovations?"

He brought Sketch to the edge of the cliff. "Well, they do have a science fair. Ready?"

"We're going to get the staff, I know it," Haven said resolutely. "Begin."

Sketch finished his lunge, which landed him over the edge of the cliff. He screamed like a baby and clutched the edge of the crumbling rock, clawing to pull himself up.

"Where am I?"

Haven stepped closer. "Tell me where the staff is and I will get you out of here."

Sketch started crying as he held onto the cliff. "I— I— don't know what you are talking about."

"Liar," Haven said as she crouched down to look into Sketch's tear-filled eyes. "If you want to get down from where you are, tell me!"

"I don't know!" the man whimpered as he looked to the deep chasm below.

"That's too bad," said Haven. Her hair blew in the fake wind as she pried one of Sketch's pinkies off the edge of the cliff. He whimpered and tried to scramble back. "I guess you'll have a fun ride to the bottom!" she pushed another finger over the edge.

"I don't have a stinkin' staff!" he screamed as he tightened his grip on the ledge.

"Then how come you stole it from the Giant's Innovation locker?"

"The Giant's what? Are you crazy?"

"That doesn't tell me anything," Haven continued.

"I didn't steal no staff," Sketch cried, trying to hold onto the ledge.

"I saw you, Sketch, when you took it," she said, pushing another finger back and watching as he kicked desperately, holding on and trying to crawl up. "It wasn't me!" he replied, his voice wobbly.

Haven paused. Sketch wasn't lying. She could see the terror in his eyes. He wouldn't lie at a moment like this. But there was one thing he did do.

"Why did you try to kidnap us?"

Sketched stopped crying and stared at Haven. His hand slipped slightly and he gasped. "If you tell me, I won't let you fall thirty feet to the ground."

"I—I wanted to get the ring you have. Someone offered to pay a lot of money if we delivered you and it to my shop."

"Changeover is coming!" Levi's voice clearly rang from the other side of the door.

Sketch looked around to figure out where it came from.

"It's time to go," Asher said softly to Haven.

"Tell me who wanted it or I will push all of your fingers over the cliff," Haven shouted angrily. She started working on the other hand, finger by finger.

"It was a cranky old man with a motorcycle," he cried. "Volker, or something."

"Vidor?" Haven stood up.

"Yeah!" Sketch started to slip. "Vidor. A crank with a cane. Now get me——" Sketch's fingers slipped and he screamed, thinking he was going to fall into the great chasm below. After two feet, he hit the ground and clutched himself sobbing uncontrollably, happy to be alive.

"Stop," Haven said, and time froze. *Vidor, the lead council member, wanted the Indigo? Why would he try to get it from Haven in such a terrible way?*

"We gotta go!" Levi yelled.

Asher picked up the Scenescape and grabbed Haven, who was still shaking from her talk with Sketch. They bolted out of the shop. In the distance, a deep red line began to trace the edge of the landscape as it neared where they were.

"We're not gonna make it!" Liora yelled.

"Yeah, we are," Haven shouted desperately. "Aiden, come! We have thirty feet to go, run!"

The group took off towards the archway, no longer caring about the people in front of them. They pushed the squishy statues aside as the red line moved at a rabbit's pace, tracing the line of the trees, the buildings, the cars, and the people until it reached the group. The archway was two steps away, but it was too late.

18:11:22

RUNNING

Silence filled Haven's ears. No living thing moved. The only thing she could feel was her own chest when she took quick breaths, crouched on the ground, holding Aiden. Aiden.

"Am I dead?" Finn asked, slowly standing up.

"We must have bit it together," Fletcher said.

"There is no way I am spending forever with you two," Liora snarked.

Haven slowly stood. They were on the same city block but at a different time. It had been crowded and light out a second ago but now the streetlights were on, no one was on the sidewalk, the shops long since closed.

Asher peeked in one of the windows. "Midnight," he said.

"The day reset?" Haven asked.

"Yes," Eutychus spoke.

Everyone turned toward him, wide-eyed.

"Oh, uh, hi, Dad," Asher grinned sheepishly.

"Of all the times to test the Changeover Theory!" Eutychus started in as he helped them into the viewing room, hugging each child with relief as they stepped in. Well, except for Liora;

no one ever hugged Liora because she wouldn't let them. "Bringing these young children with you? I could have lost you! Your mother is angrier than a glow bird right now!"

"I know, I'm sorry," Asher said as his father hugged him a little too long. The teen's arms hung by his sides until Eutychus finally let him go. The gateway shut like a silently spinning circle behind them.

"I was the one that did it, sir," Haven confessed. "I had to find out who has the staff, and I didn't want to involve you. Both you and Merry have been through so much."

Eutychus laid both of his trunk-like hands upon Haven's shoulders. "Haven, we are in this with you. I know you are used to doing things yourself, but you are one of us. We help each other."

Haven looked down and nodded. Her body relaxed. Eutychus was a safe adult; he only wanted the best for her.

"But we did find out something . . . er, weird," Asher said, glancing at Haven. "Vidor paid the three men to kidnap Haven."

Eutychus shook his head. "That's impossible. He is the most loyal Time Server of them all. The things he has done for our city; we watched him save thousands of us from disappearing. I would wager my two family Sapphires it wasn't him. Maybe they made a mistake."

Haven thought about it for a minute. Sketch did seem positive it was Vidor. And he did describe him accurately. But if it wasn't him, was someone pretending to be Vidor?

"Uh, Eutychus?" Levi asked. He was standing over the center orb, which was uncharacteristically dark instead of its glowing, sky-blue.

Eutychus crouched underneath the center pedestal and flicked the switches.

The crystal wall of direction dimmed, flickered, then went out. They stood in complete darkness.

"That's never happened," Asher's voice came from the corner.

"Get out," the older man's voice rose in a panic.

"Hold on, Dad. Let me get a light for us to see," Asher said.

"No time. This isn't right. Go!"

They clamored up the stairs as Haven whispered to the walls, "Light, please."

Veins of golden green and yellow light emitted from beneath the stairs so that each footprint remained a few seconds after they passed.

"Haven really does have mind control powers!" Finn exclaimed. Behind him, Levi's bubble board hit the wall every few steps.

The group spilled out onto the pavement, illuminated in the early evening light. Haven could make out the outline of a crowd surrounding the entrance of the viewing rooms. Among them were three R&M Sentinels. One with deep gray prismatic crystals growing out of his right shoulder stepped forward and roughly grabbed Eutychus.

"We are here to arrest you for crimes against Time Server City," he declared.

"Dude," Levi said, glancing at Asher, whose face was stone-gray.

"What crimes?" Eutychus demanded.

"Your viewing room has been tracked in every instance of the disappearance of people and buildings of the other world. You will be held in Magma Prison for trial," said the Sentinel.

"What?!" Asher said. "No! He didn't do anything!"

Haven's heart beat a thousand times a minute. She was going to throw up. No wait—she was going to pass out. She wasn't sure which, but at that moment, one of those would be better than watching Eutychus get arrested.

"And you, wearer of The Indigo." A second Sentinel, the one

with deep green streaks of malachite bubbling up from his chest, spoke gruffly. "You're to be detained."

"She is in training," Eutychus bellowed. "She has nothing to do with this evil plot."

"We'll see." The green Sentinel looked at her suspiciously. "Otherworlds create evil easily." His arms had patches of deep green and blue crystals intermixing. If his attitude weren't so threatening, Haven would have thought him a beautiful creature.

Another Sentinel, one who resembled a roughly hewn prism the color of pumpkin, stepped towards Liora. "All Otherworlds in Time Server City are to be relocated."

"Relocated?" she said, glaring at him. "Where?"

A grey Sentinel with crystals that looked like serrated knives growing from his shoulders spoke. "That is for us to decide." His tone was devious. Haven feared one errant move would surely slice one of them up like an apple.

"We're not going with you!" Liora insisted as she tried to pull back. Just then, Levi threw a Gobbled Grape on the Sentinel, which promptly expanded six feet wide to surround him.

"Run, boys! To the dino slide!" Haven called out. She knew they would go to the Hubbles' house. The twins took off on Levi's bubble board, grabbing Aiden and pulling him up with them. Three Sentinels tried to keep up, but with no success.

Eutychus's coat fell open amidst the struggle and a can of De-ruster fell, the blue foam slightly spraying as it hit the cobblestone street. Haven grabbed the can and emptied the entire thing, filling the air with a bright blue mist. The Sentinel holding Eutychus erupted in a coughing fit and let go of Eutychus.

"Go, Haven!" shouted Eutychus. "There is nothing hidden that will not be made known!"

"No! I can't leave you!" she yelled, but she was unable to spot her mentor.

"You must. And if you don't, the Indigo will be turned for evil! Don't let us down!"

On her hands and knees, Haven grasped at the cobblestone street until she could find her footing, and then took off in a full run. She glanced behind her to see the blue dust billowing into the air clear, as Eutychus pulled out shoe strings from his jacket and looped them around two discombobulated Sentinels. She turned back and focused on running. After a mile, she paused in an alleyway to catch her breath and leaned against the wall.

Haven couldn't believe this was happening. Eutychus arrested. His family, his life ruined because she had arrived at Time Server City with the Indigo. A slow panic crept up from her stomach. Then she realized that she left Liora, Levi, and Asher behind. *Oh no.*

"Haven! Wait up!" Asher's voice was breathless.

"I told you she could run fast." Liora said as she joined him with Levi in tow.

Relieved, Haven stepped out from the alley and saw that both Liora, who had a torn sleeve, Asher, who had a glob of blue foam hanging from his ear, and Levi, who untangled part of a shoelace from his wrist, were doubled over trying to catch their breath.

"Eutychus?"

Asher shook his head. "He was tangled up with those shoelaces and told us to follow you."

Liora glanced around nervously. "We need to go."

"The Hubble House," Haven said. "I told the twins and Aiden to meet us there."

The group moved swiftly down the street, which became more deserted by the minute.

"Where is everybody going?" Asher asked.

Haven slowed her pace and glanced around. The tables in

front of the usually-busy Scoffee Shoppe were the stacked upon each other as if it were closed.

"Why is Harmony's store closed?" Haven asked.

Asher paused at the storefront. "This isn't right," he said.

"Psssssst," came a whisper from behind the blinds. It caused all four of them to look to the left.

"Pssssssst," said the urgent whisper again.

Haven moved toward the sound and could see Harmony's tiny fingers parting the blinds of her little cottage next to her shop.

"Miss Harmony?" she asked, crouching down to the window sill.

"Oh, dear girl, you are in trouble," she said with urgency. "R&M Sentinels were sent to the Hubbles' house one turn ago."

"What?" Asher asked, his voice suddenly panicked.

"Oh, my sweet boy," Harmony whispered through the crack of the blinds. "I am so sorry."

"We need to move," Levi said. "If they are looking for us, we can't stay in the village."

"I have to get to my mom," Asher said as he took two steps through the city streets.

"Wait! Go through the Briny Pass," Harmony urgently whispered. "It's the most direct route through the woods. If the Sentinels are guarding the streets, you'll have a better chance getting past them."

Haven nodded as she wiped her palms on her overcoat. She was trying to stay calm, but panic kept coming in waves in the form of a painful stomachache. "Thank you, Miss Harmony."

"You are most welcome," the tiny woman paused for a moment and reached out her childlike arm to grasp Haven's sleeve.

"I want you to know," she said with a quavering voice, "there are those of us that are for you no matter what color stone you wear."

Haven considered the woman for the first time. "Thank you," she breathed. Her stomach felt a little less achy.

Harmony's hand disappeared back into the blinds, as the tiny meow of a cat clip was heard somewhere beyond the blinds. Esther.

* * *

"Stop, I tell you!" Merry yelled at a flamingo-colored Sentinel with swirls of white about his right leg. "The Otherworlds are not here!"

"Our orders are to search the house," he said coldly.

Hidden behind the trees, everyone watched, including the twins and Aiden, who arrived minutes before. Furniture, clothes, and toys were strewn across the lawn. More Sentinels threw items out of the windows of the upper floor. Haven could see her beautiful bed splintering as it hit the ground.

"Stop, berating bullies!" Charity yelled as she pounded her fists on one of the Sentinels carrying another item out of the house. The khaki colored creature pushed her forcefully to the ground.

"You scoundrel!" Edmundo rushed to Charity's aid, helping her up. "Leave my darling alone."

Schorl stepped toward the flamboyantly dressed Time Server, crushing part of a rocking chair. His onyx-colored body marred by streaks of yellow on his face; a hornet ready to strike.

"If you continue to get in our way," he warned as he towered over him, "you will end up in Magma Prison for harboring wanted fugitives." His oversized hands grasped Edmundo's shoulder and pushed him down.

Asher broke free from the clump of trees to fight, but Levi

pounced and wrestled him to the ground, pulling him out of sight.

"No!" Levi whispered. "You can't help them."

"Get off!" he said. "My mom, she needs me!"

"What did your dad say to you before we followed Haven?" Levi asked, pinning his arms to the ground.

Asher struggled for a moment, "I don't care what he said! If he saw what they were doing—"

"He knew what they were going to do!" panted Levi, wrestling to hold his friend back. "He said it himself. 'No matter what happens.'"

Asher stopped struggling. Silence filled the gap between them and the crackle of breaking furniture off in the distance.

"What did Eutychus tell you?" Haven glimpsed back and forth from Levi to Asher.

Asher ran his hand through his hair, much like Eutychus did when he was thinking, "He said that the best way to serve him was to serve you, no matter what happens."

"He . . . did?" Haven asked with a shaky voice. She leaned back against a tree and slid down to sit. Her hand flitted down to her sparkly high tops, the ones Eutychus and Merry traded for her. "Why?"

"If my dad, who is being taken to Magma Prison, told me to follow you, then he knew it, too." Asher looked more upset than anything.

A sob caught in Haven's throat as she traced the laces of her shoes. The first father figure that actually trusted her. Aiden curled up next to her and slipped his hand in hers.

"What the next move?" Finn said as he appeared on their left and balanced confidently on the bubble board.

Haven paused for several moments before she spoke. Her stomach hurt and she felt too weak, but she had to move. Aiden gripped her hand tightly, which reminded her of many memories made at Haven's Place. It was like those times of being weak and hungry and scared at the dump prepared her for this moment. "All right," she said, taking a deep breath and willing herself to stand. "We need a hiding place to make a plan. Eutychus says Vidor wouldn't pay someone off to kidnap us, and I believe him. So, if it wasn't actually Vidor—"

"—then someone was pretending to be him." Asher finished her sentence and again, ran his hand through his hair like Eutychus did.

"The Field of Memories," Levi said, looking at Asher.

"Yeah," Asher nodded resolutely. "No one will find us there."

AN HOUR OR SO LATER, the canopy of the trees whispered as the gentle breeze rustled their thick green leaves. Everyone was silent, as the sound of breaking furniture was replaced with the sounds of the forest. Haven took a deep breath to fill her lungs with the fresh air and the sweet scent of flowers. She tried to guess which ones but the only person good at that game was Hannalee.

Hannalee.

"I hope Hannalee is okay," she said, as Aiden swung her hand back and forth. Even though he had just seen their house destroyed, he seemed to just be content as long as he was with her.

"She is with a wild unicorn; nobody will hurt her," Levi said. "Those beasts are forever loyal to the people they trust and scary if you try to hurt their owners."

Somehow that made Haven feel better.

"Maybe we should find one then," Haven joked to Asher.

Asher nodded but didn't say a word. Haven could tell he wanted to be back with his family.

"Hey," she said softly to him. "Thanks for being with us."

Asher continued to look ahead, his breathing heavier than normal. Finally, he said in a throaty voice, "It's the best way I can serve."

They trekked up the slope until the canopy of trees cleared and the night sky shone above. Asher jumped up to a ledge of rock that overlooked an endless valley. Haven followed his lead and caught up next to him. Planted below were millions of flowers, and the starlight shone over each one, illuminating their petals.

"The Field of Memories," Asher said, after the moment had been filled to the brim with awe. "Every time a person from our world goes to the Star People, a flower appears that contains a piece of the real person, the memory of them."

"You mean when they die?" Fletcher asked.

"Yeah," Levi ruffled his hair. "When they die."

"Hey," Haven said as she stopped the twins and Aiden. "You guys okay? I mean after losing our home . . . "

"Listen boss, we've lost our homes loads of times," Fletcher said with a wave of his hand.

"Yeah, as long as we're together, and crush those bad dudes in the end, we're cool!" Finn agreed.

"Like Superman!" Aiden added.

"At the end of the show, the good guys always win," Fletcher agreed.

Liora looked away, as if she wanted to shrink into the side of the hill.

Haven sighed, "Okay then."

"Watch your step!" Asher called.

The twins began their descent on stone steps hewn into the side of the bluff, taking two and three at a time.

"There must be a hundred steps here," Liora said.

"One hundred and fifty-three," Levi replied.

"You've counted?"

"More times than you know," he said, his voice tinged with sadness.

When they reached the bottom, the smell of the bevy of flowers was so overwhelming that Haven had to see which one gave off each scent. She ran her fingers through the tops, delicately touching each petal as she walked by.

"Come on!" Levi said as he took off, boarding through the rows. The twins laughed and followed.

Suddenly, balls of light shot up from the flowers as their resting place was disturbed.

"Firelights," Asher whispered. "They're tiny flames but they're harmless. Fun to watch, though."

The twins and Aiden ran in circles as the multi-color Firelights chased them. They laughed as the lights followed when they switched directions.

"Watch!" Levi said as he took his bubble board, swooped into the air and did several loops. The Firelights followed to make the shape of an ice cream swirl.

"Whoa!" Finn called.

"Me, next!" Fletcher said.

The Firelights had grown in number, illuminating the flowers in a brilliance of colors. A tiny ball of liquid violet flame cast a bright glow and landed on Asher's shoulder. He gently caught it and handed it to Haven. Amazed, she peered into his hand, her face illuminated by the glow.

The creature floated upward, hovering in front of Haven's nose, and paused for a minute, causing her to feel the warmth that the tiny flame emitted. Then, as if being called somewhere else, it moved away from her face to another part of the field.

"Wow," said Haven as she stared off. She held out her hand as a blue Firelight rested on her palm.

Asher crouched down to study three Firelights chasing each

other, as Haven watched two in her hand roll around her palm lazily as if they enjoyed being there.

"You know," Haven said, taking a deep breath and feeling a new sense of hope. "We're gonna figure this out. We're gonna get Eutychus out. Your dad believes we can find the truth. He trusts us."

Asher surveyed the field. The Firelights flitted around each flower, moving as if in a dance. After a moment he touched her arm softly, "Tag."

"What?" Haven asked, furrowing her brow.

"Tag!" He said, moving two feet back.

"Are you kidding?" she said with a half-smile.

"Dad always says to do your best thinking you've gotta have fun. So, tag." Asher began to run from Haven, as did everyone else. Everyone except Liora.

"What if I step on a flower?" Haven yelled at her crush who was halfway down one row.

"Haven, these flowers never die! Don't worry and have fun!"

"Bestie is it!" Aiden squealed.

She giggled, just how Hannalee did when playing tag with Finn and Fletcher. Haven ran after Asher, who made his way down the next row and ran twice as fast as she did. She quickened her pace and let the perfumed air fill her lungs as she pushed her legs to move faster than she had before.

As Haven picked up speed, she let everything go that she had been holding onto: Jairus leaving, Hannalee in the woods, Eutychus getting arrested, the pressure of having the Indigo, the worry she had of losing everyone she cared about. Her feet dug into the fertile soil and left footprints behind. She chased after the twins, Aiden, Levi, and Asher. After expending all her energy, Haven stopped to catch her breath and knelt down in the soft earth.

"Out of breath already?" Asher asked. Behind her, his gray eyes glinted in the glow of the Firelights.

"It just . . . " she felt a loss of words. "It just feels so good to be free."

Aiden plopped himself next to Haven and dug in the dirt, "Hey! I see a flower person."

Haven glanced down to see a flash of a miniature man with a slight build and black hair appear over the flower. "That's cool," she said in awe. "It's like the person is wrapped in the flower."

Asher knelt next to her, "Each flower represents someone. It is the flower's way of helping us remember."

"Why is there a big hole over here?" Fletcher called.

Haven and Asher glanced at each other, then moved to where Fletcher and Finn were using the hole as a jumping point for their dirt war.

"That's not normal," Asher said. "It looks like someone dug a plant from the ground. Why would they do that?"

"Huh," Haven said, leaning closer. Poking out from the ground was a tiny root with a name engraved, "Seeley Slickerson."

"Hey, Levi!" Asher called, looking like he was about to put the last puzzle piece in.

Levi jogged to the gathering group as Asher pointed to the root. "There's no way. He works in the Joyless Hospital. How could he be . . . "

"Dead?" Asher asked, wide-eyed.

"He's a ghost!" Finn said.

"One that comes back to clean stuff?" Fletcher asked. "What a raw deal."

"No way Seeley is a ghost," Levi said. "I've seen him eat a whole cake before. No ghost could do that."

Haven pursed her lips, "Then that means someone is

pretending to be Seeley and is trying to hide it by stealing their memory flower."

It was as if the excitement of electricity filled the air and struck every person on the field.

"But who?" Asher asked.

"Yeah, and why?" Levi answered.

"Levi, can you get us into the Joyless Hospital?"

Everyone looked at Haven.

"Now we're talking," Levi said with a grin.

THE JOYLESS HOSPITAL was silent at such a late hour. The cookie cart was covered—put away after a long day; the help desk was dark as the koi slid silently underneath. Stars flashed brilliantly overhead, and the soft snores of a fat cat draped over a low branch echoed in the garden.

Levi motioned for them to follow and held his hands to his lips as two workers passed them, not knowing they were hidden amongst the trees. They reached the dormitory and padded softly down the darkened hall decorated with flowers and over-sized fountains.

"This is his room," Levi whispered.

"Is he a patient?" Haven asked.

Levi shook his head. "No, he has no place to go. No family."

"That happens when you're dead," Fletcher said.

Liora rolled her eyes. "So, we are just going to burst in there and what? Jump him?"

Haven hadn't thought about that. She dug into her pockets to find anything useful to catch someone. Asher handed her a thick coil of licorice.

"Licorice Loop," he said quietly. "Lasso him and it will shoot a bubblegum barrier."

Haven smiled, "You really are great at this Time Serving stuff."

"Ewwww . . . girl compliments," Finn whispered. "Gross."

Haven's heart pounded in her ears as she pushed Finn aside playfully and readied herself. Levi grasped the handle as Asher pulled another innovation out of his pocket.

The door silently opened.

Haven slinked into the room, gripped the doorway, and disappeared around the wall. A moment passed and Aiden let out a small sneeze. Liora sternly put her finger to her lips.

Haven's head popped back out while everyone else gave a slight jump. "No one is here," she said, stunned.

They scrambled into the room and searched. It looked as though nobody had spent any time in there in years. Dust had gathered on the tables, the bed was perfect, uncreased. The pillow, stiff.

"Are you sure this room is his?" Haven asked Levi.

"Positive. I see him come in here when I check out after my night shifts."

"Maybe he *is* a ghosty!" Aiden said, "Here ghosty, ghosty!"

"Shhhh," Liora hushed. "Seriously, Aiden!"

"Let's *quietly* search the hospital for him," Haven said, collecting her thoughts to make a plan. "I'll take Aiden and Liora. Levi, see if he has checked in at the employee station. And Asher, take the twins and guard the front to make sure he doesn't escape."

Everyone scattered through the building in stealth mode.

Haven's crew began with the hammock garden. Dozens of hammocks, ranging from miniature to immense, looked like sails of an old ship, their silhouettes shining in the moonlight.

Suddenly, one moved in the distance. Liora grabbed Haven's arm and tightened her other grip on Aiden's hand.

Haven pointed for Liora to go to the left so they could fan out, but Liora shook her head vigorously. Haven pointed again with more force. Again, Liora stood her ground. Haven sighed.

She crept closer to the swinging hammock, and Liora and Aiden followed close behind. Together, they ducked under a large striped hammock, but Liora accidentally entangled her arm.

Like a silent air dancer, Liora fought the hammock. Aiden suppressed a giggle as Haven stopped Liora from moving and untangled her friend. By now, they had made so much noise, Haven was sure that if the pretend-Seeley was there, he would have heard them..

Not to be deterred, Haven moved to the side of the hammock that continued to swing. She peeked her head around.

"Haven!" Levi said in a loud whisper from across the garden, startling her.

She let out a breath of frustration, as a lynx jumped from the swinging hammock and slinked away. Apparently, all their skills to sneak up on Seeley were the worst. If he was there when they arrived, he wouldn't be now.

"What?" she whispered, irritated.

Levi jogged over to the girls and Aiden, easily dodging each hammock since he had memorized their positions long ago.

"I checked the records to see when the last time Seeley worked."

"Yeah?" Haven said.

"The records are gone."

"What?"

"I don't know how, but they have been erased."

"Are you sure?" Liora asked suspiciously.

"I have been volunteering in records since I was seven. I

know how the system works," Levi said, holding Liora's gaze. "Somebody erased all of his records."

Haven let that thought sink into her brain. No records of Seeley.

"Shhhhh," Aiden said.

Haven looked at him with surprise. "Ai—"

The young boy put his chubby hand over Haven's mouth and pointed.

Everyone let the silence of the hospital wash over them. Then she could hear it. A soft sobbing lilted from the garden.

As they wove through the clearing toward the sound, the tall statue of the woman loomed overhead. The soft sobbing continued.

"I'm sorry, my Violet," the gravelly voice said. "Our son. I am so sorry, I couldn't . . ."

Haven paused. There was something familiar about that voice. She peered through the garden. Sitting at the base of the large statue, she saw a figure hunched over, softly crying.

"Ahhhhhhh!" Fletcher ran full force, followed by Finn. The boys jumped on top of the person and began to wrestle.

"Ow! Stop! You whipper-snapper!" the voice came from beneath the pile.

"Stopping's for sissies, and I ain't no sissy, you fake Seeley!" Finn yelled as he grabbed a stick and started to hit the man on the head.

"That's mine, youngin!" the person said.

"Vidor," Haven breathed.

She ran to help as the old man pulled three innovations out of his pocket. He threw two bouncy balls at Fletcher which caused his right hand to continuously bounce on his chest unable to break away. He then whipped a web at Finn who stuck to it halfway upside down, struggling like a fly.

"What are you youngins trying to do to me?" Vidor growled.

206

"You tried to kidnap us on our turf!" Fletcher tried to lunge for Vidor, but his hand bounced against his chest, which then forced him to fall down.

"Poppycock! Kidnap?"

Maybe Eutychus was wrong. Maybe it was Vidor and he had everyone fooled. Haven felt an odd sense of calm. Vidor wouldn't be able to escape and she could get an answer out of him if she pressed him with the right questions. After going through what she did with Sketch, she felt a certain power. Like she was more in control of the things around her than she ever had been before. She stepped toward Vidor.

"We know you hired Sketch."

Vidor paused and stared at Haven.

"Sketch told me that it's you who is collapsing the buildings and sucking people into the earth," she continued. "The man with the Indian Four Motorcycle, a crank with a cane. He mentioned you by name."

Vidor started to tremble. He put his hand on the statue and backed up.

"Nope," Haven said firmly, jumping toward him. She pulled out the Licorice Loop, lunged, and threw the lasso, missing him by inches. Instead, she crashed into the statue. The old man threw marbles that expanded to pillows around the statue, successfully blocking the others from advancing.

He turned to Haven, "Yer the worst Time Server battler imaginable," he cackled. "Yer throwing arm is like a wet noodle."

Haven rubbed her head as she lay sprawled on the ground. She knew she was a terrible thrower. But she couldn't give up. She reached for the statue to help her stand and saw that just above her hand loomed the tiny Freedom symbol engraved in the stone.

"Freedom," she whispered, her heartbeat picking up speed again.

The statue trembled and Vidor's eyes widened. The gray stone panel behind him shook and then slipped through a slit below like a heavy curtain, opening up a wide hole behind him. Caught off guard, the man fell through the dark hole, grasping for anything to grab onto. Levi threw his bubble board to Haven as she dashed after him.

"Lights!" she said, and instantly a long slide lit up that led deep into the earth. Vidor was halfway down it and trying to grasp the edges to stop himself. At the bottom, long shards of crystals pointed toward the slide, ready to slice anyone who landed.

"Girl!" he cried, "Don't let me be skewered!"

On the bubble board, Haven picked up speed, ducking her head to gain an extra second. She took hold of the thick rope. *You can do this Haven.* She flicked her wrist and the rope looped around, but she missed Vidor and snapped her own foot in the process.

The white room with the Indigo chair appeared. Frustrated, Haven tried to get out, she was right in the middle of catching Vidor! But she couldn't will herself away. Once again, choices loomed before her, and the screen that was the brightest was of her *speaking*, not throwing.

"Crystals, flatten!" she called with authority as the white room disappeared. Instantly, the crystals crumbled and Vidor slid over the fine sand to the corner of the room.

His breathing was hard and labored. "Thank—thank you," he mumbled.

"Tell it to the Sentinels," Haven barked as she took the Licorice Loop and hog-tied Vidor's hands and feet and part of a stone bedpost in the corner. "You won't get anywhere, and if you try, I'll make sure the walls hold you here forever."

"Awwww, confident now that you know how to use the Indigo, ain't you?" Vidor sneered.

Haven looked around. She was in a grand stone meeting room lined with glass panels. Pictures of people, plans, and maps hung from each one. A makeshift bedroom with a mussed bed was in the corner and on a messy worktable, a picture of Violet, the same woman of the statue above at the entrance of the Freedom Room. A thirty-foot banner of the previous Indigo Owner draped all the way to the floor with the words 'Freedom For All' woven within the Freedom symbol. In the corner, Haven saw four Memory Flowers lying against the wall shriveled to a crispy brown.

She knelt by one of the plants and saw the memory of Seeley—the real Seeley—with kind eyes and spectacles. Next was the girl Giant who had grinned eerily when Haven first stepped into Time Server City. She had spiked green hair and popped her gum every five seconds. On the third plant was the old librarian from the Book Exchangery, Mertle Sloskiaya. She waved at Haven, noticeably thankful her plant was to be rescued. At the last plant, Haven paused. It was none other than their new neighbor, Cricket. He jumped up and down to let Haven know his plant needed water.

Haven saw a half empty jug of water and gently poured it on the roots of the plants. "More," she commanded, and water continuously flowed over the roots to give them a good soaking.

"Cool!" Aiden slid down along with the twins.

"A secret clubhouse! Let's take notes for our next pad," Fletcher ordered Finn.

"Cricket?" Asher asked as he knelt next to Haven.

"Yeah," Haven replied. "Looks like Vidor over here used these people as his disguises to keep an eye on us."

"Smart," Asher said. "Since they had all gone to be with the Star People so long ago, no one would really recognize them, and just think it was a new person who showed up in town from another area of Time Server City or Giant Metropolis."

"Look—Seeley lived over two thousand turns ago!" Levi exclaimed.

"Whoa, that's a really old dude," Fletcher said.

"It is probably why Vidor stole their plants," Haven agreed.

"Not a bad copycat," Levi exclaimed as he stood at the center worktable. He held two outer shells of the copied Disguise O Meter. "This one almost looks like it, but you messed up on the spelling here, Vidor."

"Haven's Place," Liora murmured. "You tracked us."

Haven inspected the map of the city with marked locations where she lived. Pictures of their shanties at the dump hung in the corner. Next to it was the card of Twigette's Treasures n Things, and a receipt, for Indian Four Motorcycle parts. *The leathered man.*

"Wait, where is the Memory Flower for the guy I met at Twigettes?" Haven asked Vidor. "The guy with the goatee?"

Vidor began to tremble.

"Look," Asher said, pulling a worn paper off the board. "A list of viewing room numbers. Dad's room is on this list. Vidor? Why would you set him up? He was so loyal to you! Even after Sketch said it was you, my dad was certain it wasn't!"

"They are down the darkened slide," Otokar's voice rang from above.

"Gigglity Goobers, are you sure?" Charity's voice joined him.

"I will be the brave one, my darling," Edmundo cried as he slid down the cavern, rolled his landing and jumped up waving his arms as if performing a dance solo.

Charity and Otokar soon followed. When Otokar saw Levi, he began to blubber and rushed to his nephew, grasping him tightly. He then rushed to Asher and held both boys in a headlock.

"Disappearance was not a correct action," he tried to scold them, but he could not contain his relief.

"We were so worried," Charity grabbed the twins who already had given in to her warm bubbly grasp. "Eutychus arrested, you gone. Breeping Brownstones, you had given us a fright. I must tell Merry. She is beside herself."

"Vidor?" Otokar asked, letting the boys go. "Why are you on this ground like a little piglet?"

Edmundo rushed to his aid as he batted him away, already free from the Loop without Haven realizing it.

"Haven has discovered something we, my friend, have been searching for all these years," Vidor said as he rubbed his rump. He wobbled and pushed himself up to stand.

Otokar looked around as if noticing for the first time. "The Freedom Room."

"You have been searching for this room?" Haven asked.

"Tell her," Vidor said quietly.

"But we were sworn—"

"She might as well know being the protector of the Indigo."

Haven was taken aback. *Protector?*

Otokar nodded curtly and cleared his throat. "There is a group called S.C.A.T.S.," he leaned in close, "Secret Coalition Association for Time Servers."

"Longest name ever," Liora mumbled.

"Yes, this group formation was during the Great War. We spied on the Indigo wearer during his riots, trying to capture him."

"So the rumors about a secret group were true," Levi said wide-eyed. "You were part of it?"

Otokar slapped Levi on the back, "Oh, ho! Didn't think old Uncle Otokar could do this fighting?"

"I didn't . . . no, actually, you're so . . . *old*," Levi said.

"Age is perceived weakness," Otokar said. "You can do great things no matter how old," he leaned next to the twins, "or how young."

"Get to the good part, mustachioed Czech!" Vidor said as he waved his arms, wobbled, and then gripped the stone bed.

"S.C.A.T.S. won the war. But evidence showed others tried to keep the Freedom movement alive with rumors of them, the enemy, hiding in a Freedom Room. We have been looking for this room to uncover what they know for years; this is where they kept their plans! All they needed to continue this evil movement was . . . "

Everyone looked at Haven.

"Me," she said.

"You are correct, another wearer of the Indigo to wield its power over people just like the last wearer did. It was not only a symbol of evil, but a symbol of power and greatness among every Time Server. The interesting part is, the Indigo wearer turned out to be what the evil Freedom movement was against, an Otherworld; or you, my lovely lady," Edmundo said.

"I bet they were knocked off!" Finn said.

"More than we realize, this I am knowing," Otokar said.

"You were in S.C.A.T.S.?" Haven asked Vidor.

"Actually, he is our leader," Charity added. "Every day he is fighting to help find any person who wants to destroy the Time Server way of life. He has trained me, and Edmundie Pooh, along with dozens of others. If it weren't for Vidor, we would have lost the war."

"You didn't hire Sketch to kidnap me to get the Indigo? You aren't disguising yourself as Seeley?" Haven asked.

"Girl," Vidor said softly. Haven was taken aback; she had never heard him speak that way. "I'm not the one who did those things."

By the look of Vidor's somber face, she knew he was right.

"You know who it is," she said.

"Yes," he took a handkerchief and blew his nose. "It's my son, Fane."

VIDOR'S tiny house was more of a rabbit hole than anything else. It was at the edge of Europe East, burrowed within the woods of acacia trees. The hut itself smelled of cabbage and corned beef, but it felt cozy. Haven sat on a chair covered with a hand-stitched quilt and watched tiny specks of crystal white sand clink to the bottom of the hourglass that she had given Vidor on Giving Day. A large bowl filled with lollipops sat in the corner while the twins and Aiden fished for their favorite colors.

In the kitchen, Vidor busied himself cooking a feast for his guests. Otokar insisted he help, but Vidor kept kicking him out, throwing kitchen utensils after him.

"Vidor, the baskets come with cooked food," Charity called from the other side of the living room.

"Fairies," Vidor rolled his eyes, "I like to cook my own food, dag-nabbit. Don't trust nothing that I don't cook myself."

Charity sighed and continued to put plates on the table as Levi entertained Aiden and the twins by teaching them how to do loops on the bubble board.

Liora propped her feet on the opposite chair, staring off as she braided a lock of her own hair.

"You okay?" Haven asked.

Liora turned her head towards Haven not really looking at her.

"Liora?"

"Huh? Oh, yeah," she said, still staring off into space.

"Liora!"

"What?" she answered grouchily.

"Are you okay?" Haven asked.

"Yeah, Haven, I'm fine. Why are you always so worried about me? Stop being concerned with everyone else and think about yourself for a change."

Haven was stunned. She opened her mouth to say something but shut it. She couldn't retort.

"Feastin' time!" Vidor called, as the twins raced to the table. They had already shoved food in their mouths when the old man snapped their hands with two stretchy, sticky fingers. "Wait until we say thanks, youngins."

As Haven sat, the smell of the feast wafted through the house. Fried squash, cornbread muffins, green bean casserole, and chicken and dumplings were just the main course. Haven saw chocolate satin pie in the corner, along with candied pecans and ice cream.

"Vidor, this looks phenomenal!" Charity eyed the food. "You cooked all of this?"

"My mama taught me when I was a youngin. She's from America North, and ain't no one gonna cook for her . . . but her."

"Indeed," Otokar said. "A rigid woman, this fact I know."

Vidor snorted and patted Otokar's back. Haven thought they both must have gotten in trouble by her many times.

After everyone was settled, Vidor stood and said a blessing

over the feast, while the twins' hands hovered over the squash. He finished the blessing and winked at the boys.

"More muffins please!" Aiden said, stuffing three into his mouth at once.

"Can we have the chocolate pie now?" Finn said, trying to reach behind Vidor.

"Do it and I'll put the Shrinky Doo on you," Vidor growled. Finn brought his hand back and grumbled. He stuffed a few chunks of fried squash and a pork chop in his pocket instead.

"I think this is a good time to talk about what you plan to do next, girl," Vidor said to Haven once everyone's plates were full and they were happily munching away.

"I have taken the room numbers from the Freedom Room," Otokar said. "Scientist Irving will travel to help us."

"Yes, Edmundie Pooh and I are willing to do whatever you want, Haven. I can open a viewing room for you, give you any of the innovations that I have stored. I can even help you restock your coat if you would like."

Haven paused mid-bite. Her face flushed. Did they expect her to be their leader?

"To the rightful owner of the Indigo!" Edmundo raised his mug in the air and everyone followed.

"I . . . you think I am the rightful owner?" Haven asked.

"I know this is the big shocker," Otokar put his mug down, fluffs of foam sloshing out of the side. "Most Time Servers do not trust you."

"But you are the only one that has been able to handle the Indigo better than anyone," Charity said. "You make houses grow, you can see the Room of Choices, you can even turn things more beepity beuatifuller than before!"

"You are surely correct!" Edmundo agreed. "The best of the best."

"The Tippity of the Top!"

"The—"

"Hush, you three are scaring the girl," Vidor said with a wave of his fork that scattered a few peas across the table. "Girl, it took you three months to uncover what it took us years in all of our attempts. You are the only one that has discovered where the Freedom Room is, and you've discovered the clues to a plot more developed than we knew. You use the Indigo with deep talent and serve others without thinking about yourself. You are the true owner of the Indigo."

"But I did these things by accident," Haven said. "I mean, sometimes people helped me, but finding Seeley's memory flower, opening the Freedom Room, growing things . . . I didn't mean to do them."

"And yet here you are," Vidor said. "Don't matter if you meant to do them. You successfully dodged several attacks and have gotten closer to finding my son than I have. Accident or not, girl, you still come out with answers."

Haven sat still, sweat beading on her forehead. Asher reached his hand under the table and squeezed hers. It comforted her knowing that he was with her. They all were.

"So, what we're asking you is," Vidor said, leaning closer. "What are you planning next?"

Haven glanced around the table. The twins had a wild look in their eyes, Aiden's face shone with excitement, Levi leaned back and sported a half-grin, and Asher continued to hold her hand. A smile grew on her face until she couldn't contain it anymore.

* * *

"FANE WILL TRY to take down more buildings to create an even greater panic in Time Server City," Haven said. She commanded the room, which was now filled with everyone, plus Scientist

Irving, who arrived during a downpour after their meal. "From what I know, he likes to create mass panic, so if anyone sees me, they will immediately find a Sentinel."

"Yes, that is true," Edmundo spoke up. "Panic has risen amongst us."

"If they see her, she is toast," Fletcher agreed, as he munched on one of the tea cakes that Scientist Irving made for the twins.

"We need to catch Fane in the act," Asher added to the conversation.

Haven nodded and addressed Asher. "You found a list of viewing rooms that Fane had, right? Since he isn't assigned to a room as a Time Server, I think he is using those to access our world."

"We can monitor these rooms with Scientist Irving innovations," Otokar said, gesturing to the scientist who had stretched out his long legs into the middle of the room. His polka dotted converse shoes tapped Asher's knees across from him. Everyone turned their heads to the white-haired scientist, waiting for a response.

"Oh, me? Yes," he cleared his throat. The Giant held out his hand and unraveled his bony fingers to reveal four silver bugs no bigger than a fruit fly. "I call them Fly On The Wall or FOTWs for short," he smiled.

Haven squinted to try to get a closer look, "What do they do?"

"Oh, just about anything, man," Scientist Irving replied. "Mostly video and audio work, but you can speak through them and cause things to move in our world. It is as if you are standing right there. They also give off the coordinates of where they are, so locating them is a snap."

"How do they move?" Asher spoke up.

"You tell them what their assignment is. So, say you want

them to follow Haven. They will do so until you speak the preset code."

"So, they would just follow me forever?" Haven said.

"Until they run out of power, which I guess is about three years."

"The point of these?" Vidor growled, sucking on a neon blue lollipop.

"No one will believe that Haven isn't the one that is collapsing the buildings unless we have proof," Charity said, pacifying the grumpy old man.

"These will be our proof. I've programmed them to stream video to all the viewing rooms in Time Server City when you give the signal: Cabbage and Carrots."

"Cabbage and carrots?" Finn asked, making a fake barfing sound. "What about jellybeans and chocolate?"

"It was Fane's favorite baby food," Scientist Irving said as he glanced at Vidor.

"Ugh. Seriously?" Fletcher asked as he joined in on the barfing sounds.

"Liver and onions was mine," Vidor said with neon blue lips from his lolly.

He was answered with more retching sounds from the twins.

"When can we dispatch them?" Haven asked.

"Right after the rain clears. They don't do well in heavy rain."

Otokar stood up and slapped his hands together. "When we find his usage room, we will send our team immediately. If a video stream is captured of him destroying human buildings, then we capture him hastily."

"I'll confront him, and get him to confess," Haven said. "I've talked to him before, at Twigette's, and at the Book Exchangery, when he was disguised as Mertle; he is too prideful to not admit he was behind it. Especially if he thinks it is just him and me."

"Who else goes with the owner of the Indigo?" Vidor asked.

"Me! I'm prepping her!" Charity spoke up, almost spilling her mug of hot chocolate.

"Yes," Otokar scratched his chin, "This is an exponential idea to give her this fighting chance."

"If Haven is going, I'm going," Asher spoke up at once. "My dad told me the best way to serve him is to protect her."

"No arguing with young Asher," Otokar said, slapping the boy on the back.

Otokar nodded and looked at Edmundo and Levi. "You two will serve?"

Levi nodded as Edmundo stood up and clicked his heels, "It will be of great service to my family to fight."

"The boys here," Vidor shoved the twins with his cane. "They are smart. Can cause a ruckus. That will be of some use."

Haven started to protest and Liora stood up, "I've got them, Haven."

* * *

LATE THAT EVENING, Vidor sat on the back porch sucking a different colored lollipop, watermelon green, watching the rain cascade down the eaves of the roof into pools of muddy water below. He grasped the hourglass as he rocked back and forth on a worn rocking chair.

Haven noiselessly sat down next to him and took in the scent of freshly watered plants whose soil had overflowed from their pots.

"You're good rain-watching company," Vidor quietly spoke, rolling the sucker around in his mouth.

Haven stared at him as he chewed the last of the candy and sighed. Sand continued to drop through the tiny opening of the hourglass Vidor desperately clutched. She wondered what he was keeping track of, for it looked like the end of sand from the top bowl was coming near.

"It's keeping track of when I get to speak to my boy again," Vidor eyed her.

She spoke softly and put her hand on his forearm: "I am sorry that your son is involved."

Vidor took a handkerchief, blew his bulbous nose and stuffed the handkerchief back in his upper pocket. "Yup, my dear girl, me too. It would hurt his mama, for sure."

Haven remembered the conversation Fane had with her at the Book Exchangery when he was disguised as Mertle. "He had said he wanted the Indigo to go visit someone with the Star People. That they were taken too early. Is that true?"

Vidor stopped his rocking and sat still. "Girl," he said finally, his voice unsteady. "I have to show you something that will help you understand more about who you are facing." The old man gently placed the hourglass on the table next to a frayed picture album. Some of the pages looked like they were about to fall out. He gingerly slid the book off the table and handed it to her, his hands slightly trembling.

"Here," he said.

Haven nodded politely, but was secretly quite eager to look at the book. It had worn binding, and bits of leather string hanging from the inside of its pages were flung carelessly over the edge.

Vidor opened the book, which crackled loudly as if it hadn't been opened in a lifetime, and turned to the first page. On it was a picture of a woman Time Server. Her long black hair shone in the sunlight, and she held a brightly smiling baby. Underneath was written in perfect cursive, 'Violet and Fane: Festival of Feasts.'

"These were the two most precious things in my life," Vidor said. "My wife, whom I loved the first time I saw her, and our son," he ran his withered finger down the edge of the photograph, then decidedly flipped to the next page.

"Wait," Haven said. "Violet? Violet Krankerton? The statue of the lady in the Joyless Hospital?"

Vidor nodded, a watery smile on his face. It struck Haven as odd that the statue of Violet was the entrance to the Freedom Room. Maybe Fane really was doing this because of his mother.

Vidor turned the page. She could see the same boy, a toddler now, grabbing onto the edge of a younger Vidor's beard.

"My son wasn't always the first to get things," he chuckled, "but when he did, he made more of what he discovered. Spritely whippersnapper, he was."

Vidor turned through a couple more pages to one where a teenaged Fane was sitting next to a flower in the Field of Memories.

"Violet's passing day," Vidor said, more softly than ever. "It was hard for Fane. He and his mother were very close. She went to the stars too early, in my opinion," he finished.

"He said the same thing when I talked to him, as Mertle, of course," Haven said. He sniffled, took a deep breath, and turned to a page that had one photograph on it of a young man staring sternly back at the camera.

"Graduation Day," Vidor said. "Violet passed before the great war, and after that, Fane didn't care much for Time Serving. Matter of fact, he didn't care about anything. I, being the lead council member, had many connections with people, so I made arrangements for him to work at the Joyless Hospital, to get him on his feet. Serve like his mother used to serve at that place."

Vidor looked at the photo and touched the corner as if to try to reach out to his son.

"It was then that I lost him. He kept ranting about how Otherworlds took away the freedom of the Time Servers by having us serve them all the time. We were overworked, he said, no one thanked us, he said. His ideas about Otherworlds were fueled by what he saw in the hospital with overworked Time Servers.

"I tried to persuade him otherwise—to see the beauty in serving others without them knowing it. The joy it brought. But he wouldn't listen. He grew angry and distant, and finally left our home and me."

Vidor pulled out a letter from his coat pocket with a picture to go with it. He handed Haven the letter first. In short, scrawled writing, it read:

Vidor,

My time is short, so I write this for you to reflect during tough moments. Our son is special; you know this. Please take care of him when I leave. I've always told him that he will do great things if directed the right way. I love you to the stars and back.

—Violet

Haven wiped her eyes and handed the letter back to Vidor. In return, he gave her a very worn photograph of an older Vidor and his adult son who, by this time, had a goatee, and wore a leather jacket and boots.

It was the man Haven had seen the day she went to Twigette's with the Indigo, in search of medicine money for Aiden.

"That is my son, the one you are fighting against."

Haven sat there, unable to speak.

The withered man glanced at the hourglass and watched more of the sand clink down into the depths of the bowl. After a moment, he looked back down at the paper with frayed edges: "I look at this letter and picture every day, wishing I could have done something different to help him, until I finally realized that no one can help him unless he wants it." He shook his head as if to try to get the memories to abandon his thoughts. "He never wanted it."

Haven looked up into the man's tearful, red-rimmed eyes.

"Be careful, dear girl. No matter what, I still love him."

It was two agonizing days until the rain stopped and Scientist Irving could release his tiny silver bug-spies. He gave each person on the team a specific room number, and told them to stay there to watch for Fane Krankerton.

Irving then sat behind a wall-sized screen as the four little flies buzzed through Time Server City.

To pass the time, Vidor trained Haven on how to use the Giant's innovations more effectively.

"You're throwing too fast!" Vidor commanded. "Like this, or else you'll catch yourself on the sticky trap of the Stickier Stuck-Fast. How on this green earth have you been able to train so well without being able to throw the innovations correctly?"

It took both days before Haven could master throwing three out of the dozens of innovations that he had on the table.

"Yer gettin' better . . . at least you don't hit me anymore," the withered man said. He nodded when Haven successfully threw Fuddy Puddy underneath Aiden, who then bounced on it with glee.

"Do you know how to use all of these?" Haven asked.

"A Time Server's gotta know their tools for the field," Vidor said. "In the years I have served, there ain't one innovation I can't use." He took a square piece of paper, blew into it, and caused a great bubble to form, lifting himself and Aiden off the training circle.

Just then, Scientist Irving ran out of the room with his white hair flopping around as he yelled: "We've got some activity, folks! Room 567B50!"

"Fane's activity?" Otokar asked as he stood so fast that he knocked over the rocking chair he was sitting on.

"Looks like he is setting up to make another building collapse," the Giant said as he ran back to the room and went to work on the screen. "If you hurry now, you may be able to catch him."

"Can you call a fly to follow him?" Haven asked as her heart pounded. Even though she felt nervous, she was determined to catch this guy.

"I'll do better than that," Scientist Irving replied as he typed on his massive keyboard. His fingers punched in way more symbols and numbers than letters. "I'll get *all* the flies to that room."

"It's time," Haven said resolutely. She looked at every person in the room. The twins grinned eagerly while they hung on Levi, who sat on his bubble board. Otokar and Edmundo helped load up everyone with innovations. Liora hunched in the corner as she grabbed a few of the innovations herself. Asher winked at her as he pulled on his boots and picked up a Sticky Trap that had fallen out of his pocket. Scientist Irving tapped quickly on his keyboard, and Vidor helped Haven get her indigo overcoat on as Charity checked her pockets. She felt like a team, a family, one that sticks together, and fights together. Even though she felt the weight of what could happen if she messed up, she felt like she belonged to something good. She had found purpose.

"Everyone, get to your viewing rooms and check in from there," she commanded. "Oh, and watch out for Schorl; he is still after me, which includes anyone that gets in his way."

Otokar grasped Haven's shoulders much like Eutychus did that final time in the viewing room before he got arrested. "I am sure Fane will seek you first because you have the Indigo." He paused and looked directly into her eyes with great urgency. "Do not give it to him."

"What if I don't have a choice?" Haven asked, glancing around the room. Even if she felt like she had purpose, that old familiar fear of losing those she loved crept back in. "I don't want to lose any of you."

"You always have a choice," said Charity. "Lose us or not, we are here because we believe that *you* are the right choice. You have the strength to not give in."

"Well said, my beautiful flower," Edmundo smiled and bowed. "We need this Indigo in trustworthy hands or else we may all be with the Star People faster than we thought. Do not give away our only chance to survive."

"You *are* strong enough," Asher said in Haven's ear.

"Thank you," she said, and then took a deep breath in and out to release some of her stress. Haven felt a sense of strength and honor emanating from her friends. If they believed she was strong enough in the face of risking it all—including losing her friends—then she had to be.

Vidor hobbled to Haven and handed her a piece of paper. "If you talk to my boy, give him this. Maybe," he paused, searching for the right words. "Maybe if he remembers his mother, and the words she spoke over him, he'll come out of this crazed notion of shutting down the Time Server operation."

Haven looked down at the letter that Violet had written to him. She patted Vidor's shoulder, gently tucked the letter in her indigo-colored coat, and crouched down to hug Aiden. "You'll be safe here. You stay with Mr. Vidor, okay?"

"But—" Aiden whined.

"Please," Haven urged. "I don't want to lose you, too."

"Be brave, Bestie," Aiden said. He slipped his hand into hers and she felt brave all over again.

* * *

CHARITY STUFFED innovation after innovation into the pockets of Haven's overcoat as she chatted incessantly about each one. Haven tried to remain calm. She glanced at Asher, who pulled a small tube of what looked like travel toothpaste out of his coat. He squirted a clear gel rectangle on the wall from the flattened opening of the tube.

"Flubbery Bunny Bumper Babies," he spoke.

The gel instantly came to life with a blue glow and then flickered, as if someone were turning on an old television set. An image of Scientist Irving came to the screen.

"All set?" he asked.

"We have arrived with no Sentinel problems," Otokar called, fiddling with the center console in his room.

His viewing room, which always smelled of potatoes and sausages, was similar to Eutychus' room, except Otokar had a Time Server Coat of arms and a picture of his family hanging on the wall.

"Is this your family?" Haven asked Otokar, who stood nearby. Charity turned Haven slightly to continue her work at stocking her overcoat. The Fairy stuffed two Licorice Loops and a Fuddy Puddy into her right corner pocket.

Otokar glanced up from his work, looked at the picture again, and then looked solemnly back down. "My children. All gone from the war."

"Except for Levi," Asher said to lighten the mood. "He's with you."

"Yes," Otokar nodded to Asher. "Levi."

"Okay, Miss Indigo wearer," Charity smiled brightly, "you are all set. You have every innovation I can think of to fight bad old Fane. And just remember, if things do go higglty pigglty odd, running will do the trick."

The screen flickered again, and now half of it showed Edmundo, Levi, the twins, and Liora in the other viewing room.

"We're up!" Levi said over his shoulder, apparently the one who had the tube of Flubber Bunny gel.

"Super obvs," Liora said as she shook her Ropey Roo out just enough for her to be ready. To Haven, it seemed that she was almost too calm.

"But obvious is good, right?" Levi winked.

"Sometimes," Liora busied herself with the innovation while Levi gave a thumbs up to Asher. Haven laughed.

"I just checked on our plotting friend and he is in Florida," Scientist Irving said. "I posted the coordinates for you, so you shouldn't have any issues finding him."

"Is he alone?" Otokar asked through the Flubbery T.V.

"He is," Scientist Irving said before he paused, " . . . but I wouldn't let that put you at ease."

"Why?" Haven asked Scientist Irving, just as Edmundo was busy at the helm of the other viewing room.

"Because his behavior is erratic. He keeps talking to himself, then changing appearances, then changing back. It's freaky, man."

"Hmm," said Levi. "A degradation of Time Server thought life."

"What does that mean?" asked Liora. She wandered away from her task toward Levi, clearly more interested in what he was saying.

Levi's face fell and his tone took on a somber one. "Any Time Server that has moved far enough away from living in joy has this affliction. It is a terrible state, one wherein the worst cases, they can be physically dangerous."

"Have you seen this before in the Joyless Hospital?" Haven asked.

"Very few times," Levi said, moving toward the screen. "But, in those that I have, it has been really hard to bring them back to SOJ. State of Joy."

"You are good at helping these Time Servers." Otokar stated.

"Yeah, it's the way I like to serve," Levi said, his gaze pointed downward. Otokar stared at his nephew through the screen as he smoothed his mustache.

"Since he is acting crazy, maybe we should try to capture this guy instead of just getting proof," Haven said thoughtfully. "There are more of us than him."

"This is incredible thinking," Otokar beamed.

"Yes," Edmundo pointed his finger high in the air, "let us surround this ruffian and obliterate his dastardly plan."

"We'll cause a distraction and catch him from behind," Haven said as she leaned against the wall of direction. The orange glow of the crystals illuminating her face revealed her spark of excitement. "But I have to first get a confession that the FOTWs can record. No one is going to believe me if we don't have that."

The twins saluted her, "We got the distraction part."

"With my help," Levi grinned.

"Communicatears," Charity said as she placed a piece of tiny pea-sized putty in Haven's hand.

"Place in your ear like this," Otokar said as he placed the same thing in his ear. As he did, the pea-sized innovation seemed to melt to fit and cover the exact size and shape of his real ear. It almost looked like it had completely disappeared.

"You can remove when we are completed," Otokar said, urging her to hurry.

Haven placed the putty in her ear and felt a warmth spread to the earlobe. She could hear Otokar saying to her, "Now you hear us communicate without your mouth movement."

Haven marveled that Otokar never moved his lips.

"Think of who you want to talk to and they can hear it through these," Charity spoke, yet only in Haven's head. "Of course, they have to have a communicatear, too!"

She looked at Asher who was smiling at her.

"Can you hear me?" she thought.

"Yup," he communicated back. "And I must say you look beautiful today," he winked at her as she weakly smiled back at him.

Okay, now's not the time to flirt with the boy you like, Haven tried to concentrate on making sure Asher did not hear that thought, but his smile widened.

"Ready?" She asked everyone as they communicated back affirmatively.

"Time to Serve," she spoke to the screen.

They stepped out into JW Johnson Park in Jax, where the main fountain sprouted water into a perfect spray in the air, but was frozen in time. Untethered festival fliers were paused as they blew in the wind. The Skyway Station loomed above, and Haven could see that many people had gathered for the Art Walk in the park. It was 6:00 pm and lighted booths of crimson and blue lined the street, as many people were paused in their shopping for handmade jewelry, handmade candles, and hand-painted jars. None knew that Time Servers were among them for even a second of their evening.

Otokar peeked his head around a large teal and gold painting that read 'Duuuuuuuuuvvvvvvalllll!' in one booth, to check for any signs of Fane amongst the crowded park.

As the team stealthily moved around the booths, Haven could see that Levi and the twins had climbed to the top of the Skyway to get a bird's eye view of things. And Liora, Edmundo, and Charity had gone into the library to watch through a window.

After everyone was in place, Haven heard Otokar through her Communicatear: "You have much bravery. Show us."

Haven drew in a deep breath, closed her eyes, and blew out her angst. She was going to do what she had to do. As she moved through the park, picking her way around a booth selling a life-sized portrait of Einstein with his tongue sticking out, she surveyed the scene. Jam-packed street, illuminated buildings around, street filled with shoppers. She couldn't pick Fane out if she wanted to.

Just then, a loud crash reverberated and a trash can rolled across the Skyway's track, fell down the concrete stairs, and rolled to a stop on the landing.

"Oooops," Finn said into the communicatear.

"That's unfortunate," Fletcher said.

"Was that necessary?" Haven thought.

"Just practicing!" Finn responded.

Haven shot back, "Stop—"

But before she could say another word, a cackle erupted throughout the square, its sound careening off the frozen buildings and booths. Startled, Haven searched for the source, but couldn't find it amongst the confusing echoes. Nobody and nothing moved.

Again, there was a cackle, only louder now. This time, she felt it was nearer, which caused the hair on the back of her neck to stand on end. It was unsettling.

"Cool yourself," Otokar's voice was unmistakable in her head. "This is bait; he is trying to give you much fear."

"I wouldn't blame her," Liora said. "That is creepy."

Haven took a determined, deep breath and looked around.

"You plot in your little Freedom Room, disguising yourself as old dead people, and now you can't even face me?" Haven yelled, glancing up to the Skyway.

Once more, the mirthless laugh rang through the streets with no sign of its source. Haven climbed a smaller oak tree to look around.

"He must be using an Ventrilloquator," Edmundo spoke. "It bounces sound off of everything, making you sound as if you are in a dozen different places at the same time. Very effective."

"Try something else, Haven," Asher urged. "The stakes aren't high enough for him to show himself."

Haven thought for a moment. *What would get Fane out of his hiding place?*

She jumped down from the bottom branch of the tree and moved to the fountain. "I know why you want the Indigo," Haven yelled. "Why you've made these buildings disappear."

The eerie sound of anticipation filled her ears.

"Violet. I know who she is," Haven paused. Surely that name would bring him out of hiding. She took another breath to relax her tense nerves. "I know you want to see her again. I spoke with your father about her and . . . you."

To her left, Haven saw something move. Amongst the sea of frozen people, a man who leaned against a parked Indian Four motorcycle and wore a crooked flower pot for a hat moved towards Haven. *Cricket.*

After Haven spotted him, his form changed into the giant girl with green spiked hair. Her long legs stepped over a cement barrier as she moved closer to Haven. After two steps, the figure popped down into the shriveled old librarian Haven encountered at the Book Exchangery. Her flowered muumuu swayed as she hobbled closer to Haven, moving effortlessly around the shoppers.

"Fane?" Haven asked, confused.

The old lady laughed as she moved closer to Haven. The next moment, the woman imploded and was replaced by the leathered man with the goatee and heavy boots. The one who showed up that first day in Twigette's store.

Seeing each disguise, the Giant Girl who sneered at her the first day she walked the cobblestone streets of Time Server City, the old woman who tried to convince Haven to give her the Indigo that night of Giving Day, and the man with the flower pot hat who seemed to always be ever present. One thing was clear. Fane had been following her the whole time.

"You, little girl, know nothing of my mother," he growled much in the way his father, Vidor, did.

This snapped Haven back to Fane.

"I have a letter that says otherwise," Haven said, as she worked to steady her voice. Realizing that Fane could have been anyone she spoke to at any time freaked her out. Slowly, she pulled out the faded paper, keeping one eye in him in case he decided to change into someone else. She unfolded the letter and began to read.

"Vidor, My time is short so I write—"

"Stop, you selfish girl!" His voice spilled out in a near-squeal. His hands shook as he continued to move toward her. "I have come to arrest you for crimes against Time Server City!"

Fane struck the ground with his heel and a bubble large enough to swallow a bus formed around himself and Haven. Then he spoke low enough for only the two of them to hear: "Thought I would use this, so none of Scientist Irving's FOTWs could catch the truth."

Haven gasped. He knew what they were doing.

He cackled again. "You think you know more than you do, but you have no idea the plans for you."

"Plans can be changed," Haven said, her voice as calm as she could muster. She stood her ground as Fane moved closer, and the bubble stretched to envelop them both. Even though her voice sounded steady, she was freaking out. She thought about what Fane had just said. Plans for her. *What kind of plans?*

Clearly, he could hear her thoughts. "You mean the plans you have to keep your friends safe?" He climbed a wildly painted van and stomped on the roof, the metal slightly buckling under the force. Haven looked up. Through the window, she could see two figures tied up in a Ropey Roo, struggling against the glass. *Vidor and Aiden.*

"No!" she screamed, but only her and Fane could hear, as the bubble blocked out all communication.

"Your selfishness has cost you your friends," he sneered.

"My selfishness?" Haven screamed, throwing the letter at him, "Your selfishness, Fane! You caused all of this for what? The power to see your mother?"

He cackled again, almost losing his balance on the van that held Aiden and Vidor. "You really think that is what this is about? Me seeing the Star People? The girl who could figure anything out, the genius of her friends, can't even see what is right in front of her face!"

Haven paused and stole glances around the park. She saw Asher and Otokar moving towards the bubble.

"You are the selfish one. Pretending to be the one who serves everyone, putting others first," he spat upon the ground. "But I see you, Haven. You're afraid."

"You think I'm afraid?" Haven realized Otokar was trying to break the bubble and wanted to keep Fane busy. "Of what?" She added.

"Of losing the people that are closest to you."

Heat rose to Haven's cheeks.

"Oh, but that makes the plan so much better for me. Selfish girl wants to keep everyone safe so she feels safe. It will be tough for you when the other Time Servers see that you are the one that ends up putting them in the ground. Then off to Magma Prison you go, alone. And the Indigo will be free to the one who knows how to steal it. Time Server city destroyed, you gone, and me, with the most powerful stone of all."

At that, Haven lunged at him, unable to contain her anger. He pulled a chain out of his pocket that sparked with an electro-current and flicked his wrist. The chain elongated instantly and tried to wrap around Haven, but she ducked on instinct. It hit the bubble with a crackle just as Fane jumped to the car Haven had crouched upon.

He kicked her over to the side and she fell with a thud on the ground. The bubble popped in the process.

They wrestled on the street between the booths. Haven was surprised at her strength against an adult. They always made it seem that they were stronger than kids. She elbowed him in the knee and heard a crushing sound as the man groaned in pain. She dove for his hand to release it from the electro chain he had swung around again.

The chain missed Haven by inches, but she heard Otokar's cry and a crack and she knew it had found a target. On contact, Otokar's foot was frozen. By this time, Haven had jumped on top of Fane, threw her weight backward over the hood of a car, rolled him over, and pinned him.

"You don't have to do this!" she panted, sweat dripping down her face.

The flap of his pack opened, revealing the staff. Haven grabbed it and it clattered to the ground. Instinctively Haven leaped upon it and Fane on top of her, forcing her hand over the handle and jamming the end of the staff in the ground.

He cackled as buildings swayed, booths crumpled, the frozen shoppers fell into the abyss that opened wide to allow for the whole park and the surrounding buildings to be swallowed.

Haven was thrown to the side of the car as the road pitched to the left. The staff fell with a clang. Fane grabbed the golden rod and made for his gateway, nimbly jumping over falling benches and lampposts in the street.

"Get going!" Asher's real voice yelled in the din of the breaking glass of the buildings as he pulled Haven along.

"Aiden! Vidor!" Haven yelled as she tried to get to them.

"I've got them, Haven!" Liora yelled from across the abyss.

Edmundo, who held a rag to a large cut on his head, helped Otokar to the opposite gateway. Levi and the twins were on the other side of the block. They tried to get to the other four, but the City Hall building collapsed and blocked their path.

Haven looked toward the bus where Liora was supposed to be helping Vidor and Aiden but couldn't get herself to move. Half of her leg was wedged inside a huge crack in the pavement, which sank quickly with a car, taking her with it.

"I can't!" she yelled to Asher who looked down to see her predicament.

He searched around in desperation. They were the only two on that side and he had nothing to help her.

"Snake String!" Jairus shouted as he came out of the gateway.

He threw a small coil of bright green leather to Asher, who seemed to know immediately what it did as he wrapped it quickly around Haven's leg.

The leather slid around her calf as a snake would its prey, although it wasn't squeezing her muscles. As a matter of fact, it was lifting her leg up as the rope went deeper into the ground and freed her from her trap.

"Let's go!" shouted Jairus above the roar of folding buildings and falling glass.

Haven's leg was freed.

The trio maneuvered around the booths and trees, climbing a few sinking ones to the gateway they first entered. As she passed the sinking people, her heart went with them as she saw so many innocent lives falling into a pit in the ground.

Haven, Jairus, and Asher jumped through the gateway and watched it shrink until the doorway to the Otherworld was closed.

The whole city block finished caving in on itself. Buildings, cars, streets, and people—hundreds of them—all buried underground, all because Haven activated the staff. A new city block took its place and time restarted, the occupants somehow unaware that hundreds of people were gone, frozen in the ground below.

"Did they make it?" Haven breathed as she lay on the ground out of breath.

Jairus adjusted his pack, looked at Asher, then looked down on the floor.

Haven forced herself to the screen and pounded the wall as she yelled for Liora, Aiden, and the twins. Finally, someone hobbled to the screen. Edmundo's face looked grim.

"No!" Haven shouted. She fell to her knees. "No!" she sobbed.

She tore at her hair and struck the ground. She tried to tear off the Indigo but it wouldn't budge, which made her strike the Indigo fiercely on the rough stone floor. If she had never found it, they all would have been safe. Her makeshift family, Liora, Jairus, Finn, Fletcher, Hannalee, and Aiden at Haven's Place, playing freeze tag and laughing in the days to come.

She lay there crying and screaming over her loss, while Asher gently sat by her side until she couldn't scream anymore.

"It's gonna be okay," he said to her as he tried to rub her back to soothe her. It didn't work.

"No, it's not. I lost them. It's my fault." her voice cracked. "I —I thought I could catch Fane. I was *so* sure."

"We all believe you can, we just underestimated him."

"I am so stupid. I can't—"

"Stop," Jairus said firmly. Haven raised her head. "This isn't you, Haven. Crying because you failed at something."

Haven sat up and rubbed her face, her eyes dull.

"What do you do when something doesn't work out on our contraptions?" Jairus asked.

"This isn't some contraption, Jairus! This is our *family*," she cried, her face red and scrunched up in heartache.

"Same principle. What do you do?"

Haven hesitated for a moment and then spoke. "I try again." She wiped her hands across her face to dry the tears, but they kept arriving.

Jairus calmly reached into his pack and pulled out several rolled-up documents. Haven saw the freedom symbol on each one. "I stole these from the Freedom Room," he said. "They are plans of the staff, and it looks like what he did back there can be reversed. We just need to get the staff from him."

Haven felt immediate relief, "How did you—?"

"I've been following you. Didn't think I would actually leave you guys here to fend for yourselves?"

"Yeah," Haven said bitterly. "I did."

"You don't know everything about me," he teased. Haven let out a snotty half-laugh. "Haven, you can do this. Watching you take charge—I was . . . "

Haven smiled through her watery eyes and Jairus tried to hide his. Seeing his confidence in her gave her strength. It was good to have her thinking partner back. "It's okay. I'm just glad you didn't leave."

"Never," Jairus said quietly.

"So how can we reverse it?" Asher asked, as he picked up a pebble off the floor and threw it into the corner.

Jairus bristled. "Why do you care?"

Asher paused and glared at Jairus. "Because those were my friends back there, too. And my dad's innocence depends on whether or not we catch this maniac."

Jairus and Asher stared daggers at one another.

"Jairus, Asher," Haven said softly. "I need both of you to catch Fane. One can figure stuff out, and the other knows more about Time Serving than me. Please?"

They both broke their angry eye-contact, nodded toward Haven, but didn't say anything more about it.

Then, the white-haired scientist popped into view, his complexion looking similar to his hair. "Haven? Asher?"

"Did you see what happened?" Asher asked.

"Yup," he said running a hand through his wild hair. "Unfortunately, everyone in Time Server City saw it too."

"What?!" Haven asked incredulously.

"I thought that since Fane was engaging you, Haven, that he would collapse a building or two. Maybe even catch you saving the buildings and show how truly heroic you are."

"But you caught me collapsing the buildings instead," Haven said dryly.

"Affirmative," the scientist said looking down. "Looks like you have to get the staff to reverse what he did no matter what. If you come up empty-handed, he wins, and you go to Magma Prison."

"Is he still in the viewing room?"

"That would be a yes. Looks like he is trying to make it to Antarctica. Not many people come out of those viewing room stations."

Jairus and Haven zeroed in on each other. Without hesitation, Haven said, "Asher, can you follow his coordinates?"

He jumped to the helm, "On it."

"Scientist Irving, is there a way you can send them to Asher?"

"Already in the corner of the screen."

"We are following close behind you!" Otokar came on the screen.

"Yes, we will catch the scoundrel of scoundrels!" Edmundo said.

Asher continued to steer while monitoring the screen.

"I need some sort of ladder or something to climb," Jairus said.

Haven pulled out a square piece of metal, shook it, and a ladder unfolded.

"That's cool," Jairus said, trying to contain his awe and interest.

"Giants' Innovation. Told you their stuff can do anything. You'd fit right in with them."

Jairus didn't say a word but busied himself with the ladder. He ushered Haven up so she could peek her head over the wall of the viewing room. The wind from the speed of the viewing room moved her hair and made Haven feel like she was flying over the edge of the earth's surface.

"Don't knock her off the ladder," Jairus said to Asher.

Asher nodded as he captained the room and took direction from Jairus. It caught Haven off guard, the two working together without arguing, but noticing Asher's determination and Jairus' intelligence gave her more confidence. She was going to right every wrong Fane had done.

"Almost to him," Scientist Irving boomed from below.

Jairus climbed to the edge of the wall after Haven to get a look. Both of them lay flat and watched the surface of the earth speed past beneath them.

"Jairus?" Haven asked.

"Yeah?"

"Thanks."

He tried to contain a grin and looked down. His long eyelashes covering his piercing blue eyes.

"Up ahead!" Asher called.

Haven saw another viewing room ahead, zooming erratically. It was Fane and the golden staff.

"He is flying fast," she called out.

"Ease up. Let's go behind him," said Jairus.

Asher nodded and moved slightly slower than Fane's room. "Steady."

Jairus edged his way to the front of the room and had readied himself to jump when Fane caught sight of the boy atop the viewing room wall and crashed his room into theirs, causing Jairus to nearly fall off the edge.

"He's spotted us!" Haven yelled as she grabbed Jairus' arm to pull him back in.

There was another loud crash, which caused the room to spin out of control and both teenagers went sprawling over the side of the wall as Asher hung on below. He grabbed the center console and righted the room. Haven and Jairus clung to the wall with no ladder to support them. Jairus pulled his foot over the side to get a better view of where Fane was, and Haven found footing on the Lost Items opening ledge.

"Left!" Jairus yelled as Asher immediately responded.

With no mercy, Fane crashed into them once more, sending the room into another dramatic quaking.

"I've got an idea!" said Haven as she hung onto the side and let herself drop into the room. " We need to dodge him this time."

Jairus understood and climbed back up the wall to bark orders at Asher, just as Haven crossed the room to the other side. She lay flat on her belly, grasping the edges as if she were glued to the spot.

"Back!" he yelled, and Asher responded, almost knocking Haven off the wall.

Fane's Room cut in front of theirs, so Haven took a deep breath, and jumped with perfect timing.

"Girl!" he growled, as she landed with a thud in the corner. He moved the room swiftly to the right, trying to throw Haven. She grabbed onto a crystal circle on the Wall of Direction and her legs flew out from under her.

Fane spun the orb the other way, turning the viewing room in a circle, but Haven was strong enough to stay put. He lost control of the room because he wasn't prepared for another crash against Asher's room. The collision knocked Fane off his feet, and he rolled backward like a bowling ball headed for its pins.

Haven let go, jumped to the orb, and stopped the room. She turned towards Fane but instead she saw Aiden.

Haven paused. "Aiden?"

"Haven! The scaredy guy went upstairs!"

Haven glanced up the stairs but didn't see a shadow.

"Come on, Haven!" Aiden cried as he grabbed ahold of Haven's arm. As she did, a glint of an ebony ring with a winged gear for a band caught Haven's attention. *Wait. Aiden isn't a Time Server. He doesn't have a ring.*

Haven took the fake Aiden's hand and twisted it until the figure was brought to their knees. The Disguise O Meter fell from Fane's coat pocket and flew across the room, causing the fake Aiden to implode and Fane to appear.

They both lunged for the device, but Haven kicked Fane in the chest. She knocked the wind out of him, reached the innovation first, and stomped on it, crushing the entire thing so all that was left was a few sparks and pieces of the freedom symbol.

Fane pulled himself up slowly. He had a long scrape on his forehead and was holding his left knee. Haven made a move to grab the pack behind his back, but he threw his electro-chain out at her. It grazed her back and right arm, and she fell to her knees. Haven couldn't move, as it felt like her upper body was asleep with pins and needles.

The injured Fane limped up the stairs right as Jairus jumped down from the wall. A loud pop and a cloud of purple, glittery smoke followed Fane as he disappeared up the stairway.

Jairus jumped clear of Haven to pursue Fane, who by now, was halfway up the stairs.

Then, from atop the viewing room, Asher called out: "Haven!" And he jumped down the wall much in the same fashion Jairus had.

"She is fine," Otokar said, using the Lost Items slots to neatly climb down the wall. He knelt next to the teenagers.

"Can you feel your fingers?" he asked Haven.

"Not my first two," she admitted.

"This Electro Chain is meant to stop you but not permanently harm you. You will get feeling in your hand again soon." Otokar helped her up. "You must go, now!"

Otokar pulled Haven up and pushed her up the stairs with Asher on their heels. Haven fought for each breath as the dizziness threatened to overtake her. The thick smoke filled her lungs.

"What—" she coughed and sputtered.

"Cover your breathing tools and move!" came the voice of Otokar in Haven's earpiece.

She covered her nose and mouth and felt her way along the wall until she could finally see the clearing of daylight. Hundreds of Sentinels surrounded the entry courtyard. It was Jairus, Otokar, Asher, and Haven . . . against all of them.

"For the Way of the Time Server!" Edmundo shouted as he and Charity flew in from the left. He on a bicycle, and she using her wings, dropping goopie gloop on ten Sentinels at once.

Haven took that chance to take the Flourishy Floss out of her pocket and shoot it across dozens more Sentinels, entangling them in a web of dental floss that wouldn't come apart. Asher tossed Jairus three more innovations and they went to work on the Sentinels to the left.

The battle continued as innovations were used against the Sentinels' strength. Some were shot into the air, others stuck to the ground. But for every Sentinel they took down, three more took their place until the entire courtyard was filled with colorful crystal and stone. The battling crew began to lose.

"Haven!" Jairus hollered. "Get the staff, it has a reversal switch underneath the handle. It's the only way we can get Liora, Aiden, and the twins back."

Haven nodded and searched the crowd to see Fane weaving through the Sentinels. The staff stuck obviously out of his pack.

She dodged a Sentinel, but another grabbed her leg. Then she heard faint meowing coming closer, as barrels filled with scoffee crashed onto the Sentinel, causing him to let her go. Haven looked up and saw Esther perched over the second story window of the Scoffee store. Next, Esther rolled two more barrels over another Sentinel who had just lunged after Haven.

"Indigo wearer!" Schorl's rough voice boomed behind her. "Your crimes are done."

He grabbed her arm, his tight grip squeezing the life out of it. She struggled as he lifted her up so that she was eye to eye with him.

"I knew I would catch you," he said, with both anger and calmness balanced in his voice. His black glossy eyes contorted to express cruelty. "*Failure.*"

Haven watched Fane disappear into the forest trees. Her breaths caught up to her as she slowed them down. *Think, Haven.* Then she smiled.

"I never fail unless I give up," she said sweetly. "And I don't give up."

With her free hand, she pulled the Licorice Loop out of her pocket and whipped it into the air. It circled around Schorl's head as he watched it descend like a thick, springy snake, encircling the needles on his feet and twisting so the Sentinel lost his balance. As Schorl fell, he dropped Haven and the Loop coiled back into her hand as if it were her pet.

Schorl jumped up as Haven ran, his long strides and heavy footfalls coming after her. Haven pumped her legs as fast as they could go when she saw something gallop up next to her.

A unicorn.

"Grab my hand, Haven!" Hannalee yelled. The spunky girl shone like a hero as she effortlessly rode the Unicorn. Hannalee had strapped her stuffed one to the front, its knitted hair flapped in the wind. Sentinels from all sides tried to grab her and it, but the magical pair dodged every one.

"Now, Haven!"

Haven did as she was told and grabbed Hannalee's tiny hand, and the unicorn bucked, allowing Haven to fly onto its back. Schorl lunged but the unicorn kicked out and knocked the Sentinel down.

"I'm riding a unicorn." Haven muttered to herself in disbelief. "I'm riding a unicorn?"

"This is Unie Junior," Hannalee yelled proudly as two more Sentinels dove for them and the Unicorn hoofed each one. "Hang on, we will get you away from these meanies."

"Where have you been?" Haven asked, relief filling her.

"Finding Jairus," Hannalee said as they came to a canter when the Sentinels were far enough behind them.

Haven laughed. "Will you take me to the forest over there? But you have to stay hidden cause I don't want Fane to get you."

"Who is that?"

"Just a bad guy I'm going to catch."

THE CHOICE

"FANE!" Haven screamed as she tore through the woods. "I know you're here!"

She ripped through the trees, searching for the leathered man. A wave of cackling echoes bounced off of each trunk.

"You selfish coward!" Haven shouted. She paused and clutched the stitch in her side, her heavy breathing now the only thing heard amongst the trees. She eyed the darkness ahead, trying to push down the bit of nervousness that threatened to bubble to the surface.

"Right behind you, girl," Fane said quietly.

Haven whipped around. Leaning against the trunk of a withered oak tree with half of its branches missing was Fane, bloodied knee, electro-chain softly buzzing. It sparked slightly in anticipation of its next victim.

With the speed of lightning, she reached into one of her pockets and pulled out a wad of tin foil. She threw it at him and it expanded into a silver sheet that was bigger than a house. Fane threw up a handful of sand and disintegrated the sheet above him on contact.

"Try again," he growled, limping to the left.

"She grasped another Licorice Loop in her lower left pocket and Fuddy Puddy in her right. Haven dive rolled and threw both. The Loop encircled Fane and shot up a bubble gum barrier while the Puddy inside made him rebound as if he were on a trampoline.

As Fane bounced on his back, he whipped his electro-chain, slicing the thin barrier in half.

He cackled. "You don't deserve to wear the Indigo." As he caught his breath, he added: "Your weak attempts to use innovations from the Giants are easily conquered. You have the *Indigo*, girl, and you're not even *using* it!" He almost toppled over in fits of laughter as Haven stood there, her face flushed.

He was right.

She pursed her lips and put her hand on the ground. "Rise."

The ground shot up thirty feet and threw him high into the air, his electro-chain buzzing after him like a hissing snake. He pulled something out of his coat pocket and a bubble appeared and surrounded him, helping him to land gently on the ground.

Haven again asked for rocks to form underneath which had Fane lose footing and slide down the hill in front of her. She covered her mouth to stifle a giggle as she watched him try to right himself, looking like an octopus out of the water.

The electro-chain whipped toward Haven. She jumped to avoid the crackling chain, but it caught one of her legs then jerked her to the ground. Haven landed hard on the rise of a grassy knoll with a thump, unable to move because the numbing effects of the chain overpowered her. She watched Fane, helpless, as he coiled the chain back into his leather-gloved hand.

"You'll never be able to steal this from me girl," he paced with a slight limp, and the banyan tree behind her swayed slightly. "But," he went on, "I will trade."

Haven took quick short breaths as her body buzzed from within. She glanced at the Indigo.

"Yes," he whispered. "I'll give you the staff in exchange for the Indigo. They can't arrest you then. You're not a threat to Time Server City. You can get your friends back. And you won't be alone anymore."

Haven squeezed her eyes shut, as she willed the effect of the electro-chain to wear off. Her chest felt heavy from the weight of losing Aiden, Liora, and the twins. Losing them was worse than losing her own life.

Her white room appeared, where a vase with dahlias rested on a glass table. The soft indigo chair invited Haven for a sit as the screen flickered on.

Only one scene played, showing her keeping the Indigo and standing up to Fane. The R&M Sentinels then came to drag her away and throw her in the Magma Prison with white hot lava flowing around her as she sat frozen in time, alone. That was the choice she needed to make to serve selflessly.

"No!" she screamed at the screen, willing it to turn off. "I don't want this! I don't want to serve right now! Where is the screen where I get my friends back? Where is that solution?"

The screen flickered on, the same image, her keeping the Indigo and standing up to Fane, and then being frozen in Magma prison. Haven's breathing picked up. Her chest felt like it had a million porcupines attacking it. She grabbed the vase with the dahlias and used all her might to throw it against the pure white wall, watching it shatter into a billion pieces. The dahlias lay limp amongst the shards of glass on the floor. She knew she was supposed to be the owner of the Indigo. She knew it wasn't right to give it to him. But she didn't care. She wasn't strong enough to be without her chosen family, and she didn't want to be alone.

"All. . . . all . . . right," she stammered as the room faded. "I'll give it to you. Just give me the staff."

With a trembling hand, Haven removed the ring with its curling vines and the ornate dahlia that cupped the stone. The leather of Fane's glove cracked as he opened his hand to receive the Indigo. He tore off his other glove with haste, revealing his own Time Server ring, with an ebony stone encircled with skulls. He slipped the Indigo on his finger, and the band widened to fit as the bright purple stone shone on his forefinger. It was no longer Haven's sweet treasure found in the trash, but now used for Fane's selfishness.

Then, spitting upon the ground and cracking his knuckles, Fane jammed the staff in a rock jutting from the hill overlooking Time Server City, looked back and sneered as he spoke, "Time Server City must be buried. Now." Fane pulled the handle down.

Trees snapped. A crack in the ground opened like the mouth of a monster, and the staff shook then tilted. The houses on the outskirts of each village began to fold down. Haven heard yells of fright and surprise as Time Servers moved like a school of confused anchovies unsure of where the predator was coming from. No matter where they went, the hole was too large for them to escape.

Haven clutched at the grassy ground and her heart picked up speed. All of her Time Server Friends. They were in terror right now. All because of *her* selfishness.

Fane grabbed the staff that looked like the leaning tower of Pisa, hobbled to Haven with a look of satisfaction spread over his crooked face, and threw the staff towards her. It landed on the earth with a clang. *Such a beautiful thing Clarence created, but used to destroy everything, even his own brother. If only Scientist Irving could reverse this,* Haven thought.

The reversal switch! Haven desperately grasped for the staff. Underneath the handle was a minuscule switch, hidden by an ornate freedom symbol. She flipped it.

Nothing happened.

She flipped it again, and nothing happened. Fane laughed, slapping his knees as if someone told him the funniest joke on earth. He crouched down so that Haven could see the glint of the Indigo as if it called for her to save it, "I destroyed the switch, girl. You have too much trust."

A pang filled Haven. Jairus. Right before they entered the gateway for the first time, he said the same thing.

As the villages folded in on themselves like accordions, the center of the city began to crumble too. Fane stood up as he yelled with glee when the council building crashed to the ground. Haven caught her breath, she knew Jairus, Asher, Otokar, Charity, and Edmundo had to be there somewhere. The clocktower, the large tree that Haven and Asher swung under during Giving Day, the scoffee store where Harmony and Esther served, the Joyless hospital where Merry and J.J. were now . . . it was all gone. Folded like paper beneath the earth.

"Help. Please," Haven looked around for anyone to take out Fane as she watched helplessly. The feeling of her legs came back in tiny prickles, as the effects of Fane's electro-chain wore off. The rough dirt scraped her cheeks, knuckles, and bore under her nails as she gripped the earth, wishing everything to stop. Everyone she cared for was gone and she, in her selfishness, had helped Fane to destroy it. She was truly alone.

"You and I aren't so different, *selfish coward*," Fane spat.

"Stop," she barely could utter a whisper.

"Oh! Not so easy to take, is it? But I'll tell you one thing, girl. Your choice today has freed us from the slavery your world had on us. You Otherworlds are on your own."

"Stop!" she yelled.

Fane cackled with glee, as he saw the rise out of Haven. "Your words have no power over me," as he kicked the staff and limped toward the flattened land that was now where Time

Server City used to be and yelled as if everyone could hear him, "Freedom!"

Haven covered her face with her hands, screaming into her clenched fingers. She had become who the Time Servers feared: the one who would be responsible for all of their deaths. It was worse than what the other crazy Indigo Wearer did. She demolished the whole city by thinking only of herself.

As she continued to scream into her hands, her voice grew hoarse. Her heart felt like it had imploded then exploded over and over again.

The wind blew, and as she quieted, it sounded as if the trees were singing to her. Higher pitches then lower as the strength of the wind increased. She paused and squeezed her eyes tighter. She wished she could speak tree.

"Haven!"

She glanced up. A tall figure in a red hooded overcoat stood in front of her. Her inky hair was in a bun, nails painted a cardinal red, a bo staff in her hand, and her name described her build.

"Twigette? What—? How—?"

"The Choice Maker," She folded her arms across her chest. "He knew where to find you."

Haven's thoughts went wild. *Twigette, here in this world. How could she be in this world? Wait, of course she would be in this world. She freaked out when she saw the Indigo for the first time. Has she been the one following me this whole time? Was she in the Choice Maker's office the night of Giving Day?* As Haven pulled the threads of reason together in her mind she realized one thing, "And you are the List Collaborator?"

"Yes," Twigette said. She firmly took hold of Haven's arm and pulled her off the ground, Twigette's strong presence helping Haven cling to a wave of calm. "Come on, my favorite trader, we need to get you up. The Choice Maker knew you would be here, he saw the thread of choices, and he sent me before Fane could do anything else."

Haven felt a knot in the pit of her stomach. "How much does the Choice Maker know?"

"Everything, sweet Haven," the Choice Maker said as he made his way through an opening between two great oak trees that seemed to bow with the wind as he passed. Haven trembled as he teetered up to her. He wrapped his arm around her in a warm hug and squeezed tight.

Haven broke. Her tears flowed with no barrier; there was no reason to stop them now. Tears for Aiden, Liora, Jairus, the Twins, Hannalee, Asher, Eutychus, Merry, and JJ. For Charity and Edmundo. All the people she had grown to see as family. Gone because of her selfishness.

"Oh, Haven, we all make bad choices sometimes," he comforted her.

"You're the Choice Maker!" she sobbed. "You're appointed to make good choices."

"Ah! But that is only because I have made the bad ones first, so I learned from my mistakes."

Haven paused and looked up.

"Forgiving yourself, and moving on to make a better choice is the only thing you can do."

Haven sniffed and wiped her nose, much like Hannalee often did, which made the tears nearly return.

"Now, let's have a think. Haven, you are a fantastic problem solver, how can we solve this little . . . " the Choice Maker wriggled his pinky, "problem of ours?"

Haven laughed watching the old man wiggle his pinky. She took a deep breath, blew out her stress, and closed her eyes.

Fane had the Indigo, and as long as he had it, there was no hope of Time Server City being recovered. No one else would take the Indigo except for her. She couldn't force it from him because of the purple goo and being electrocuted. The only way to get the Indigo would be if Fane were put in Magma Prison, or if he was to give it to someone willfully.

She knew Schorl was after her. It had become his personal mission to see her end up in Magma Prison, so there was no convincing him to arrest Fane; he'd think that Fane was the hero! It seemed now that the only way for her to get the Indigo would be for Fane to give it to her willingly.

Who could convince him to do that?

Haven opened her eyes and smiled.

"You have the solution," the Choice Maker said.

"Can we use a Fairy Induced Idea on him? Would it work on a Time Server?"

The Choice Maker looked at her, as a smile formed. "Dear Haven, what do you mean?"

Haven tapped her lips much like Jairus did when he almost solved a problem. "I mean, that the F.I.I. can put ideas in people's heads. Does it work the same for a memory?"

Twigette and the Choice Maker glanced at each other.

"Which memory, my favorite trader?" Twigette picked up the staff and slipped it in her belt.

"How about one of his mother? One to remind him of who he truly was before she left for the Star People?"

"And what would that do?" Twigette furrowed her brow trying to track what her favorite trader was saying.

Haven continued. "I mean, Vidor said to me that Violet was the only person Fane listened to. After she went to the Star People, he never listened to anyone else. In the Book Exchangery, there was a moment when I asked him who he would like to see, and he mentioned his mother. In Violet's letter to Vidor, she wrote that she always told Fane that he would do great things if directed the right way. He freaked out when I tried to read him the letter at the park, so I know she still matters to him. If we can remind him of what she said to him, how she saw him, maybe . . . just maybe, I can convince him to give me back the ring."

"And how would you do that?" The Choice Maker had a twinkle in his eye as he mischievously raised his eyebrows twice.

Haven glanced at Twigette, then at the ground. "I know what it is like to feel angry and abandoned. He and I are no different, we just decided to *do* different things afterward. I'm not exactly sure what I would say, but I know how he feels, and that may be enough for me to convince him."

"Hmm," The Choice Maker said. "The Choice thread did lead through your decisions." He tapped his lips that were curled into a half-smile almost as if he knew this exact moment was going to happen. "Let's try it! Twigette? I assume you have a sphere that works on a Time Server?"

"Yes, back in my shop, only one left."

"Let me get my inspector-glasses," the Choice Maker said as he reached in his overcoat and fumbled around. "Oh, cheese nuggets! I should organize these things more."

"Left side, top pocket." Twigette shook her head as she pointed to his coat..

"Oh," he chuckled. "Yes, my loyal friend. You do seem to know where everything is amidst the chaos. Even sweet Haven in the Otherworld."

The Choice Maker winked as he pulled out a golden periscope that elongated after putting it to his eye. It went over the tops of the trees, managing to avoid every branch and leaf. Everything was left undisturbed. "The Memory Tree fields still look intact. Fane wasn't foolish enough to try to bury those!"

FINAL MEMORY

IN THE DEEP NIGHT, the Memory Tree trunks and branches glowed a soft blue every time the surviving trio passed one of them. Once they were a distance of twenty feet away, the tree would dim down to look like a regular old tree. It was as if the Memory Trees were begging Haven to come closer, to look at the memories stored deep inside, so she could know the secrets they were so willing to give.

Twigette kept an eye on her watch, or on the wrist-device that *looked* like a watch. "We are almost to his tree . . . about thirty paces to the right."

"She always knows exactly where things are," The Choice Maker marveled.

Haven thought about Twigette's trading shop and how she seemed to know where everything was stored. "Yeah, you should see her shop!"

"Here," Twigette said, pointing to a withered elm tree whose bark looked like the veins of a hundred-year-old man's hands crawling up the side.

"Haven, since this is your idea, why don't you choose the memory?" The Choice Maker suggested. "Twigette—?"

Twigette stepped up to the tree and whispered something to it. It was a lilting language, something Haven hadn't heard before. Almost as if Twigette were letting the wind out of her lips in puffs, first strong, then soft with three short bursts at the end. Then, like finishing at the end of an exam, she lifted her thumb and pointed back to the tree, "All yours, Trader."

Haven paused.

"Come on," the Choice Maker gently pushed her forward, "go up to the tree, put your ear to it, and let the tree give you its secrets."

Haven crept up to the tree with trepidation. She was sure that at any moment Fane would jump out from somewhere and stop her.

"He doesn't know we are here. As a matter of fact, it looks like he is trying to access—never mind. We're safe," The Choice Maker assured her as he gently lowered the periscope.

How does he know what I am thinking?

"I would have thought the same thing," the Choice Maker smiled, shaking his head. "Now go on."

Haven knelt. She leaned her ear against the tree and closed her eyes. A sigh escaped from the trunk, and then Haven heard a soft whisper. After a moment, the whisper grew until she could hear Fane's voice, much calmer, and steadier than what she was used to. Pictures flashed in front of her. She could see herself from his point of view, cowering, giving him the ring, and him feeling triumphant. She could see him jumping from the city destruction into the viewing room and feeling the stabbing pain in his leg.

"Violet," Haven whispered. "Show me Violet."

Things blurred in front of Haven's eyes, the years passing

backward until Fane's voice was younger, almost matching Jairus' teenaged-tone. She heard him share about his thirteenth birthday party where his mother accidentally spilled his cake on the floor. Haven saw him help her clean it up as she smeared some of the frosting on his new leather jacket for fun. Haven felt his happiness as Violet hugged him and whispered that he will do great things with his life. Time whirred back again until Fane's voice became a young boy of about Aiden's age. Violet knelt in front of young Fane, who stood in front of his mother's broken hourglass.

She spoke lovingly to him. "You are always my son, no matter what."

"This," Haven opened her eyes.

Twigette moved quickly as she took out a calculator, the same type that Eutychus had on her first day of training and placed it against the tree. The code of the memory was entered by the tree. Twigette whispered something soothing to the tree as the calculator was released.

"Now what?" Haven asked.

"Now we go back to where we began," Twigette adjusted her glasses.

* * *

Dust floated in the beams of light that shone through the cracks in the back of Twigette's Store. Shelves that reached three stories high stretched along the walls and were stuffed with knick-knacks from all eras of Otherworld time. The Choice Maker led them through his own Room of Choices that smelled of earthy sandalwood and was filled with an old suit of armor and fairy paintings—one of which had a door etched into it. When you allowed yourself to be sucked into this fairy painting, the door could transport you straight to Twigette's Store.

"It's how Twigette would report to me," he winked at Haven when her mouth had popped open.

"You sure it is okay that we are in real-time?" Haven asked, trying not to be worried about Fane.

"All of the viewing rooms are now buried underground, dear Haven," Fane doesn't have access to them unless he unearths them again, and Twigette has the staff."

"Plus, I have this time freeze detector," Twigette added. She motioned to the row of bobble head dolls that Haven had always felt creeped out by. "Whenever someone enters a second of time near this store, they all freeze, and record what happens in that frozen second of time. I just have to slow the recording, but I can see what has been done in here."

"Doesn't that creep you out?" Haven said with scrunched up eyes. "I mean, they could do anything to you!" Haven thought about the dirty diaper that was put on Sketch's head.

"I am always notified beforehand if someone is serving on the block," she called as she walked through a row of radio parts. "Plus, normal Time Servers respect privacy, remember? It's in their promises."

"It's true," The Choice Maker said as he stumbled over a bicycle wheel that was rusted from the rim. "Ooof," he said, and plopped down on a pouf chair while feathers and more dust ejected into the air.

"Sphere. Sphere. Sphere," Twigette muttered to herself as she went down two more aisles, looking up and down.

Haven looked around, idly. She didn't know what to do with herself, so she glanced up at the chandelier with leaf-shaped crystals that hung from the ceiling.

A crash of empty soup cans four aisles away turned Haven's attention back to Twigette, who was now head-first in an extra-large moving box. Her legs kicked much like the Fairy who dug in the trash the first time Haven saw time freeze.

The Choice Maker Chuckled, "You know, my friend, you should really think about organizing this place."

"Chaos is organization," Twigette mumbled amidst the box's contents. " . . . if you have the key to decode it." She pulled herself up from the box, and in her hand she held a tiny glass sphere, much like what Eutychus used on the mother who lost her son in the amusement park. A glitter-blue Chrysanthemum settled inside as Twigette tapped it carefully. "The last of the memory flowers for a Time Server."

Haven wrinkled her brow. "Are there different memory flowers for Time Servers?"

"After the big war, the memory flower fields for Time Servers were destroyed. We found it had been used to influence too many in the wrong way. The Memory Tree Fairies had been harvesting them to give to the Freedom Fighters. They were sent to Magma Prison."

"Except this baby," Twigette pushed her glasses up her nose. "I kept it for insurance. Now let me encode this memory into the dust—"

A cackle echoed through the room. Haven froze. The Choice Maker casually looked over his shoulder. Twigette kept encoding the dust.

"You three afraid of what I have done to Time Server City, that you decided to hide in here?" Fane cackled as his ghostly figure seemed to appear through the same doorway they had just come through . . . the one in the Fairy Painting in the Choice Maker's Room of Choices. "Oh, don't worry, little girl," he assured Haven. "The Indigo must really want me to destroy you. As I was testing my new powers, I happened upon a room with a screen that showed me exactly how to find you." He limped toward the Choice Maker. "And. Now. I. Have."

The Choice Maker remained seated as if an old dog sauntered into the room. He yawned, batted at a fly that was buzzing around his head, and then snuggled into the chair a little deeper.

Irritated with the reaction, Fane took an old-time television and pushed it off the shelf onto the floor. "You'd better be afraid of me, old man," he growled as he faced the Choice Maker. "I've heard stories of your cowardice."

The Choice Maker flinched, but remained seated, and the fly deciding to rest on an old coffee mug.

Haven glanced at Fane's boots. He didn't realize it, but he was about to trip on the cord of that television that had been pulled tight when it hit the floor. Haven calmly pulled the Gumlocker out of her side pocket and unraveled it one-handed. If she could only get the sphere, and spray the memory dust in his face . . .

Fane spoke. " . . . you mention how these rings are meant to help people, and this one did. Helped me to finally take all of you out."

He whipped around and lifted his Indigo-clad hand toward Haven as she stepped toward him. He tripped. Haven threw the Gumlocker to the floor as he fell with a thud.

"Not a fair trade!" Twigette yelled, and Haven threw her hand up to catch the sphere as it sailed across the room, the blue chrysanthemum glinting as it passed through the beams of light.

Fane struggled against the Gumlocker but it held him and his arm to the floor.

"Fairy Induced Idea, please," Haven whispered as she took the sphere, and squeezed the dust into Fane's face. He struggled for a moment, and then went wide-eyed and limp.

Haven knew what he was experiencing. His mother, her smell of lavender, her soft caress against his face, the shame that he felt for breaking his mother's hourglass. The one Violet had told him was passed down a thousand generations ago. He felt like he was the worst person in the world. He was so angry with himself. And then her words were spoken so softly, so lovingly, "You are always my son, no matter what."

Then Fane broke. Not physically into a billion pieces, of course. But he began to cry. As first, they were blubbery, wet tears, but it wasn't long before it turned into howls. He was reminded that he was forgiven by the most important person in the world to him: his mother.

Twigette stared at him wide-eyed. Haven knew feelings weren't really her thing, and she kept crossing her arms, then uncrossing them. She grabbed a sword, and then decided Fane wasn't a threat so she leaned it against the bookshelves.

"Mama! Oh, Mama!" Fane sobbed. "Mama, I'm so sorry."

The Choice Maker looked like he was crying silently along with Fane, for he took a flowered handkerchief and dabbed his eyes.

Haven felt moved. She knelt in front of the mourning man and patted his head. "I'm sure she would tell you that she forgives you."

At that, Fane began to sob all over again, letting the years of anger and anguish pour out.

"Big baby," Twigette rolled her eyes. She found another chair, sat down, and leaned against the hilt of her sword.

"You don't understand, I tried. I just tried to see her again with the Star People, but the Indigo . . . I couldn't . . . it wouldn't . . . "

At once, Haven understood. Fane wanted to see his mother again. In all his anger, he destroyed Time Server City, but after that, there was nothing else he wanted except to see her. Haven's eyes welled up with tears. She wanted that, too. Aiden, Liora, Jairus, Hannalee, the twins, Eutychus and Merry, Asher. She would do anything to see them again, and then she understood. The desire to see someone you've lost is so strong, it can make you do anything.

"Fane," Haven said softly. "I have a deal to make you."

He growled and tried to turn his head, but he was still stuck to the ground.

"I'll help you see your mom again if you give me back The Indigo."

He looked at her out of the corners of his eyes and huffed. The fly took flight again and buzzed to the Choice Maker's hand who eyed it carefully. "You know you're going to Magma Prison girl if I give this back to you."

"I know."

"You know everyone is going to blame you for what happened, even if this batty old man of a Choice Maker says differently."

"I know."

"Frozen. For the rest of your life."

"I know."

"No friends. All alone."

Haven took a deep breath and let it out trying to blow out her stress. "I know."

"Then why take it back?"

"Making a better choice is the only thing I can do," Haven repeated the words the Choice Maker said only hours earlier.

"You mean to tell me that I give this back to you, then I get to see my mother?"

"I promise, on my honor as a trader," Haven looked at Twigette, who straightened her posture.

Fane groaned. He looked at the Choice Maker who sat a little too smug in his seat.

"Girl, you may have a little more crack than I first thought." He struggled slightly to the right and was able to roll over to his side, although the Gumlocker still had part of his leather jacket. "The Indigo is yours."

Haven held out her hand as he placed the Indigo in it.

Warmth filled her body, the happy kind, and she slipped the Indigo on with no problem.

"Choice Maker, can I *really* access the Star People?" Haven squinted at him.

"You didn't know if you could do it? Sticks and Smoldhorts —" Fane muttered. He tried to jump up but was still slightly stuck to the ground.

Twigette laughed so hard that she knocked over two barrels of eyeglasses. "Ah! So, I have taught you something! Bluff through the trade!"

The Choice Maker smiled as he put something in his coat pocket, "You indeed have the power and only if you use it self-lessly. It may be a bit fuzzy but I have found that occasionally, when they want to be reached, you can."

She took a deep breath, closed her eyes, and whispered softly, "Violet . . ."

* * *

"I have the Indigo Wearer!" Schorl announced and he dragged Haven by the hands.

The crowd of Time Servers yelled in appreciation and stared as she was brought through the city streets.

"Send her to Magma Prison!" they shouted.

Through the slit in her swollen eye, Haven could see Esther following her, ducking through the crowds and unnoticed by the others. Esther was not yelling; in fact, her face remained stony. The lavender-haired young girl stopped when she reached her aunt. Several of the Time Servers remained solemn, Asher, Otokar, Edmundo, and Charity amongst them. She knew Jairus must be hidden somewhere. Vidor, Aiden, and Liora were with the Choice Maker, hidden in the forest after she unearthed them with the staff. Haven smiled, causing the slit in her eye to completely close.

Then she felt something wet hit her face. Then another something. This time, she noticed it was red and sticky: Gloopie Glop. Then, a Licorice Loop grabbed her ankle and tugged her left and directly through some Unicorn dung. The Time Servers were throwing whatever they could at her, glad for her capture. Schorl continued to drag her through the streets, a spectacle of proof that the time to fear was over.

A Bubble Hooper landed on her chest, making her rise from the ground about seven feet so the people in the back could see Haven's misery. But she wasn't miserable. She was happy. She was relieved. She was thankful. The city block in the Otherworld had been unearthed. Time Server City was restored. And all her friends were alive.

"The Indigo Wearer is not a threat anymore!" The Clock Watcher's voice could be heard over the roar of cheers. "Your society is safe once again."

○○:○○:○○

CHANGEOVER

THE GLOW of the orange-red rock was comforting to Haven as she sat, frozen in time. It was strange to her, not being hungry, not needing anything her humanity usually signaled, but also being aware of what was going on around her at all times. For the endless time she had been there, it could be maddening if she let it.

She saw Schorl and his cronies march through the chamber halls, giving a sneer to Haven as they passed a few times each day. She was their trophy, the next generation of evil Indigo Wearers, frozen in Magma Prison. Other than the Sentinels, no other visitor came.

Haven was alone with her thoughts. All that had happened to her flashed in front of her forever-frozen eyes like a movie played on repeat.

Twigette being the List Collaborator, her commanding presence giving Haven peace when she had made her bad choice.

Aiden and his sticky sweet hands cupping her face when he wanted her attention.

Liora, and the way she grumped when she was made to do something she didn't want to do.

Jairus, and his ability to figure out the toughest problems, and how he never gave up on any project.

The twins, and the laughter they brought.

And Hannalee, *how in the world did she get a unicorn to let her ride him?*

Eutychus. Haven realized that she didn't see him in here when she was brought in. *Maybe he hadn't been locked up?*

Asher, and the way his warm, thick hand surrounded hers and helped her feel supported. He gave up protecting his family to help her because he had believed in her that much. *And now . . . well, at least the Indigo wasn't in the hands of a madman anymore.*

She was grateful that her friends had been freed from the frozen park square in Jax before she went to Magma Prison; the Choice Maker helped her with that. Her thoughts went to the woman in the country house in which Haven was almost buried the first time Fane tried to get the Indigo. She hoped the woman was freed from the underground trap as well.

Then Haven heard it. A scuffle, scuffle, and a swish down the hall. It wasn't the same as the heavy-footed steps of the Sentinels. The sound moved slowly but determinedly towards her. Haven was not able to turn her head, so she waited patiently. She had learned that was all she *could* do. Wait, and watch.

A woman made entirely of white crystal stood before Haven, her train dragging behind her. The crown of crystals made Haven think she was royalty. The woman stared at Haven and Haven stared right back at the woman. Her expressionless face made it difficult for Haven to figure out what she was thinking, but Haven knew she was giving her a hard look. After some time, the woman turned, and with her long train making the *scuffle, scuffle, swish* sound, she moved down the hall and out of the chamber.

Schorl entered next. Haven knew from the sound of his needle-like crystals tinkling as he walked quickly to her chamber. Without saying a word, he took two flat stones and put them in the side panel to unlock Haven from the frozen bonds. Instantly, she felt a release. Her shoulders slumped, her chest moved with her breath, and her eyelids blinked. *What was going on? Were they executing her? Wasn't being frozen forever bad enough?*

"Come," he said without helping her up.

Haven tried to stand on her own but was unable to after having sat frozen for months. She half-crawled, half-walked down the chamber as she looked at the other inhabitants. She saw an older man with a shock of white hair interrupting black on the sides, sitting in much the same position as she had sat, knowing he was watching her as she had watched the others. He looked strangely familiar, but she couldn't remember where she had seen him.

The last occupant she passed before exiting the chamber was none other than Fane. His leather jacket was ripped, and his face still cut from the fight she had with him. Haven suddenly felt light, even though she worked through the heaviness of being frozen for months. *How was Fane in here? Did they know he was the cause of Time Server City collapsing?*

Schorl and Haven wound through cavernous hallways, and the heat of the lava passing them caused Haven to sweat. She grasped onto rocks jutting from the sides, gaining strength until the last few steps when she was able to walk slowly, dragging only one foot.

"Stay," The Sentinel ordered, and left her in a large marble room with chaise lounges and pillows that looked like marble but were soft to the touch. Exhausted, Haven sat and felt relief upon impact; the quiet of the room was nice compared to the low rumble of Magma Prison.

"Yes," she heard the Choice Maker say. "And thank you."

Haven sat up straighter and peered around the corner. The Choice Maker and the same crystal woman who had looked at her moments before were speaking to each other. He bowed to her. As the Choice Maker turned to enter the room, the woman caught Haven's eyes, tilted her head to one side as if studying her, then moved away with the same *scuffle, scuffle, swish* she had made before.

"Ready to leave?" The Choice Maker asked with a spring in his step.

"I—I'm going?"

"Yes, you are," he said. He took Haven gently by the elbow and led her through the room and out into a large archway hewn into orange sandstone and white lines of quartz. "I know you have questions, but let's leave and then I will answer as many as I can."

Haven smiled weakly. As usual, the Choice Maker knew what she was thinking before she could even ask. He led her up many steps that opened to a station carved in the cavernous rock. A thousand bubbles under a green net held a glass-encased dirigible.

"Haven!" Aiden's tiny voice echoed in the ornate entryway as he tackled her.

Haven could not contain her smile as she breathed in the boy's scent of earth and lollipops.

"Bestie," she whispered as she hugged him back.

Jairus and Asher ran to her aid, picking her up on either side while the twins and Liora stood by. They helped her into the glass house, while Hannalee fed Unie Junior who had a garland of flowers around his neck.

After she was set down, Levi appeared and leaned over her to check her pulse. "She's gonna need a few quarts of scoffee to fully come out of sitting in Magma Prison for months," he said.

"Listen to my nephew!" Otokar hollered. "He is a phenomenal Joyless Hospital material!"

Haven raised her eyebrows at Levi, who gave a slight smile.

Eutychus pushed him aside and gave Haven a bear hug. "Thank you," he whispered as he blubbered. She could barely breathe under the strength of his hug.

"All right, you ninny!" Vidor hit Eutychus with the cane to push him back. "Ezra needs a word with Haven. You get back so they can have privacy!"

"Aww, man!" Finn said. "We didn't even get our turn to check in with the boss!"

"You'll get your turn, youngin'! Now, git! Someone's gotta help Edmundo steer this contraption or else we might end up in Giant Metropolis. Again!" Vidor squeezed Haven's shoulder as he pushed the twins up the steps. There, Haven saw Charity waving to her and heard Eutychus singing a song about Dragons and shoelaces.

"Haven, dear girl," the Choice Maker began, as he leaned on the edge of the observation deck and looked out onto pointed rock towers jutting up from the desert. "I want you to know how very proud I am of you and what you have done for our city. After seeing what happened from Scientist Irving's Fly On the Wall, all Time Servers saw how they had been tricked. I think you will find many gifts for you when you arrive at the Hubbles'."

"What do you mean, the Fly On The Wall? I thought it recorded me destroying JW Johnson park and all of the buildings around it."

"Ah, yes, it did. But it also recorded Fane's confession in Twigette's store that night, you accepting the Indigo back from Fane, even though you knew you would be arrested for crimes you didn't commit, and showing mercy to him by calling Violet from the Star People. All things that prove that you are truly a person that serves selflessly."

Haven looked down and fiddled with her fingers.

"To deny your utmost desire to save us from a terrible fate is monumental. All of us owe our lives to you and the selfless choice you made."

Haven looked up into the man's deep brown eyes as he patted her hand. They were filled with kindness and made her feel so loved. He reached into his front pocket, grasped something small, dropped it into her palm, and held his hand over it. "This, my dear girl, is yours."

He lifted his hand away and there was the Indigo. She was speechless. She didn't think anyone would be allowed to wear it after what happened.

"The head council deliberated a long time to decide the fate of the Indigo. Eutychus, Twigette, Otokar, Edmundo, and Charity among others, were your biggest supporters. After months of going over every possibility, it was decided that the correct choice was to give it back to its rightful owner, you."

"Mr. Choice Maker?"

"Ezra, dear girl," the man said through a smile.

"Mr. Ezra, do you agree with them? I mean, do you think I should have the Indigo?"

He chuckled. "Haven, I am one of the ones who fought the most to have you keep it. As a matter of fact," he turned towards her and clasped her hands, "I want you to consider something."

The elderly man's hands felt warm around her cold ones. The fall weather arrived and the wind whipped, causing her to shiver.

"After seeing the gifts you have displayed with and without the Indigo," he carried on with a smile on his face, "the council has come to the same conclusion myself and Twigette have. We want you to consider training with me to be a Choice Maker."

Haven felt unsteady and held on tightly to the Choice Maker's hands. *Her? A Choice Maker? Why her?*

"Don't ask yourself why," he winked, "as I did the first twenty years I served at this post. If you are controlled by fear, you will never reach the full potential of your purpose. We need you, Haven. The Time Servers, they . . . we are your family."

She laughed through her now freely flowing tears.

"Do not give an answer now," he said. The Choice Maker reached into his pocket and brought a handkerchief with smiley faces embroidered on it. "Please take your time to consider what you want, for a Choice Maker's life, although fun, can be a great amount of selfless serving and tough choices."

Haven thought about the tough choices she had had to make in her life. All of them eventually led her and her friends to this place. She thought about her first big choice to keep the Indigo, despite Fane trying to get her to give it to him, and then she realized Twigette was the first one to convince her to keep the Indigo. *Do not give it to anyone else*, she had said. Haven realized there was one more question that wasn't answered. One that should have been answered from the beginning. "Mr. Ezra . . . why was Twigette in the Otherworld?"

"Because, my dear child . . ." He sighed and looked off into the distance. "I sent her to look after you. Your life and the lives of those around you are more tied to this world than you think."

* * *

"Did you pick out china patterns?" Liora teased Haven as she made her way to the rest of the group.

"Yes, and they have dahlias on them," Haven quipped. "Geez, I find out you are accepted into Fairy Fighter training next month and all of a sudden, your snarkiness has bloomed."

"Whatever, genius," Liora snorted as she threw two Skitter Fiddles at Levi, who caught one and raised his eyebrows at her.

"Show off," Liora scoffed as Levi laughed.

"Haven does have some new hardware though," Jairus said as Haven settled in her seat.

Aiden turned around from the seat in front of her. "Bestie has her Indigo. It's Haven's Indigo! You gonna be a superhero?" He asked in earnest.

Haven ruffled the boy's soft hair. "We'll see," and she winked mischievously.

Jairus rolled his eyes. "Of course she is. What, you going to stay home while the rest of us do something with our lives? It'll drive you crazy."

"You should talk, Mr. I'm-going-to-Giant-University-for-geniuses," Liora said as she leaned against the chair and propped her feet on the edge of the table.

"University of the Giants," Hannalee corrected Liora. "Jairus is a smartie! Isn't he, Unie Junior?" she asked the unicorn as she fed him some Popper Petals.

Haven smiled and nudged Jairus with her elbow, "You decided to stay?"

"Yeah, yeah. Gotta do something with myself now that I've done my duty to protect you," Jairus answered. He glanced at Haven and then out to the rocky desert. As they soared over the cliffs of Edoar heading back to Time Server City, she remembered poor Sketch who thought he was actually hanging off one of them. Even as they were hundreds of feet above, the depths of each crack between the cliffs looked terrifying.

"Didn't need to protect me!" Fletcher announced.

"Jairus only needed to protect the skirts," Fletcher added.

Haven tossed Popper Petals at the boys, which snapped with a sugary spark when each hit them. One hit Asher and he grinned at her, and she returned the grin more goofily than ever.

Unie Junior, who had been sitting quietly next to Hannalee like a trained Great Dane, began to snap at the other petals flying through the air. The twins kept throwing them to see if the great unicorn could catch five at a time.

"Finn!" Hannalee exclaimed as she stood and put a hand on her hip. Her knitted unicorn dangled to the side, while she patted the real unicorn with the other. "Don't mess with Unie Junior!" She took a handful of Sour Flowers and pelted him with the few that escaped Unie Junior's quick bites, like a dog earning his reward.

"Don't start a candy war," Liora warned.

"She'll disguise herself into Schorl and scare your socks off," Levi said, wriggling his fingers at Finn and Fletcher.

"Awww, that Disguise O Meter won't fool me even if it is fixed," Fletcher scoffed, "Besides, that's back in the museum."

"But I know how to borrow it!" Haven poked him.

"Yeah, now that my Bestie is a hero, she can do anything, better than Superman." Aiden beamed a recently-toothless grin.

"That is sure the truth," Asher said as he put his arm around Haven and squeezed her quickly.

She reached to put her arm back around him but he had already dropped his, so her mis-timing caused her to hit him in his nose.

"Ow!" he said putting his hand to his face as his head rocked back.

"Sorry!" she said wincing. *Oh my gosh, I haven't seen him in months and this is how I act?*

"Haven?" Aiden asked, picking up a few Popper Petals from Jairus' bin. "Are we still family even if we don't see each other lots?"

Haven looked at Liora, her loyal, fiery friend, then Jairus, the curly haired intelligent boy. She saw Hannalee straighten the flowers in Unie Junior's mane, and Finn and Fletcher tossing Sour Flowers into each other's mouths. A smile erupted from deep within her, fueled by the joy that she felt spread across her face.

She leaned in close to her Bestie, and whispered, "No matter what, we're family."

* * *

HIS LONG FINGERS drummed the marble desk. He adjusted the clock as light from an opened door streamed in.

He motioned for them to enter and they did so silently, shutting the door with a soft click.

"She doesn't suspect me."

"Good," he said. "Keep it that way."

ACKNOWLEDGMENTS

Thank you to the King of Kings, the Alpha and the Omega, my Savior for entrusting me with this story. It was you who answered me with this idea within twenty-four hours after I asked you with a heartfelt desire to write stories that would capture people's hearts and honor you.

To my husband, who listened to every plot twist, every idea, and walked with me through the highs and lows of rejection and open doors. You always told me I could do it.

To my oldest daughter, the person whom Haven is modeled after, your encouragement and editor's notes kept me going when I wasn't sure the story would resonate with your age group. This book needed you, and so did I.

To my son who listened to the iterations of this book with kindness and patience and gave me hugs when I needed them most.

To my twinsie who played with her little sister so I could write and left me encouraging notes at my desk, on my night-stand, on my writing chair . . .

To the baby who kept me connected to the world.

To Agata, my very first book editor. Your insight and ideas brought depth to this book I didn't even know possible. You are the real deal, and anyone who knows you knows that is a fact.

To Lizzie, your kind notes and sharp insights gave this project fire again! A million times thank you; for your trust, and for your hard work.

To my RTC family who encouraged me as a writer and editor. I learned so much working with all of you, and am thankful for you allowing me to create alongside you.

To Danielle, the world's most awesomest coach, you told me to speak out what I wanted. It was so real that I believed this day would come and it has! Thank you for encouraging me.

To Alisa, my dearest friend, thank you for your prayers. And more prayers. And more prayers.

To my beta readers Kaitlyn, Jude, Ethan, Malia, and Arden. Thanks for giving me feedback, it gave wheels to the book's journey.

To Pamela who was the first reader to lay eyes on the manuscript. You told me there was a lot of love in here, and it meant so much.

And last, to the readers of this book. I wrote this for you. I have prayed that these stories would touch you, and I am so grateful you gave up a piece of your life to spend it inside a world I took part in creating. I feel appreciative, obliged, honored, and about a dozen other words to describe being thankful.

ABOUT THE AUTHOR

Sarah Byrd is a proud wife to a man working on the frontlines in a trauma one hospital in the city where the first scenes of *Haven's Indigo* takes place. Together, they have four children whose ages span over eleven years. Fueled by Jesus, coffee, and lots of prayer, she is an author, editor, and collaborative writer, and has worked in publishing for almost five years. This is her debut novel.

www.ingramcontent.com/pod-product-compliance
Lightning Source LLC
Chambersburg PA
CBHW061615190726
48288CB00007B/2337